Memoirs of a Dragon Hunter
"Bursting with the author's trademark zany humor and spicy romance . . . this quick tale will delight paranormal romance fans."—*Publishers Weekly*

Sparks Fly
"Balanced by a well-organized plot and MacAlister's trademark humor."—*Publishers Weekly*

It's All Greek to Me
"A fun and sexy read."—The Season for Romance
"A wonderful lighthearted romantic romp as a kick-butt American Amazon and a hunky Greek find love. Filled with humor, fans will laugh with the zaniness of Harry meets Yacky."—*Midwest Book Review*

Much Ado About Vampires
"A humorous take on the dark and demonic."—*USA Today*
"Once again this author has done a wonderful job. I was sucked into the world of Dark Ones right from the start and was taken on a fantastic ride. This book is full of witty dialogue and great romance, making it one that should not be missed."—Fresh Fiction

The Unbearable Lightness of Dragons
"Had me laughing out loud. . . . This book is full of humor and romance, keeping the reader entertained all the way through . . . a wondrous story full of magic. . . . I cannot wait to see what happens next in the lives of the dragons."—Fresh Fiction

ALSO BY KATIE MACALISTER

ACROPOLIS
NOW
A BILLIONAIRE ROMANTIC COMEDY

KATIE MACALISTER

FAT CAT BOOKS

I hereby dedicate the dishy guys herein to Lisa Lypowy, who came up with the title for this book in what I can only describe as a feat of brilliance. Thank you so much, Lisa!

ONE
TWENTY-FOUR YEARS AGO

"Hey, Sacajawea, you look like you're on the warpath. What gives?"

I stopped to glare at the speaker, who was standing next to one of the residence buildings of St. Anne's College with two other people, both of whom cast me swift glances before turning away. I was used to the British students treating me like I was a lesser species of newt infringing upon their sacred citadel of learning, but I really hated it when my own countryman treated me with the same disdain.

"Knock it off, Esker," I told the young man, clutching my laptop case tight to my chest, hoping against hope the drowning feeling would let up and I could draw in a breath. "You know that's politically incorrect, and ignorant to boot. Sacajawea was Shoshone, and my mother was Navajo. Besides which, calling me Sacajawea isn't at all a slur. She was an awesome woman, brave, a gifted explorer, and possessor of the infinite patience needed to drag a couple of clueless white men from Missouri to the west coast less than two months after having given birth. So the next time you want to insult me, try using the name of some lame-ass white man whose daddy bought his way into Oxford because he didn't have the grades to get the scholarship on his own, like the rest of us."

"Fuck you," Esker snapped while the two Brits laughed.

I gave him the finger as I hurried off, brushing the incident from my mind. I tried again to get some air into my lungs, but anxiety seemed to wrap around me with iron bands. I had to talk to Neo.

"Morning, Kamil," I greeted the porter as I ran past his desk, heading toward the building where Neo roomed.

"Good morning, Beam," the stately, gray-haired man answered as I hurried to the stairwell. "You looking for your young man? He asked me to tell you he was going to the library."

"He is? Dammit. OK, thanks." I spun on my heel and rushed across to the library, making a beeline for the back wall, where Neo liked to claim a long table hidden by some study carrels. Relief filled me when I saw his familiar dark head bent over his laptop, the pressure around my lungs loosening just enough for me to take a deep breath. I glanced around, but students seldom came to this side of the library, since it was made dark by several large chestnut trees nestled up against the side of the building. "Thank the goddess I found you."

"I told Kamil where I was," he answered without looking up. "How did you do on Tormesson's group project?"

"Fine," I said, dumping my case on the table next to him before pulling a hard wooden chair up beside him. "But it doesn't matter. Not now."

I hated the throb in my voice, hated that I was so close to tears, but ever since I'd gotten the news, my emotions felt raw and bleeding.

"Of course it matters. You may not have to break a sweat for good grades, but the rest of us have to work our asses off for first-class honors."

"Neo." I put my hand on his arm, swallowing down the lump of tears that made my throat ache.

He must have heard the emotion in my voice, because he looked over at me, his gray eyes normally filled with humor, but now questioning. "What's wrong, sunshine?"

I almost broke down at the nickname he'd absurdly given me the first time we'd met, six months earlier at the international students' orientation.

"I have to go home."

He made a face and glared at his laptop screen. "I understand. I wouldn't want to help untangle this mess of code, but I have to turn it in tonight, so we'll have to call off date night until it's done."

I took a deep breath. "I don't mean I need to go back to my room … I mean that I have to go home. To New Mexico."

He frowned, his eyes once again turned to me. "The term isn't over until the middle of June. That's almost two months away. Why would you want to go home now?"

I slid my hand down to his fingers, clinging to his hand and praying that I wouldn't break down. Not in public. I couldn't stand it if others saw me sobbing. "My cousin died this morning."

"Oh, Beam, I'm sorry," he said, turning in his chair so that he could pull me into a hug, his arms warm and strong around me. I leaned into his chest, my face pressed against his throat, breathing in the lemony scent of his soap. "So very sorry. You must be devastated. My poor little sunshine."

I clung to him for a few minutes while he murmured words of support, before finally pushing myself off him to wipe angrily at my nose and eyes with a tissue. There was still no one close to us, but I didn't need people to see me having a breakdown in public. "I think I must be in shock, because it doesn't seem real."

"What happened? I assume this is the cousin who took you and your sister in when your mother died?" he asked, his hand warm on my back as he drew little circles.

My shoulders slumped as I leaned into his hand, wishing I could hit a reset button and restart the day. "Two years ago, yes. I didn't know her too well, but she was nothing but nice to us. The local police called to tell me she went into the hospital for what she thought was a chronic cough, but she had pneumonia, and after four days …" I hiccuped back another painful lump of tears, blinking rapidly to keep them from falling. "Anyway, the police said that Autumn was being held by child welfare services, and that I had to come home to take over guardianship—otherwise she'll be put into the foster system."

"How old is your sister?" he asked, his eyes darkening with shared pain.

"Fifteen." Cold crept over me, making me shiver despite the relative warmth of a sunny spring day. "I can't let her go into the system, Neo. Not because of who our parents were, but because the system is bad. Bad for *anyone*."

"And your family … ?" He let the question hang in the air.

"There's no one else. Calypso was our only cousin, and my grandparents died before I was born. There's the tribal chapter, the local government, but since our father was white—a deadbeat, but white nonetheless—the local chapter doesn't bother themselves much what happens to us. I *have* to go back."

Neo was silent for a few minutes, his thumb stroking over the back of my hand. "Yes, I can see that you do. You can't leave your sister to fend for herself. Have you spoken to Gargle?"

"No," I said, not even smiling at the popular student nickname for the academic advisor who monitored my time at Oxford. "But I know what she's going to say—going back home will forfeit the Whaddon Scholarship. I'll be kicked out. I might even have to pay back the money from the scholarship that's already been spent on me. Oh god, I don't want to go home! You don't know what it's like there. …"

The words dried up as the reality of life in New Mexico came all too readily to my mind. My mother had raised us to be proud of our heritage, mixed as it was, but that didn't stop the fact that there were few opportunities available to poor girls with no family support.

"You can bring your sister here," Neo said suddenly, his eyes narrowed on nothing in particular as he obviously tried to find a solution to my problem. "You'll have to move to a flat in town so she can stay with you, but I'm sure that can be arranged. Just tell Gargle you have to go home for the funeral and to get your sister, and I'm sure she'll excuse you for a week or so."

I was shaking my head even before he finished speaking. "Even if I could do that, how am I going to afford to support Autumn? The Whaddon people don't give you much wiggle room when it comes to money."

"If she lived with you, in your room, that wouldn't be any more expensive than now," he protested.

I gave him a watery smile. "If I didn't love you so much, I'd point out just how out of touch you are with what it's like to be poor. Living situation aside, I'd still have to feed her. And clothe her. And get her to a school, and I'm not even sure I could get a visa for her to be here long enough to go to school. And, oh, a hundred other things. I'd have to get a job, and my visa prohibits that."

"Well …" His jaw flexed a couple of times. "What if you said to hell with the Whaddon Scholarship? No, hear me out. If that's what's giving you grief, then you can simply go home to fetch your sister, come back, and finish your degree without them."

"Paying for Oxford how?" I asked, feeling like I was slowly sliding down into a pit of mud. Life-sucking mud.

"You could work under the table," he suggested.

"I could," I said slowly, aware the lung vises were tightening. "But it wouldn't pay much. And it doesn't explain how I'm going to pay for airfare to and from England, not to mention dealing with my cousin's hospital bills. No, don't offer me money. I won't take it. I know your mother gives you lots of money to spend, but I have my pride, and I'm not going to leech off you like so many others have."

"I wouldn't consider a loan leeching, but yes, I know full well you won't let me help you out despite me being happy to do so." His beautiful gray eyes were grave as he lifted my hand to his mouth, kissing my fingers. "Given your pesky pride—"

I pulled my hand away, frowning. "Hey! Some of us cling to our pride because we've been harassed our whole lives, and it's pretty much all we have left."

He reclaimed my hand, and pressed a loud smack to it before pushing back the chair, and kneeling next to me. "There's only one solution, then. Marry me."

I stared at him, wondering if the shock of the news had finally turned my brain into mush. *"What?"*

"You'll have to marry me," he said. "That's the only solution. If you marry me, you can stay in England, finish up your degree, and we'll be able to take care of your sister."

"That's ridiculous," I said, trying to pull my hand back.

"Why am I ridiculous?" A little flash of pain in his eyes had me sliding off the chair until I was kneeling in front of him.

"You aren't." I leaned forward to press a kiss to his lips, his delicious, wonderful lips. "You are fabulous. Marvelous. Sexy and smart and funny. I've loved you from the first time I saw you, looking as lost and alone as I felt at the new-student orientation. But your idea is crazy. For one thing, you're Greek, not British."

"I'm both. My mother was born in Edinburgh, so I have UK citizenship as well as Greek."

"That's very cool, but still, the whole thing is unthinkable," I said.

"Why? Why don't you want to marry me?" he asked, pulling me onto his lap.

"I never said I didn't want to marry you," I answered, breathing in again the wonderful scent that clung to him. "I'm head over toes in love with you. But because I love you so much, I'm not going to marry you until the time is right."

His black brows pulled together, giving me the irresistible urge to smooth out the little wrinkle between them. "That doesn't make any sense."

"It does—you're just letting your heart dictate to your brain." I gave him a sad smile, one that I hoped expressed just how much I regretted the situation I was in. "Maybe if we were at the end of the degree rather than having just started it … but it doesn't matter. I have to go home. You will stay here. Maybe after you graduate, you can look me up, and—"

"To hell with that," he said, his mouth closing on mine, his tongue doing a little dance in my mouth that made me melt against him. By the time he pulled away, my head was spinning, my lips felt bruised, and the band around my lungs had tightened to the point where it hurt to breathe. "You love me. I love you. We're going to be married someday, so we'll just do it now. No, don't bother arguing, Beam. You are more important than any degree. We'll get married. You can bring your sister here. We'll get a flat, and live together, and you can get back into the program without the Whaddon people breathing down your back. We'll live happily ever after, dammit."

I couldn't help it—he looked so indignant, I laughed. "You're the only man I know who can look simultaneously pissed and romantic while proposing." A thought occurred to me, even as I considered what he had offered. "But … what about your parents?"

His gaze flickered away, but not before I saw a flash of doubt in his eyes. "What will they think of us getting married? They'll love you. You're entirely adorable."

I allowed myself to cherish the glow of his praise for a few seconds. "You may think so, but I'm not so sure that they'll be thrilled at the news that their only son and heir has married a woman with no money, no family, and no prospects."

"One ten times smarter than me, who has managed to gain a prestigious Whaddon Scholarship, and is a borderline mathematical genius with an analytical mind that can untangle even the most obtuse code. No, sunshine, don't protest." He gave me another kiss, this one swift and fast before he shifted me off his legs so he could stand. "This is the only thing that makes sense. We'll get married, you'll go back to the States to get your sister, and while you're gone, I'll find us a place to live. It's going to be simple, just you wait and see."

I looked up the long length of his body, my heart feeling like it was made up of butterflies fluttering in my chest. For the first time since I'd heard of my cousin's death, I took a long, shaky breath, finally filling my lungs. "Are you sure?" I asked him, something in the back of my mind warning that this was not the solution that I needed.

"Of course." He smiled as he held out his hand to help me up, brushing back a strand of hair that had clung to my mouth. "Everything will work out, I promise."

Misgiving slowly filled my stomach, but I pushed it aside, desperate to find a way to have my cake and eat it, too.

You know that never works out, a pessimistic voice in my head pointed out. I ignored it, just as I ignored the other doubts that gathered around me like personal storm clouds.

Neo was right—everything would work out. Maybe his parents wouldn't be thrilled with me, but I trusted his knowledge of his family. We'd be happy, Autumn would be safe, and our lives would be filled with happiness and love.

Anything else would be a crime.

TWO
FIVE DAYS LATER

"OK, that was awkward."

"Getting married at the registry office?" Neo hauled my overnight bag up the last of the stairs to the floor where his room was located. "I thought you wanted that. If you had said you wanted a proper wedding—"

"No, I'm perfectly happy with getting married in town. I meant telling Kamil that we got married."

Neo waggled his eyebrows at me. "It wasn't awkward. It was romantic. He wished us well."

"But I bet you he thinks it's odd that we got married."

"It doesn't matter what anyone but you thinks. And speaking of that, welcome home, Mrs. Papaioannou." Neo set down the bag and carried me over the threshold of his room, pausing just inside the door with an indescribable expression on his face. "That sounds so odd. Mrs. Papaioannou is my mother."

I slid down his chest when he let go of my legs, a shiver running down my back at his words. "That's just creepy, Neo. I'm so not your mom."

He smiled, and my insides melted, both at the wattage of his smile and at the steamy glint visible in his gray eyes. "I agree, you aren't. How about this, then … welcome home, Mrs. Moonbeam Swiftcloud Papaioannou née Nakai?"

"Goddess, that's worse," I said, giving in and kissing the tip of his nose before plopping my overnight bag onto his desk. His room was a chaotic mess of clothes, books, laptops, three electric guitars, and assorted other electronics beloved by young men of eighteen with a hefty disposable income. "I really wish Mom hadn't been so firmly entrenched in the hippie movement when I was born. I like the native names in her family, but nooo, she had to name me Moonbeam."

"I like Moonbeam," he said, his hands on my waist as he pulled me close while moving his hips suggestively against me. "I like that it's not traditional. It fits you."

"You call me sunshine," I pointed out, various and sundry body parts immediately interested in what he had planned. My nipples became highly sensitized strumpets, demanding freedom from my bra, while my belly was suddenly filled with little butterflies that made me feel incredibly feminine.

"That's because you bring light to my life," he said, kissing my neck in a way that had my knees turning to mush.

I slid my hands up his chest as he moved us in a slow, intimate dance to music only he could hear. "And what about you? You have a pretty unique name, too. Do you like it?"

He grimaced. "I don't really think much about it. It might be different in England, but Neo is hardly a nontraditional name in Greece."

"I like it nonetheless. It's better than being named after an intangible object."

"What I like is you. Let's have our wedding night!"

I glanced out the window, laughing as he shuffled us over toward where his bed sat dominating most of the room. Neo had redecorated the room with some of his own furniture, something that was not standard policy at Oxford, but I gathered that the more upper-crust you were, the more the officials were willing to look the other way. "We can't have a wedding night, Mr. Papaioannou. It's only two in the afternoon!"

"I believe we can, my sweet, sexy sunshine." He toppled me onto the bed, following me down, his hands seemingly everywhere at once. We were both suddenly desperate as our garments went flying, each trying to help the other, ending with us in a naked, needy tangle on the bed.

I pushed Neo onto his back when he tried to do the same to me. Although we'd been lovers for only four months, I knew that he loved being on top. "Oh no, I'm a bride, and I get to say who goes where. You get to be my bucking bronco."

"Oooh," he said, his hands going straight for my breasts, which was exactly the plan. "You're going to be aggressive?"

"I'm a married woman," I said with a toss of my hair, but that was quickly followed by a moan when Neo pulled me down to take one nipple gently in his teeth. "Married women ... hoo ... married women ... no, do the other one. It's hurt that you don't love it as much. Married women are bossy that way," I said, a little breathlessly.

He paid due attention to my lonely breast, making me squirm as I straddled his thighs. "I like you bossy. You may boss me anytime. Would you like to impale yourself on me now? Because if you don't, I might end up disappointing you."

"You could never do that," I said, leaning down to kiss him, his mouth infinitely sweet and hot and everything that I wanted a mouth to be.

His hands slid down my belly, and his fingers curled into me in a way that had me rising up on my knees as I stared down at him. His eyes were filled with dark intentions. Sexy dark intentions, ones that warmed me to my toenails.

"Like that, did you?" he asked, and for a moment, I was so overwhelmed with love for him that the world seemed to stop spinning. Everything froze, and in the space of time between heartbeats, I knew that my life would never be the same.

I saw stars, rocking my hips against his dancing fingers. "Oh, goddess, yes. Let's wedding night, Neo. Let's wedding night like no one has ever wedding nighted."

He laughed, shifting me so that his penis rubbed against flesh so sensitive that just the feeling of him, warm and smooth and velvety hard, made a ripple of excitement spread from my belly outward. "I fully intend to make you the most wedding-nighted wife in existence. Are you ready?"

"I was ready months ago. Years. Centuries. Eons," I said, stroking my hands down his chest. He had lovely bands of muscles on his belly, not quite a six-pack, but not far off it, either. "I love your chest hair."

He paused in the act of positioning himself at my party zone, blinking a couple of times. "I'm glad. I like your chest minus hair, too."

"I mean that I like your particular hair." I let my fingers trail through the soft hairs, enjoying the tickling sensation on my fingertips as I followed the narrowing line of hair that moved down to his belly button, a thin line proceeding southward until it led straight to his penis. "It's so soft."

"Beam?"

"Hmm?" I let my hands go crazy on his belly, moving over to the thick muscles of his flanks. He was slightly ticklish here, so I made sure to keep my touch firm rather than teasing.

"Is there a reason you aren't making me your bucking bronco? Because I'm quite serious that if I'm not inside of you in the next ten seconds, it may well all be over." His fingers were back, curling into me again, two fingers making me arch and clutch him as my sensitive inner flesh poised on the edge of an orgasm.

"I don't … Neo, that's not fair … No, don't stop, do it again … I don't … what did you say?" I was having a hard time forming words as his fingers continued to stroke me. But when he pulled his hand from between my thighs, I started to object before suddenly squawking as he managed some sort of sexual ninja move that flipped us both over, leaving me flat on my back, with Neo coming over me, pulling my legs up and around his hips.

"If you don't want me to be the bronco, then you can be it."

He thrust into me, not a gentle movement of a lover wooing, but a man claiming a woman. My hips rose to meet his when he thrust again and again, his mouth on first my collarbone, then my neck, then finally my mouth.

Our bodies worked together, straining for the one shining moment when we embraced the passion that had flared between us since the first time we'd met.

"Too … hard?" he asked in panting gasps as he continued to pound into my body.

"No. Harder. I want all of you," I said, moaning as my body welcomed the invader. I clutched his back, feeling the dampness that told me he was working hard to bring us both to pleasure, the salty taste of his skin as I bit gently on his shoulder. It was all too much, too many sensations, and I gave myself up to an orgasm that left me shaking with its intensity.

Neo was thrusting wildly now, short, hard, fast movements that rocked the bed—then for a moment he froze, his pupils huge in his eyes before he collapsed down on me, his hips making little bucking movements a couple more times before he completely relaxed.

"Jeez Louise, that was … man, it's never been like that before, has it?" I managed to ask, kissing his neck and wrapping my arms around him, relishing my ragged breathing almost as much as I was pleased by the fact that he was still panting, obviously trying to draw breath into his lungs.

His breath was hot on my shoulder for a few minutes before he managed to roll off me.

"No. If this is what being married does to you, then I'm going to have to start going to the gym every day, because if I don't, you're going to kill me," he said, still panting.

He stared at the ceiling, his body splayed out on the big bed like the Greek god he was.

I felt incredibly warm, safe, and happy, and curled up into his side, one hand possessively on that chest despite the fact that our lovemaking had evidently stripped me of all my bones.

"Yeah, I have a feeling I'll be signing up for one of those Pilates classes. I need to work on my stamina," I agreed, and wondered how life could be so wonderful.

A song burbled from his phone.

"You don't have to work on anything," he said, picking up the phone. "You're perfect in every—hell and damnation."

I propped my head up on my hand, watching a frown pull his brows down. "I hope that last wasn't directed toward me. What is it?"

His jaw flexed twice before he said, "My mother," just before sitting up to answer the call.

I debated staying next to him to provide support, knowing he would tell his parents that we'd been married a few hours before, but a general sticky feeling gave my dislike of confrontation the motivation to scoot out of bed with a whispered, "I'm going to get cleaned up," before I made a dash for the en suite bathroom.

The shouting started five minutes later. I'd taken a swift shower, and was using Neo's blow-dryer when I heard the muffled sound of his voice over the roar of air next to my head.

I switched off the dryer and, wrapped in his silk bathrobe, moved over to open the bathroom door.

Neo was striding around the room buck naked, his hands gesticulating as he spoke loudly. His phone was evidently on speaker, because I could hear the high-pitched woman's voice slicing through the air even before I had the door opened fully.

"—utterly ridiculous to think you're old enough to make these decisions for yourself. Who is this woman? Why did you allow yourself to be coerced into marriage? Is she claiming to be pregnant? If she is, I can assure you that it's a trap, and nothing more."

"No one coerced me into marriage," Neo yelled, his back to me as he now stood with his hands on his hips, glaring at the phone lying on the bed. "In fact, the situation is exactly the opposite. I had to convince Beam to marry me. She didn't want to at first. She thought we should spend more time together before we got married, but I convinced her that she's the woman I want."

"An Indian?" Neo's mother said in a voice that made my skin crawl. "Neo, my darling, I've heard about such people. They're all desperate for a sugar daddy, and you—"

"Stop it!" Neo bellowed, running a hand through his hair, the long, silky lengths of it falling effortlessly back from his brow in a way that never failed to make me want to swoon. "You're not listening to me, not to mention the fact that you're being hateful toward Beam's heritage. The term is Native American, and no, she's not looking for a sugar daddy. Hell, she's at Oxford! How do you think she got here if she was so poor?"

I was about to reach out for him, but hesitated, pulling my outstretched hand back, a little pang of pain stabbing into my belly. Neo knew full well that my mother had worked hard to provide for my sister and me, and that we didn't have much money left over for anything extra, like higher education.

If I hadn't gotten the Whaddon Scholarship, I'd never have been able to scrape together enough to be at any good college, let alone one overseas.

"Neo." A masculine voice spoke now, obviously his father, because the man rattled off several things in Greek that I didn't understand.

"I don't care," Neo said, and even from where I stood behind him, I could tell his jaw was set. "She's not at all like that. We've known each other for six months. It's not like Beam is a stranger."

I stared at the back of him, my gaze moving from the back of his head, with his beautiful, silky black hair, down to broad shoulders that never failed to make me feel feminine despite my almost six-foot, solid self. The way his back tapered down to his waist made my breath hitch, and his butt, the flesh pale compared with his legs and back, always made my hands tingle with a need to touch the swooping sides of the gently curved cheeks.

"Darling, about this, you have to grant that your father and I have more experience," his mother said in a cooing voice. "You are so young. Think of all the girls who've thrown themselves at you the last few years. We were right about them, were we not? You must trust that we have your best interests at heart when we tell you that marriage now, away from our protection, is not the action of the mature man you say you are."

Neo took a deep breath. "I told you when I came to England that I would not submit romantic partners for your approval. I won't let you destroy this relationship. You drove away every other girl who showed an interest in me, and they weren't even remotely as precious to me as Beam is. We're married. We're of age. Get used to the idea."

"Do you think we're going to allow you to waste your life on a little whore who managed to get her clutches into you?" his mother almost screamed in a shrill voice that sliced through me with the accuracy of a razor.

Neo must have heard me wrapping my arms around myself in protection from the attack, because he turned to face me, holding out a hand for me. "I've had enough of this. Beam hasn't done anything to deserve your contempt, and I won't let you treat her like this. I'll call you later, when you've calmed down."

I took his hand, my belly feeling as if it were filled with lead. Cold, clammy lead.

Neo stabbed at his phone, ending the call, before pulling me into his arms, holding me tight against his magnificent chest. "Beam, I forbid you to be upset."

"You forbid me?" I said, giving a shaky laugh against him despite my eyes stinging with tears. "Now who's bossy?"

He squeezed me tight, then pushed me back enough to give me a loud kiss. "We'll take turns being bossy, OK? Love, don't cry. My parents can be overly protective, and that comes out wrong sometimes. Don't let their comments hurt your feelings. Our news took them by surprise, but they'll come around, you'll see. They can't help but love you as much as I do."

I wanted badly to tell him that the fury I heard in his mother's voice didn't sound like she would easily accept me as a daughter-in-law, but I really didn't want to face more strife. I had enough right now, coping with everything that had happened in the last week. "Are you sure you don't want to come home with me?" I asked instead, wishing I could beg him to come with me, but knowing that he had to stay to take exams the following week. We'd agreed that he would stay at Oxford, and when I returned with Autumn in a week or two, I'd reapply for entrance to St. Anne's.

"I wish I could, sunshine," he said, brushing away a tear that had leaked from my eye. "But it'll be better this way, so long as you can cope with your sister. It'll be one less thing my parents can hold against us."

The rest of the evening was spent gathering up my things, explaining to my advisor why I was going home right at the critical part of the term, and reassuring her that I wasn't going to let the subsequent loss of my scholarship mean I wouldn't return to finish my degree.

My internal voice yakked at me the whole way home, but I did my best to ignore it. I didn't need any more negativity in my life. Now was my time for happiness.

My stomach quivered in a way that was pure warning of Things to Come.

Sixteen days later

"Do I have to stay here by myself? Can't I come with you?" Autumn's expression was apprehensive as she glanced around the lobby. "These people are so ... fancy."

I knew just what she meant. "Fancy" was my mother's code word for the affluent tourists who came around Santa Fe and Albuquerque. The people who sauntered into the apartment building where I'd come in desperation for some answers was, indeed, filled with the upper class of Athens.

"Think of this as a good opportunity to write stories about all the people you see here," I told my little sister, well aware that I was playing on her interest of being a writer to keep her out of my hair for a few minutes. "I won't be gone long. Pick the ten most interesting people you see, and by the time you've decided what their backstories are, I'll be back."

"Promise?" she asked, taking one of the leather and chrome seats that dotted the lobby, shooting another glance over at the curved, highly polished desk where the building staff stood in a group of three, watching us.

"Cross my heart," I said, giving her a smile filled with confidence I didn't feel, before turning and striding to the elevator bank, nodding at the concierge cluster. One of them detached, a young woman who could easily have been a model, following me into the elevator, using a security card to send the elevator up to the penthouse.

"Of course Neo lives in a penthouse," I said under my breath, my palms so sweaty that I had to keep wiping them on the gauze skirt of the nicest dress I owned.

"Pardon?" the woman who had accompanied me asked. Her expression was one of mild disbelief, like she couldn't fathom why Neo's illustrious family had told her to let me go up to their apartment.

"Nothing. I'm just a little nervous. I haven't met my … Neo's family before. You know how it is when you meet a boyfriend's parents … husband's parents."

She looked even more disbelieving at the word "husband," but evidently had been trained to keep from voicing the sentiments obvious by her expression.

We rode the rest of the way up in silence. Once again, I seemed to be unable to take a deep breath, but this time it wasn't anxiety that was bound around me but fear. And pain. And anger.

I tried hard to push down everything but the anger.

The door pinged open, displaying a cream-colored rug and a cream sofa set against a freestanding wall bedecked with a floor-to-ceiling abstract mural in greens, blues, and grays.

I stared at it, wondering what was behind the wall, my stomach turning over in a way that warned nausea would be the next step. My fingernails bit into my palms as I tried to calm my madly beating heart.

"Madam?" the apartment woman said, giving me a hard look. "I must take the elevator down."

"OK," I said, but it took another half minute before I could move off the elevator, my skirt fluttering slightly at the whoosh of the door as it closed.

I stood silent for a few seconds, unsure of what I was supposed to do. Neo and his family had to know I was here, since the people at the desk had to call up for permission, and yet, no one was here to greet me. Was I just supposed to go around the wall and wander through their penthouse?

My stomach lurched. I took a couple of steps forward, and called out, "Hello? Is anyone there?"

A rustle followed by the click of high heels on polished floor had me straightening my shoulders, and forcing a smile onto my stiff lips.

"So, you are here." The woman who strode toward me wasn't at all what I expected. Judging by the fight Neo had had with his mother more than two weeks before, I expected Mrs. Papaioannou to be a dragon lady, all pointed scarlet nails, narrow, hard lines, and gritty eyes.

The woman who marched toward me was tall and elegant, with long blond hair expertly tinted and highlighted, in an equally elegant sheath dress of deep amethyst.

Her gray eyes were as cold as granite, however.

"I am, yes. I'd like to see Neo, if possible," I said politely, trying very hard not to melt into a puddle before such a daunting woman.

She gave a sniff, an actual sniff, before answering. "It is not possible. Neo wants nothing to do with you. In fact, he forbade me to allow you to come up here, but I told him that I wished to meet you for myself. I wanted to see the truth of what he said."

"What ... what did he say?" I asked, clearing my throat when my voice cracked.

"Camilla? Where have you gone? The documents arrived on that woman who tried to steal from Neo—" A man rounded the corner, pausing when he saw me, but I had a feeling by the polished expression of surprise, and the dramatic pose he struck, that he'd known full well I was there. He looked like a vaguely blurry version of Neo, his dark hair curly rather than straight, and shot through with gray. "Who is this?"

"This is the American," Neo's mother said, one arm across her waist so she could rest the opposite elbow on the back of her hand, tapping one exquisitely manicured finger on her lips.

Neo's father, whose name I remembered was Aris, took a step backward, as if in horror of my presence. "No! She dares to come here, into our home?"

"I didn't steal anything from Neo," I said, wanting to simultaneously vomit and cry. "We got married is all. I'm sorry that you don't like that fact, but it was perfectly legal, because we looked up the requirements to get married in England. Is Neo here? I really need to see him. I need to know why …" I stopped, unable to go on before these two polished, urbane people who were regarding me as if I were a bit of dog poop on their shoes.

"The marriage could not possibly be legal," Aris said, shaking a sheaf of papers at me. "Neo did not have our permission to marry."

"He's eighteen," I argued, still fighting the urge to burst into tears. Of all things, verbally sparring with his parents was the last thing I had thought I'd be doing in Athens. "That's legal in England."

"Regardless, we won't tolerate this attempt to get your dirty little claws into his fortune," Camilla Papaioannou said, brushing past me to straighten up a flower in a vase that sat on the table to the left of the sofa. "The marriage will be annulled."

"What?" I stared from her to Aris, panic welling up inside of me. "I don't want an annulment."

"We're quite aware of what you want," Aris said, jerking some papers from the folder and shoving them at me. "You may think you can get away with whatever scam you are pulling, but luckily, Neo has parents who watch out for him."

"I'm not trying to scam anyone," I protested, glancing down at the papers in my hands. To my horror, they were reports clearly drawn up by a lawyer's office, reports that were splashed with my pictures. "PROSTITUTION CHARGES" headed up one report. My mouth went dry as I shuffled through the papers, confusion, mortification, and horror mingling in a cocktail of hellish nightmare. "MISDEMEANOR THEFT CHARGES" headed up a second sheet, while a third blared out "ILLEGAL SUBSTANCES CHARGES." "What is this? These have my picture on them, but I've never done anything like this."

"And yet, our lawyer had no trouble finding out the truth about you," Aris said, taking the papers from my numb fingers. "Neo was most interested to learn about the woman who had coerced him into an illegal marriage. Very interested. And disgusted, naturally, but his mother and I put that down to the skillful way you trapped him."

The world was whirling around me. I held out a hand, feeling as if I was going to fall, but after a few seconds, the black spots in front of my eyes faded. I looked over to Neo's mother. "It's all lies. I have never been in any trouble. I'm not a prostitute, or a thief, and I don't take drugs. I don't know why you have papers that say I'm the worst sort of person, but it's not true. If I could just see Neo—"

"I've told her he doesn't want to see her," Camilla said, strolling past me to stand beside her husband. "I told her that the very idea of her disgusted him."

"And yet, here she stands. Well, we might as well take advantage of the moment, unwelcome as it is." Aris pulled out a stapled stack of papers from the folder and handed it to me. "If you have any decency in you, you'll sign the annulment papers now. If not, we'll be forced to press charges against you for fraud, and you'll end up in prison."

"Prison?" I said on a gasp, trying to make sense of the madness into which I'd stepped. "For what? Marrying Neo?"

"For attempting to defraud him," Aris snapped.

"You have a sibling, do you not?" Camilla asked. "No doubt she has a hand in this whole sordid affair, but if you want to keep her out of trouble, then you'll do what's right and sign."

I looked down at the papers, wondering what had happened during the time I'd gone back to get Autumn. Clearly, someone had manufactured a false past about me, one sordid enough that it would change Neo from the loving, laughing man I'd left two weeks ago to one that now refused to see me.

"I—I want to talk to Neo," I repeated.

"That will not be happening," Aris answered, his words clipped and as frosty as an iceberg. "Sign the papers now, before we have to take legal action against you. Go back to the hole you crawled out of. We don't care what you do, so long as it's away from our son."

"Go back?" I asked, my brain feeling as if it were swimming in molasses. I seemed to be having a hard time making it work, to think, to figure out what was happening. "I can't. I spent the last of the money to get here. If I could just talk to Neo, explain to him that none of this is true, if I could understand why he left England, then we can put all this annulment business behind us."

"Sign it," Aris snapped. "I promise you that you'll be very sorry if you don't."

I swallowed back a lump of fear that rose at his not-so-veiled threat. "My mother told me never to sign anything without reading it thoroughly."

"Darling," Camilla drawled, her hand on her husband's arm. "Not that I condone the actions this ... woman ... has made, but it is true that Neo can be easily swayed by those who play on his finer emotions. How many times has he sought our assistance with some needy person or other? Perhaps if this Bean—"

"Beam. My name is Beam," I said absently, my mind still whirling around like a hamster caught on an exercise wheel.

"—touched his altruistic sensibilities, it would behoove us to provide her with the funds necessary to return to her home."

I stared at her, the words not making sense any more than anything had for the last ten minutes. "You want to pay me? To what? Sign this annulment?"

"Of course not," Aris said, his lip curling. "That would be illegal. But my wife does have a point. Neo, generous soul that he is, would not like to know that anyone was left destitute on his behalf. We will naturally provide you with the funds needed to return to your home in the States. Two thousand U.S. dollars, I believe, will be sufficient."

"Now, darling, let us not be so parsimonious," Camilla cooed, still holding his arm, the smug look on her face making me want to run away and hide. "Ten thousand dollars is more than generous, but it would be what Neo wanted."

I stared at her for a minute, then turned my gaze to Aris, anger and shame rising within me, but thankfully, the anger won out.

It was useless. Somehow, they'd lied to Neo, and he had believed it. I knew then that I would never get through to him. There was no way that I could fight these people. They had everything—power, money, influence—and all I had was humble beginnings, and a talent for math and programming. There was no way I would win against them.

"Keep your blood money," I said, letting the annulment papers slide from my fingers. They hit the floor with a soft thwap. I turned and walked over to the elevator, pressing the call button, not responding at all when they hurled abuse at me, calling me everything from gold digger to slut. The elevator doors opened and I entered, turning to face them, my body feeling numb, as if I were disconnected from it.

I said nothing when Aris, now red-faced, threatened to have me thrown into the most disgusting prison he could find, while Camilla paced back and forth, thanking god that they'd learned the truth about me before Neo was irrevocably entangled.

The doors closed just as my numbness wore off, and I collapsed onto the floor of the elevator, the tears coming at last.

FORTY-FIVE DAYS LATER

"Beam! What are you doing here? I thought you were in England with Autumn?"

I forced a smile to my lips, accepting the hug from Daria, whom I'd known since we were in grade school. "I was. We ... oh goddess. We had to come back."

"Have you been crying?" Daria looked around the hall of the dorm where she lived during the semester at the local university, then pulled me inside before closing the door. "Sweetie, what's wrong? Where's your handsome Greek?"

"Gone," I said, choking back tears. "I'll tell you what happened, but don't interrupt, because if I start crying, I'm not going to stop."

"Sit," she said, pointing to her bed, curling up on her roommate's bed. "I promise I won't say anything until you're done."

"You're going to make a great psychologist," I told her, then spent fifteen minutes detailing the hellish nightmare that my life had become.

When I was done, she said simply, "So you are divorced now?"

"Actually it was an annulment. I just got the final papers." I toyed with the edge of my blouse, hating the fact that I appeared so pathetic, but needing to tell someone friendly what had happened.

"Annulment?" Daria's nose wrinkled. "Don't they do that for religious reasons?"

"I don't know. Neo's family arranged it."

"Oh, sweetie." She moved over to sit next to me, giving

me a hug that made me feel a little better. "That's just the suckiest of all suckitude. If you don't want to talk about it, I'll totally understand."

"No, I should. I feel like no one understands. Autumn is confused. I'm going crazy trying to find a job to support us. Which makes you my sanity outlet."

"And I'm happy to be that, although I'm sorry you need an outlet. Are you OK?"

"Not really. I'm not sleeping well. I keep bursting into tears at random moments. And I'm so hurt and angry at Neo … and his parents."

"They sound like assholes."

"Worse. Rich, entitled assholes. Ones who came unglued on me when they heard Neo and I were married."

"Just you?" she asked. "Not him, too?"

"Just me. At least, I don't think they gave Neo any trouble. I don't know for sure, because he just … disappeared. We were supposed to get a flat together, but when I got back to England with Autumn, he was gone. His room at St. Anne's, the college in Oxford we attended, was empty. It was like he'd never been there at all. The only thing I got out of anyone was that he'd gone home a couple of days after we were married, while I was here to take care of the legalities to do with Cousin Calypso's death."

"I'm so sorry she passed," Daria said, giving me another squeeze.

"Me too. At times, I feel like my family is cursed."

"You're not going to go back to England? To Oxford? Is the Whaddon thing definitely off?"

"Yes. They won't let me back in, and I couldn't afford to go to Oxford without their help."

Daria frowned, looking at her hands. "This just sucks so hard. There has to be something we can do. Some way for you to get some money. Maybe Neo's family—"

"Ugh." I shuddered. "Don't even mention that."

Her eyebrows rose. "You mean they *did* offer to help you?"

"If by 'help' you mean tried to bribe me to sign the annulment papers, then yes. I didn't take their offer. I couldn't."

"No, I guess you couldn't," she said with a sigh. "I take it Neo isn't being of any help?"

"I wouldn't know. He's not talking to me. I tried to get hold of him through a couple of mutual friends, but they all said he refused to respond to me. So I figured that his parents won. They made up a bunch of lies, and told him, and he believed them."

"Man. I can't even imagine how that made you feel."

I got up, unable to stay still. My body felt twitchy, as if moving would help calm my rampant emotions. "It was so humiliating, Daria. Beyond humiliating. It's like my emotions are swamping me."

"Well, you are grieving the loss of a relationship. I imagine that makes everything seem crazy intense to you right now." She sat cross-legged, her head tipped a little to the side as she watched me.

"What hurts the most is that Neo believed them over me. He believed a pack of lies about me. *Me!* We'd been together for six months! And yet, when push came to shove, he chose his parents over me."

"Yeah, that would do a number on anyone," she agreed.

I spun around to face her, slapping my hands on my legs. "He should have known I wouldn't have done any of the things his parents said I did. He should have known I wouldn't try to use him that way. He just should have known. Oh god, I just can't do this. It's all so horrible. Everything is ruined now. I can't go back to Oxford. I have to get a job to support Autumn and me. Everything I dreamed of, everything we had two months ago, is gone. It's all turned to dust. I'll never forgive him. Them. Never!"

"Beam—"

"I can't. I'm sorry, Daria, but I just can't anymore. I'll talk to you later, OK?" I said, hurrying to the door.

"I'm here if you need me," she called after me when I ran out of her room.

I tried to outrun my thoughts, but even as I did so, I knew it wouldn't work. For better or worse, I was now bound to a past that was a bottomless well of sorrow.

THREE
PRESENT DAY

"No."

"Pleeeeease, Auntie!"

"Absolutely not."

"But you have to! My advisor said that not only could I get kicked out of the Pi intern program—I might not get into another one, and then I couldn't graduate next year."

Every atom of my being screamed. "You don't understand, Ziggy. I can't go to Greece. I told you that when you wanted the Pi internship. I told you that I couldn't help you at all with that company, and you said that was fine, you'd make your own way. You could have gone anywhere else for your internship—"

"Pi was the best! Everything they offered was a hundred times better than the next company on the list. I *explained* all this to you!"

"You did, but I still think you could have found another company—no, stop sputtering at me, Zigs. What's done is done, and you're there. I just wanted to remind you that you know full well what happened to me with that family. I made an oath years ago—"

"Before Mom died, yes, I know, but please, Auntie, this is vital! Dire, even! My supervisor, Sasha, said there's nothing she can do to help me because the order to kick me out of the program came from the board of directors."

I shook my head, rubbing two fingers on my left temple like the growing headache could be stroked away. "That makes no sense. Why would a board of a big company be concerned about a twenty-year-old intern?"

"Dunno, but please, you have to help me. If I do OK with this internship, they'll likely offer me a job next year. Sasha said that they offer ninety percent of interns jobs, and I really, really want to work for Pi."

I tried one last-ditch effort to make sense of the latest batch of shit life tossed at me. "Why is this Sasha not helping you? She has to be in a much better position to tackle the internal goings-on, since she's in charge of the intern program. Surely, she has to be able to help you over whatever glitch has happened?"

"But she doesn't know the Papaioannou family, and you do. You can talk to Mr. Papaioannou. You can tell him to make the board stop saying I've done something wrong, and to not kick me out. You can save my life!"

"I haven't spoken to anyone in that family for over twenty years. And really, I don't think it's a lifesaving matter, Zigs, so you can rein in your dramatic emoting," I told my niece, still rubbing my head. "I don't know why you didn't go in for acting like your mom instead of computers."

"Because I'm a programming genius like you," she answered, knowing exactly which buttons to push.

"That flattery would get you somewhere if I was programming these days, but sadly, accountancy is what puts bread on the table, and money in your tuition fund. Talk to Sasha. Maybe your advisor at the U of Athens could help?" I regretted the desperate note in my voice, but just the idea of me going to Greece to beard the Papaioannou lions in their respective dens made my back twitchy. Especially the thought of seeing Neo. "That rat bastard."

"Who? My advisor? She's not a rat bastard, although she does seem to think that international students are more trouble than we're worth. But that's not important. What is important is you saving me. Please, Auntie Beam, please, please, *please* talk to the Papaioannous."

"No," I said, feeling as if I were sinking in a pool from which there was no escape.

"You can come to Athens."

"Over my dead body. Recall the oath I referenced a minute ago."

"You can stay with me. I'll sleep on the floor so you can have the bed," she said, obviously ignoring my protests. "It won't cost you anything but airfare, and since you were going to use your travel points next year so we could go to Paris, that won't even cost you anything. So really, you'll be getting a vacation for free!"

"To Greece, a country that holds nothing but horrible, traumatic memories," I pointed out, wondering when my life had gotten so out of control that I couldn't deal with one little niece. Except Ziggy was anything but little—she was built like me, almost six feet tall and on the substantial side of body shapes.

"But think of this as your chance to lay ghosts," she said, making me sit up straight, blinking at the serendipity of her words.

"Why do you say that?" I asked, wondering if, somehow, she'd talked to my therapist.

"Because Mom said that you had unresolved issues with your ex and his family, and the psychology class I had last semester said it was important for personal growth to make peace with trauma points." I was silent for so long, she asked, "You still there? Zoom says you're still in the room, but since we're not on video, I can't tell if you really are or not. Did you mute yourself?"

"No, I'm here," I said slowly, my headache growing as I considered just how weird life could be. For twenty-four years, I'd been living my life without anyone telling me to lay ghosts, and now in the space of a week, Daria, who had become an excellent therapist, and Ziggy told me it was time to do just that.

They didn't know the ghosts in question, though.

"Good. So, you'll come to Athens? You'll save me from whatever nefarious plot the Pi company has against me? You'll be the lifesaver I need?"

I closed my eyes against the jagged stab of memories I'd thought were long buried. "Even if I did agree to help you, there's no way I can do anything but be generally supportive. I don't have any connection with the family that runs Pi."

"You were married to Neo Papaioannou—"

"For all of two weeks," I interrupted. "And I haven't spoken to him since the day after I left England."

"I don't care," she said, causing me to smile ruefully to myself. Ziggy was so much like Autumn—just as stubborn and full of a type of joie de vivre that I could never hope to achieve. Everything was a grand adventure to Ziggy, a romp that broadened horizons and made lifelong friendships. "I know you can help. I know you can stop the Papaioannous from picking on me."

I froze for a moment, the fine hairs on the back of my neck twitching at her words. "What do you mean they're picking on you? I thought you said it was the board of directors who took exception to something you did with the program you were working on."

"I am. It is. That is, they are. But Sasha said that it's Mrs. Zola that specifically gave the board the order to give me the boot."

"Mrs. Zola?" I asked, confused by the name.

"She's Mr. Papaioannou's mother. Her name is something with a C ... Carmine ... Carola ..."

"Camilla," I said, more long-buried memories coming to mind. A blush burned up my chest as I relived the scene with Neo's parents throwing their false accusations in my face before attempting to buy me off. "I didn't know she remarried."

"I guess so," Ziggy said, obviously indifferent to the subject. "But that's really unimportant compared to the fact that she seems to have it in for me, and I just know you can make it stop."

While she was talking, I pulled out my phone and texted rapidly to my therapist.

To: Daria

Hey. When you said last week that you thought I was not going to move forward with my ability to connect with men on an emotional level until I laid the ghost of my relationship with Neo, can that be done with me telling the Scapegoat Chair exactly what I think of Neo? Or does it have to be an in-person situation? Asking for a friend.

"What happens if I come out and there's nothing I can do to help you?" I asked Ziggy, wanting to make her understand that despite the romantic "lost love" image of my past, the reality was that there was no way in hell I'd have any influence on the Papaioannou family.

Although the idea that the evil Camilla was picking on my sweet Ziggy made me want to punch something.

"I won't blame you," she said, sighing with a sadness that was palpable even over the Zoom connection. "But I can't do anything on my own, and with your connection to the family, I just know you'll fix things."

From: Daria

Given your feelings due to having to scrap your dreams and take on a job you disliked, then yes, I believe meeting with him would be helpful. You have not had luck with the Scapegoat Chair concerning this issue in the last fifteen years.

To: Daria

Yeah, well, it's kind of hard to yell at a chair for believing its family instead of me.

From: Daria

That sounds like the Beam of the past who had not yet moved beyond hiding behind her pride.

"Auntie?"

"Give me a sec, I'm texting my therapist," I told her, madly typing away on my phone.

To: Daria

Neo didn't want me enough to fight for me. That's not pride, it's hurt, pure and simple.

From: Daria

It's abandonment, yes, both physically and emotionally, but I suggest that the fact that you have not been able to resolve the issues you feel over that abandonment in more than twenty years indicates that it is tied to more than your self-image. I believe you recognize this, since you have difficulty discussing anything regarding your former marriage with any of the tools I offer.

To: Daria

I can't help but feel weird yelling at a chair for marrying me one day, then annulling me the next.

From: Daria

Regardless, an in-person meeting, which is what you asked about, would allow you to say what you need to say in order to move on from that relationship. The Scapegoat Chair, while helpful, can only do so much. It lacks the interpersonal depths that can only be reached by seeing individuals in person, so long as it is a physically safe situation. Are you thinking of following this track to healing?

To: Daria

Goddess help me, I am. My niece wants me to go to Athens to help with some problem at Pi.

From: Daria

Pi? The numerical value?

To: Daria

Pi in this instance is Papaioannou International. That's my ex's very successful company he got to form because he wasn't kicked out of Oxford. And I don't want to see him. He thinks I'm a thieving druggy sex worker.

Ziggy whistled to herself, fortunately giving me the time I needed.

From: Daria

How do you know what he thinks? Is it reasonable for you to make that judgment without knowing for a fact it's true? You didn't speak to him after you went to fetch your sister, did you?

"Dammit, she has a point," I said, staring at nothing in particular.

"Your therapist? About what?"

"Seeing Neo in person rather than unloading years of pain on an innocent chair in her office."

"Huh?"

I made a face despite knowing Ziggy wouldn't see it. "It's something she does for therapeutic reasons. You yell at the chair when you can't process your emotions any other way. The bottom line is that she says I don't know for sure that Neo believed everything his parents told him about me, not that any of it was true."

To: Daria

You may think it's a matter of giving him the benefit of doubt, but that rat bastard never answered any of the letters, e-mails, or calls I made to him. He was the ghostiest of all ghosters. I'd say that was a pretty good indicator that he believed what his parents told him.

"Wow. Your therapist is much more fun than mine. She makes me journal everything. I don't like to journal unless I can use a bunch of anime stickers."

"There's nothing that can't be made better by fun stickers," I agreed absently.

From: Daria

But you don't know for a fact that he believes that you were deceptive and manipulative. He may well do so, but until you can ascertain that for yourself, I'd urge you to think beyond your own biases, and view the situation from his point of view at the time.

To: Daria

Dammit, I'm going to have to go to Greece. I'm going to have to see Neo. It's going to be the most embarrassing event of my whole life, including the time I almost died of shame in front of his parents.

"Are you done texting, yet? Because I'm getting hungry, and want some lunch before I have to tackle the afternoon volunteer time at the local primary school."

From: Daria

You don't have to do anything you don't want to do, Beam.

To: Daria

You say that, but I feel you thinking I should.
From: Daria
I'm going to close this conversation, unless you feel strongly about continuing it further.

I sighed heavily. "Fine. I'll go to Athens. I'll talk to your intern person, but that's it. I have no pull with the Papaio-annou family, so don't expect that to happen. Maybe I can figure out what's going on and help them over whatever the problem is, although frankly, that sounds pretty unrealistic to me."

"Yay!" Ziggy cheered.

To: Daria
You'd better clear your calendar now, because when Neo wipes me all over the ground with his scorn, derision, and all the Mean Things He Said, I'm going to need hours and hours a day to pull my crap together.

From: Daria
I have more faith in you than that. You have come far in resolving your life traumas, and I am confident you will resolve this one, as well. Let me know if you need my thoughts on any problems about which you are unsure.

After a few more minutes of me warning my niece that her expectations were far beyond anything that I could possibly achieve, I disconnected from the call, and stared blankly at the computer screen for a few minutes, trying to pinpoint my emotions. Daria was very big on identifying emotions.

"I feel annoyed," I told the monitor. "And anxious. And really pissed that Camilla would go after Ziggy. I just bet you she found out Zigs is my niece, and she's trying to punish her. If she thinks she can get away with that, she can just think again. She might have been able to push me around twenty-four years ago, but I'm not a naive eighteen-year-old. If she dares to cross me, I'll have a few cutting things of my own to say."

Brave words for someone who can't even think of Neo without hiding from those memories, the little commentator in my mind pointed out. I made a face at it—I thought of it as a snarky lady who lived in my mind, dissecting my life choices with the acerbity and cutting criticism of a Real Housewife TV persona.

"And you can just bite my shiny pink ass," I told the voice, quickly looking up the phone number of a private detective for whom I'd set up a payroll system. I spent half an hour explaining to him that I was looking for my ex, and that I had no idea whether he was in Athens or elsewhere, and although I was now freelancing as a CPA, I could authorize a moderate amount of funds to use for the search.

I sat staring at my laptop for a few minutes, my mind stuck on the irony of having to pay someone to find Neo just so I could give him a piece of my mind.

Two days later, the PI came through with the information that Neo was currently in South America, but had a ticket booked for Athens later in the week.

"I'm tired of living like this," I finally told the screen, making a decision. I viewed my credit card rewards, swearing softly to myself the whole time. I hated to spend my Paris trip points on the trip to Athens, but I'd be damned if I spent one cent more to fly to a country where the only residents I knew hated my guts.

"Daria just better be right about this," I said as I booked my own ticket to fly to Athens. I'd be getting in the evening before Neo, which suited me just fine. I'd meet with Ziggy, and deal with her situation before tackling him.

It all sounded so simple in my head. I hate it when life fools you like that.

FOUR

Neo Papaioannou was furious. Never one to keep his feelings to himself, he announced, "I'm furious."

"About what?" asked the man who'd met him as he collected his luggage. Chase was unruffled by Neo's announcement, as only an old friend could be. "Welcome home, by the way. It's nice to see you again."

"Thank you. It's nice to see you in person, as well."

"Now that the niceties are over with, what's got you in such a fury?" Chase asked.

Neo emerged from the relative coolness of the Athens airport and stepped outside, automatically bracing himself for the wall of heat that hit him with the force of a semitruck. Directly in front of him was a shiny blue hybrid car with a driver lounging against it, looking at his phone. "Everything. No, that's not entirely true. Most things. Hello, Christos. Still addicted to online gambling?"

The driver snapped to attention, his face going a dark red as he shoved his phone into his pocket, and hurriedly opened the car door. "Good afternoon, Kyrie Papaioannou. No, no, I would not think of gambling while I was at work."

"Good. The odds are never in your favor," Neo said, sliding into the back seat, his body slumping against the comfortable cushions, every iota of his being wrapped in a miasma of self-pity, annoyance, and irritation. "Lots of irritation," he said aloud when Chase got in next to him, after having overseen the luggage being stored in the trunk.

"I asked you what you were so mad about. Whew. Hot day today." Chase moved an air-conditioning vent so that the full force of air would blow on him.

"I'm furious that I'm here, to begin with," Neo said, looking out of the window, ignoring the sounds of irate airport traffic as they joined the exodus heading the thirty-some kilometers to the city center. "I wasn't ready to leave Chinchero."

"You did what you set off to do," Chase said, pulling out a tablet to tap on it, no doubt checking e-mails. Chase was a very dedicated chief financial officer, Neo mused sourly, then chastised himself. It wasn't Chase's fault that he was in such a foul mood. "You made miracles happen, according to all accounts."

"Not miracles," Neo said, mentally going over his to-do list that he'd created during the four years he'd been in Peru. "It was mostly greasing a few palms and donating to officials' pet projects. At least, that's what got the Internet access."

"The fact that you had to fight everyone every step of the way makes it a miracle," Chase said, still focused on his tablet.

"I didn't finish what I set out to do, though," Neo said, now irritated with himself. And his mother. Mostly his mother. Camilla had a lot to answer for by summoning him home for some minor issue.

"What?" Chase looked up at that, frowning in thought for a second before his brows relaxed. "Oh, the remote schools? I don't know why you're beating yourself up. You got the contracts set up, paid for them for ten years, and trained leaders in all the communities to facilitate the schooling. It may be annoying to not see it kick into action next month, but that doesn't mean you didn't do everything you wanted to do there. Speaking of which, did you want to stay in Peru for the next phase of your do-gooding, or will you go to some other godfor-saken spot that no salary in the world would convince me to visit?"

"I don't know," Neo answered, feeling petulant, an emotion he immediately quashed when he realized he was taking out his bad humor on those who didn't deserve it. He'd save that for his mother. "I haven't decided yet. There's a lot to do still in Peru, but that can be said about so many locations, not just in South America."

Chase glanced at him. "Have you thought of staying home for a change and running your company?"

"Why should I?" Neo gave a little one-shouldered shrug. "It runs itself fine. Or rather, you and the board take care of anything it needs."

"It's your company," Chase pointed out. "The board has said that they'd like it if you were a bit more hands-on with guiding Pi, since ..." His words trailed to a stop, filling the back of the car with an awkward silence.

"Since my surgery?"

"No. Everyone understood why you were out of the loop for that year. It's more ... well ... you know." Chase looked profoundly uncomfortable.

Enlightenment dawned. "Ah, since my mother has been trying to push her agenda? That's why I set up the board as it is, though. They keep her from doing any damage to Pi while my attention is elsewhere. And of course, you keep an eye on her."

"The board may have been able to do so in the past, but some of the messages I've had from a couple of people say that the power structure has shifted. A few others have apparently been on the receiving end of your mother's generosity, and ... well, to be blunt, it sounds like she's using them as a form of her own puppet regime."

"She's bribing the board?" Neo asked, more than a little shocked. His mother might be many things, but he'd never considered that she would go so far. "Why wasn't I told about this?"

"You *were* told," Chase said, quickly averting his gaze when Neo turned to pin him back with an indignant glare. "You were cc'd on all the messages between the three board members who raised concerns."

He thought. "Ah. Yes, I remember the e-mails. They were several months back, however, right as I was conducting the negotiations for the remote-learning contract. I thought I told you to take care of it?"

"You did, and I tried, although I'm not you, Neo. I'm just the CFO, and an American to boot. The board, as a whole, doesn't have a lot of respect for me."

It was on the tip of Neo's tongue to point out that he counted on his friend to deal with problems, but he had always prided himself on being an honest man. Ultimately, any problem with Pi was his responsibility. "You're right, I should have dealt with it then. The board seemed so stable the last time I was in Greece, but it has been two years since I checked on things personally. I will take care of this problem with the board, and make sure nothing like it happens again. I'll just have to spend part of the year in Athens instead of undertaking projects elsewhere."

The startled expression Chase turned on him drove home just how lax he'd been with regard to his company. He'd always been interested more in the challenges life had to offer than what he'd thought of as the mundane minutiae of running a business, even one as benevolent as Pi, but clearly, that disinterest had done some damage.

And that he would not stand for. He might have set Pi up to run well on its own, but it was still his, and he'd be damned if he saw it ruined because he was too focused on other, more interesting projects.

"Yes," he said, responding to his inner narrative. "It's time I focused on the company a bit. I'll cancel the flight next week to Ecuador, and will spend some time in Athens before I decide where to go next."

"Your mother will be delighted to have you home, I'm sure," Chase said in an oddly strangled tone.

Neo felt his lips twitch in a rueful smile. While his mother was almost cloyingly doting, she disliked the fact that the older he got, the more he proceeded without consideration of her advice. "No doubt she'll be happy for about ten minutes; then I'll start getting lectures about my shortcomings, how I should stop my vagabond ways, and finally what I owe the family."

Chase said nothing for a few minutes, during which time Neo mentally rehashed the last call he'd had with his mother, who demanded he come home to deal with a grave family problem that could well destroy all their futures. Neo was aware that his mother overdramatized things, but her confusing messages indicated he needed to intervene before she caused lawsuits to be lodged against the company.

"What's the name of the man who your mother said is causing trouble?" Chase asked, pulling up a database that Neo knew was normally available to specific law-enforcement individuals.

"Dmitri," he answered, reluctance to continue causing him to add after a substantial pause, "Dmitri Papaioannou."

Chase's eyebrows rose. "Family?"

"Distant. Well, emotionally distant. They're cousins, technically."

"They?"

Neo looked out the window again, absently noting how blue the sky was, and how bright the white of the houses that perched on a hillside. He'd missed Greece the last fifteen years while he spent time working in remote areas of New Guinea, Thailand, and South America, but the few trips he'd made home had always left him itching to be gone again after a week or two. This time, however, might be different. "There's a lot of men in my family. My father was one of eleven brothers. Only seven survived to have children, including my father and his twin, my uncle Okeanos. Their oldest living brother had two sons, Iakovos and Theodor, both of whom are in real estate. Another brother had just one son, Dmitri. Dmitri works with the other two in a green version of their development company."

"That's a lot of Papaioannous," Chase remarked.

"My father and Okeanos had a falling-out with two of their brothers. I don't remember what it was about, exactly, although I'm sure my mother will go on about it ad nauseam if you ask her. Somehow, Iakovos's and Dmitri's fathers tried to cheat my father and his twin out of a substantial fortune from their father. Dad and Okeanos broke with that side of the family, more or less disowning them and swearing they'd never have anything to do with them."

"Holy shit. Yeah, I see them now," Chase said, reading a business-paper article on his tablet. "I had no idea you had cousins as successful as you."

Neo gave another half shrug. "Does it matter? They deal in real estate. Pi is focused on helping people. Our paths don't cross very often, and when they did—this is when I was younger—my parents would simply ignore them. They don't have anything to do with us, and we leave them alone."

"According to this, two of your cousins spend part of the time in Athens. Holy shit times two!" Chase looked up, his eyes wide. "Did you know that one of them married a princess?"

"No." Neo leaned over to quickly read the paragraph that accompanied a picture of a curly-haired man with his arm around a smiling woman with round glasses. "She doesn't look like a princess."

A little pang hit him as soon as he spoke the words. His cousin Dmitri's bride reminded him for some reason of Beam. Maybe it was her dark hair, long and straight, or perhaps it was the direct way she looked at the camera, obviously comfortable with who she was.

One of the things he admired the most about Beam was the fact that she didn't play mind games.

At least, that's what he'd thought.

He sat back, aware of the familiar sensation that made it seem like his heart was encased in cement. Beam was long gone, no longer a part of his life. He wouldn't spare her even one moment of thought considering what she'd done to him.

The rest of the trip into the city was spent with Chase detailing news of his three cousins as reported in both the business and society sections of various newspapers and periodicals.

"What are you going to do about this princess-marrying Dmitri?" Chase asked when they arrived at the smoked-glass and chrome building that was Pi headquarters. Neo felt a familiar zing of irritation as he entered the lobby, remembering how proud his father was of it because it looked unlike any of the other white or cream stone buildings of Athens. At the time, he'd gone along with his father's design, but the older he grew, the more he valued the historical aspects of Athens.

"Do me a favor and see how much it would cost to re-cover the outside of the building," he said, surprising even himself as he strode across the lobby, the reception and security who guarded the access to the offices stepping back deferentially. He might not be a familiar figure in the halls of Pi Tower, but everyone there treated him with the obsequiousness that rode his skin like the thorny prickles of a spiny holdback plant that grew in Chinchero.

"Re-cover as in … recover?" Chase asked, trotting after Neo, who strode to the bank of elevators, automatically pulling out a flat card that would allow him access to any floor of the building, including his penthouse on the twenty-eighth floor. "Is something wrong with the building?"

"Re-cover as in make a new outside for it. Something that blends in a bit better with the other buildings surrounding us."

Chase stared at him in confusion for a few seconds, nimbly hopping on the elevator just as the doors started to close. "OK. I'll get my assistant on it. About your cousin Dmitri—"

"I'll deal with him." Neo made an effort to relax his shoulders, taking deep, calming breaths against the tension that always accompanied meeting his family.

"Fine, but I'm here to help," Chase pointed out. "You may pay me to keep the budget cranking along properly, but I'm still your friend. If you need help, I'm here."

Neo gave him a smile. "And I appreciate that. You're the only one who's stuck with me since my parents forced me to cut all my ties in England, leave Oxford, and go to MIT, heartbroken, betrayed, and lonely as hell. Oh Christ, what now?" This last was spoken when the elevator door opened on the fourteenth floor.

A woman stood in front of the doors, looking over her shoulder toward the personnel office, where strident voices could be heard from behind some soft brown cubicle walls.

The woman in front of them turned her head, her eyes widening when she caught sight of Neo. "Mr. Papaioannou! I had no idea ... I'm so sorry. Er ... I'll wait for another elevator."

The voices that came from behind the walls rose. Neo narrowed his eyes, one hand automatically going out to stop the elevator door from closing. "Who is angry? What's going on?"

"It's ... er ... an American lady," the woman said, edging away before murmuring something about taking the stairs.

"Probably just some visitor," Chase said, tapping on his tablet. "Looks like there's a board meeting at four this afternoon. Your mother scheduled it. Maybe we should—"

Neo, who was no stranger to people who gave vent to their emotions, growing up as he did with a very vocal father and uncle, stepped out of the elevator, marching forward with a determined set to his chin. He understood that occasionally Greeks liked to express themselves loudly, but the woman who was even now threatening to call in an army of lawyers, as well as the American ambassador, needed to be reminded that Pi was not a place for such behavior.

"—I'm not going to let you ramrod Ziggy this way," the woman said, her voice dripping with anger. "She's done nothing wrong."

Neo rounded a corner and got a view of the woman from behind, a tall, curvy woman in a green-and-blue gauzy sundress, her head topped by a straw sun hat. She stood next to an equally tall but less substantial woman who was in profile. The latter was holding up a phone, clearly recording the interaction, another fact that annoyed Neo.

"Not even close to anything wrong," the second woman said. Neo judged her to be in her early twenties. Like the other woman, she also had an American accent. "I double- and triple-checked everything. The whole chunk of code was perfect when I plugged it in to the test server. Perfect!"

"To accuse her of malicious acts is just utter bullshit," the first woman said, yanking her hat off her head, causing her hair to cascade down her back in a glorious curtain of chocolate brown touched with amber.

Neo froze in midstep, staring at that hair. A sensual memory rose effortlessly in his mind, one where hair very similar slithered across his belly, instantly arousing him.

Beam had hair like that. Beam, who destroyed him as no other woman could.

"Furthermore, I suspect that Ziggy is being unfairly targeted by Mrs. Papaioannou—"

The younger woman said something softly.

"—sorry, Mrs. Zola—due to her history with me."

"I understand that you're upset," the HR woman said, looking both frightened and apologetic. She clutched a clipboard, and periodically flipped through the papers on it as if she'd find an answer to the loud, angry woman therein. "But the fact remains that the legal department of Papaioannou Incorporated has seen fit to terminate the internship of Miss Claymore. Simply put, the code she implemented wiped out our entire test server, requiring a full reinstall, and considering that her code disabled both physical and cloud automatic backups, the entire test server department will have to rebuild it manually. That will take hundreds if not thousands of hours, since Miss Claymore's override eliminated all of Pi's storage system."

"What's this?" The woman's words broke through the misery that wrapped around Neo at the thought of Beam, and he strode forward to find out what devastation had struck his servers, intending on demanding answers and punishing those whose incompetence led to the situation. "What is—"

The words dried up on his lips as the woman with the hair spun around, her eyes huge as she stared at him. Color leached from her face, her normally warm-toned skin now tinted in gray.

He stared right back at her, the analytic part of his mind noting to himself that Beam had aged well. Very well. Where she had been lithesome and svelte as an eighteen-year-old, her skin dewy with the bloom of youth, Beam twenty-four years later was the personification of lush, a desirable goddess whose curves were meant for hands that would worship her as was her due.

"Mr. Papaioannou!" the HR woman said, her voice filled with mingled relief and wariness. "Sir, I'm afraid we have a little ... situation ... here."

"Neo?" Beam asked, taking a step toward him, one hand lifting as if she was going to reach out and brush his hair off his forehead, just as she used to do so many years ago.

"It is you," was all he could manage to say, his brain whirling around like a deranged hedgehog on ice. "I thought it was. Your hair ..."

Beam reached up to touch her hair, her mouth parted slightly, instantly drawing Neo's attention. Gods, he loved her mouth. She was sweet, so sweet, leaving him feeling as if he could kiss her all day and never come up for air.

"Neo? That's your ex?" the younger woman asked, taking a picture of him with her phone.

He had a mental image of just how foolish he looked, standing there gawking at Beam, an astounded expression no doubt plastered all over his face. His eyes widened when he took in the sight of the young woman, their similarity in appearance causing his mind to stagger to a halt. "You ...

you're …" He turned back to Beam, his heart both singing a dirge and leaping about wildly in his chest. "You were pregnant? You didn't tell me? You hid my child from me?"

"Me?" The word came out in a surprised squeak; then Beam shook her head, gesturing toward the younger woman. "No, I wasn't pregnant. This is Ziggy, my niece. My sister Autumn's daughter. She's … er …"

"Aunt Beam is my guardian, not that I need one anymore because I'm twenty, but she has been my guardian for the last sixteen years since my mom died. Hi. I've heard a lot about you."

Neo pulled himself together enough to remember who he was, where he was, and, most important, what Beam had done to him.

"What are you doing here?" he asked her, mentally flinching at the coldness in his voice.

Beam must have felt it, as well, because her hand dropped, and she took a step back. Then her chin rose, a gesture that delighted him, yet also infuriated him, because it implied she had the right to raise her chin at him, the victim in their misguided relationship. "I'm trying to help my niece. Your mother is apparently persecuting her because somehow—and I don't know how—she found out she's related to me."

"There are too many pronouns in that sentence to make sense," Neo said with what he hoped was a stern tone, but already his heart, which had for the last twenty-four years remained untouchable, was starting to come alive again.

"Yes, there were," Beam said, her shoulders slumping as she rubbed her forehead. "It's the jet lag, I think. I can't even remember the last time I slept. I think it was days ago."

"Aunt Beam flew out from New Mexico to help me," the impossibly named Ziggy told him in a confidential tone. He stared down when she scooted over next to him, one hand on his arm as she smiled up at him with eyes that were more brown than hazel. "It took her more than twenty-four hours because of some missed connection. She had to sleep on chairs in an airport in Iceland where some douchebag groped her. So then she couldn't sleep at all."

"You're touching me," he told Ziggy, his mind still feeling like it was reeling from the blow of seeing Beam, believing for a moment that she had hidden his child from him, and now oddly enraged at the idea of someone daring to touch his Beam.

Except she wasn't his. She never had been.

"Yes, I am. Do you dislike being touched?" Ziggy asked him, her eyes as guileless as he used to believe Beam's were.

He took a step to the side so that her hand dropped as he said, "No. Yes. I don't know. It's not terrible, but normally, people don't touch me. Even my girlfriends ask first."

She turned to Beam, asking, "You had to ask before you touched him? Dude. That's just all sorts of weird."

"Not her," he said quickly before Beam could answer. He gave her another one of his cold looks. "She is not my girlfriend. I meant the others. The ones who came after her."

Pain flashed in Beam's eyes, making his gut tighten. She turned slightly to face her niece, and Neo had a feeling she was putting shields up to keep him from reading her expression. "The past doesn't matter. Well, it does, but not at this moment. Right now, I'm here to help Ziggy figure out why she's being unfairly persecuted by your mother."

It was on the tip of his tongue to say that his mother would not unfairly persecute anyone, but honesty kept him from saying that. Instead, aware that Chase was standing silent behind him, he gestured toward the HR woman and said, "What exactly is the nature of the charges against—" He interrupted himself, and asked Beam's niece, "Is your name really Ziggy?"

"Yup. Mom was a bit weird that way," the girl said, grinning. "Aunt Beam told her that it would make my life a living hell, but eh. I've grown to like it. I mean, it's no Moonbeam, but still, you don't find a whole lot of women named Ziggy, am I right?"

"You are almost, but not quite, as unique as your aunt," he told the young woman, then continued with the HR rep. "What are the charges against Ziggy?"

The HR woman consulted her clipboard again, shooting him scared little glances. Neo stood silent, aware that most of the employees of Pi viewed him as some mythical being who occasionally appeared, gave the board a list of new goals, and disappeared to remote locations for another year. "Somehow, the prototype that Miss Claymore installed on the test server overwrote several safety protocols, resulting in the deletion of data on both the cloud and hard drive backups," she said, then continued to detail a story that seemed highly unlikely to him.

"You're saying the data is gone? The code exists in our source control, but the data has been wiped?" Neo asked, mentally shaking his head. There was no way that a lowly intern should have the power to access that sort of security level.

"Yes, I believe so," the woman said, flipping desperately through the papers. "That's what engineering said."

"Why was an intern's prototype allowed to have access to the data?" he asked.

"I don't know," the woman said, apparently about ready to cry.

"That's what I'd like to know, too," Beam said, the elegant sweep of her brows now pulled together as she obviously tried to puzzle out the situation.

Neo had always loved her brows. They weren't the plucked arches that so many women went in for, but nice, solid eyebrows, slightly arched, yes, but still substantial enough to give a man faith in them. In addition, they were a barometer of her emotions, varying from flat lines that warned her anger was nigh, to graceful swoops when she was playful. In short, they were eyebrows a man could rely upon.

Except her eyebrows were as deceitful as the rest of her.

"It doesn't seem reasonable that Ziggy, a mere intern, should be able to destroy anything, let alone data. Not that she would write any malicious code, but even assuming that her code was a bit wonky, it was supposed to be uploaded to a safe server. How could that affect anything else?" Beam continued, her gaze avoiding his.

He very much wanted her to look at him. He wanted her to see that he was so over her that he could barely remember who she was. He wanted her to see that he'd gotten along just fine in his life without her.

"Excuse me, Bean, is it?" Chase asked, moving to stand next to him.

"Beam," Neo corrected automatically. He took the clipboard from the HR rep and flipped through the readouts.

"I understand that you are here to assist your niece, but I'm afraid that visitors are not allowed on floors above the fourth. If you would just wait down in the lobby with your niece, we will ensure that a full investigation is made into the matter. Mr. Papaioannou has an important meeting to attend, so I'm sure you won't want to keep him any longer."

Neo opened his mouth to tell Chase that he was fully capable of dealing with the matter, but before he could speak, Beam underwent a transformation. It was as if he'd been cast back twenty-four years to when Beam lit into one of the other members of their college who took delight in picking on her.

"We wouldn't *dream* of imposing on Mr. Papaioannou's *so very precious* time," she said, her eyes alight with sparking emotion that never failed to delight him, her expressive brows a flat line that added to the emphasis she placed on words that she no doubt thought would cut him to the quick. She was meeting his gaze now, making his heart want to cheer, even if it was clear she was furious with him. "But I will not move one inch until I get some answers. I will not allow my niece to be railroaded like I was. Been there, done that, got the T-shirt."

He took a step forward, narrowing his eyes. "Railroaded? You? You're the one who railroaded me, assuming that term means deceived."

"I never deceived you," she said with a near snort of derision, taking a step toward him until they stood toe to toe. "You're delusional as well as an asshat."

He straightened his shoulders and made an effort to look down his nose at her. It wasn't easy since she was nearly as tall as he was, but he made the attempt nonetheless. "You lied to me. You told me the scholarship provided you money to live on, and the truth is you were selling drugs, as well as your ... er ... favors."

Next to him, Ziggy's brows rose, her eyes wide as she glanced at her aunt. "Wow, Mom never mentioned that."

A blush rose from Beam's chest, washing upward until her cheeks were dusky pink, but it didn't lessen the anger sparks in her eyes. "You bastard!"

The HR woman gasped and scuttled backward, glancing around as if seeking help.

Chase had his phone out and was tapping in a message, no doubt about to summon security. Neo held out a hand to stop him, never taking his eyes from Beam's as he said, "Calling me names doesn't change the truth. You were a drug dealer and a prostitute. You lied and cheated and deceived."

Beam slapped him. He stood for a moment so stunned, he almost didn't register the sting from the blow.

"That's bullshit, and you know it," she yelled at him. "The fact that you could believe something so heinous about me tells me just how wrong about you I was. I didn't deceive you—you deceived me. You made me believe you loved me—then the second your parents filled you with a bunch of lies so ridiculous that any sane person could see through them, you ran away and hid from me."

"I didn't run away and hide. You did. You knew I'd found out the truth, and you left me."

Beam looked like she wanted to slap him again, but managed to hold herself back, instead taking her niece by the arm. "I see nothing about you has changed in the last twenty-four years. You're still an arrogant, deceptive asshat who doesn't care about anything but what benefits him and his equally deceitful and asshattish family. Well, I'm not going to let your mom ruin another life. We'll get a lawyer. We're going to fight the crap your mom throws at Ziggy, and when I've cleared her name, then I'm suing your mother for trying to destroy an innocent girl just like she did to me. Only this time, she's not going to win."

Beam pushed past him, hauling a still wide-eyed Ziggy with her.

Neo's brain felt like it was on a particularly daunting roller coaster, one moment building to a climax of anger, the next feeling as if the ground had rocketed away from under him.

"I'm not arrogant," he heard himself telling Beam's angry back as she marched toward the elevator, where a group of employees were clustered. They scattered before her, hurrying out of her way. "I care about other people."

Beam stabbed several times at the elevator button, refusing to so much as turn around and blast him with her angry eye sparks.

"I'll call security," Chase murmured, holding the phone to his ear.

"No," Neo said, watching as the two women got on the elevator. Although they had to turn to face him, Beam steadfastly refused to look his way, although Ziggy, with a wary glance at her aunt, lifted her hand to wave at him.

He waved back, his mind reeling. "What just happened?" he asked, rubbing his abused cheek, still feeling like he had just crested the top of a coaster rise and was plummeting toward the earth.

"I'm not sure, but I assume that woman was from a past relationship?" Chase asked, still tapping on his phone.

"Yes." He bit off the urge to add that it was the only relationship that had mattered, but he had too much to think about to bare his soul to Chase.

His gaze sharpened on nothing as he recalled Beam's words; then he strode toward the elevator, scattering orders in his wake. "Investigate the damage done by Ziggy's code. Find out how it could have affected the servers beyond the test one. Locate the latest backup and install it. Get one of the engineers to work out just what her code did. And tell my mother I'm here, and want to have a word with her."

He rode the elevator to the twenty-seventh floor, where his office suite ran the full length of the side of the building that faced the Acropolis.

Why were Beam's accusations giving him grief? He knew that she was a liar, had hidden the truths of her life from him when they were together, and yet now he couldn't help but feel that something didn't fit.

Maybe it was the niggling doubts he'd had twenty-four years ago about how he could be so wrong about Beam's true character.

Maybe it was awareness of just how ruthless his parents had been since that time.

Maybe it was the stark pain in Beam's eyes when he hurled the truth at her. For a few seconds, her expression was as clear to him as the vision of the Acropolis. She wasn't uncomfortable, or in denial, or even self-deluded. His words had cut her to the quick, and he had a horrible feeling that he'd just done something very cruel.

"I'm not a monster," he told the Acropolis, leaning his forehead against the window. "But I sure as hell feel like one right now."

Then he straightened up, gave the complex of ancient structures a curt nod, and plopped his laptop onto his desk. He wanted to look for himself at Ziggy's code. It seemed highly suspicious that a college intern could write something so devastating.

The thought flitted through his mind that Beam was brilliant at both code and encryption, and perhaps she might have had a hand in helping her niece sabotage Pi.

"If she did, she'll pay for it. And if she didn't ..." His mind shut down at the idea that perhaps he'd misjudged her.

Another piece of the cement encasing his heart cracked and crumbled to dust, followed almost immediately by a deep, searing sense of guilt.

FIVE

"Darling, it's so good to see—oh, Neo, no! What is this you're wearing? You're nothing but wrinkles. Did Chase not tell you that we were going to a party at the embassy at six? You'll have to hurry and get changed. Lancelot, tell Mariah to lay out Mr. Neo's tuxedo." Camilla Papaio-annou Zola bustled across the living room, now done in shades of peach and cream, Neo absently noted, standing still so his mother could kiss his cheek before holding him at arm's length to examine him. "You are so handsome, just like your father, which just proves that I was right to pick the surgeon for you. I don't see so much as a cow-lick where your scar is. And how glad I am that you've come home to deal with this horrible situation. Lancelot, get Neo a drink. No, not that, he dislikes wine. Whiskey for my darling, just like his papa. Now come, sit with me and tell me everything about your time in Brazil, but just for a minute, because I promised the ambassador that I'd be ready to help him should he need introductions to all the right people. He's new, you know. One of those work-ing-class Frenchmen who rose in the ranks, but one does try to dismiss those sorts of social biases when it comes to ambassadors."

Neo resisted being pulled to the long peach couch, irri-tation niggling inside as he made a show of examining the room. The penthouse, like all of the building, was his, but his mother had long ago claimed the living space, telling him that of course he'd need a hostess, and she would be happy to fill that role until such time as she found him a suitable wife. "You changed things again, I see."

"Of course I did. You couldn't expect me to live in a room that positively reeked of the sea. Why you ever gave that designer free rein to do the room in a nautical theme is beyond me. Athens is not one of those squalid little islands. Athens is chic and sophisticated," she said with a tinkling laugh that no one had ever matched. It sounded like a stream burbling over particularly delighted stones.

It crossed his mind that Beam's laughter was much more earthy, a sound that made you glad to hear it. It was infectious, her laugh, and for a moment, he mourned the fact that she had been so cruel to him, sending his life down a path of loneliness and isolation.

Nonsense, he told himself sternly as he waved away the glass of whiskey his stepfather offered. *No one put you on that path but yourself.* "I have no intention on going to a party, ambassadorial or otherwise. What is the problem with the Papaioannou cousins that was so dire I needed to fly halfway around the world at a most inconvenient time?"

"Darling—" his mother started to say, and Neo knew she was going into what he used to call her bulldozer mode, simply plowing over any protests or disagreements and blithely continuing on her way, taking whoever stood in her path with her.

Neo stood resolute. It had been only the last ten years or so that he'd discovered the way to survive his mother's bulldozer mentality was to simply refuse to be knocked down. "What is the problem?" he repeated.

She sighed, patting the couch next to her. Neo, aware that he had to bend a little, took the seat, and was immediately encased in a cloud of his mother's favorite rose perfume.

Beam hated rose perfume.

"Your cousin Dmitri—he used to be that Iakovos Papa-ioannou's assistant, but evidently he was promoted or some-thing—he stole a piece of land from us in Sri Lanka."

"Stole?" Neo asked, a wrinkle forming between his brows. "If he stole something, then surely you can have a charge laid against him?"

Camilla waved a hand in a vague gesture. "He didn't ac-tually steal the land per se, although it amounts to it since he operated in a wholly underhanded manner. There's a de-lightful quaint little town in the mountains that Chase and I thought would be perfect for an electronics factory. You know, gainful employment for all the local natives."

His frown grew a bit tighter. "I don't think people like to be referred to as natives—"

"Later, I heard that Dmitri was in negotiations for the land, wanting to build some resort or other there, and of course, I was horrified, darling, just horrified. You know how we work day and night to enact the Pi motto of leaving the world a better place, so of course I couldn't let that Dmitri ruin the spot, as well as make all those lovely local people slaves to the rich tourists."

"Far better they should work at an electronics factory," he said, knowing full well his mother would miss the sar-casm in his voice.

She did. "Exactly! I knew you would agree that we can't stand for this. I did what I could to put pressure on the local government to rescind the sale to Dmitri, but things are at a sticking point, and I can't help but feel that it would be better if the CEO of Pi would step in to reassure the govern-ment officials that you only want what's best for the people and country."

"I see," Neo said, now having a pretty good picture of what had happened. He was once again angry, this time less at his mother than at himself. "I don't see that it's really an issue worth fighting for, to be honest. Let Papaioannou Green have the land. There must be other locations where our help will be welcome."

His mother stiffened, her lips tightening in a way that was a warning of a temper about to lash out. Neo had long lost the fear of that temper, however, and now watched her with a sort of impartial interest, wondering just how far she'd go to push this particular project.

"Let him have it? Have you forgotten what that side of the family has done to us?" She got to her feet, striking a dramatic pose, gesturing with one hand. "Have you forgotten how they treated us, your father and uncle, when all we did was try to help them? Have you forgotten how after that, they cut ties with us, and when your beloved father died, how they offered no help to me, a penniless widow with a child to raise?"

"I was twenty-eight, and hardly a child—" Neo started to say, but his mother was in full bulldozer mode now.

"Do you forget how I scraped together enough money so that you could start your empire? Do you forget what you owe to me, who sacrificed everything for you? Are you so willing to see our enemies grind us to dust?"

A little headache blossomed at the back of his head. He made an effort to relax his tense shoulders. It was odd that the whole time he was away from his family, he didn't have so much as one headache. "I don't forget any of that, but I don't see how letting Dmitri have a piece of land in Sri Lanka is going to bring about the destruction of Pi. It's far too strong to crumble over something so insignificant."

"If so, it is because you owe everything that Pi is to me," Camilla snapped, her knuckles white on the wineglass she still held. "I took your silly little software company that you swore would change the world for the better, and built it into the powerhouse is today. I've worked tirelessly to make Pi a success, all so you can indulge in your little hobbies. If I say that this deal must be squashed, and that side of the family taught yet another lesson about meddling in our affairs, then that is what must happen!"

Neo bit back a number of rude things, knowing it would do no good to argue with his mother. Instead, he countered her hyperbole with truth, which he had a feeling would put him squarely in the bull's-eye of her wrath, but he'd been in that spot before, and survived. "While I appreciate the help you've provided to Pi, it is, and always will be, *my* company. It is my vision that drives it, and the unofficial position you hold was granted to you because you are my family. You are not on the board, you do not make decisions about the direction the company takes, and you do not issue company-wide goals. Nothing about that is going to change, so in this case, I don't see a valid reason for going to war with any branch of our family."

"You dare speak to me that way!" his mother said on a dramatic gasp, waving her hand toward Lancelot, who sat silent in a chair behind her, his eyes wary as he watched the two combatants. Neo didn't think much about his stepfather, because there wasn't much to think about—he was his mother's shadow, more a lapdog in human form than a marital partner. Neo'd long since come to the conclusion that Lancelot was merely an elaborate accessory, one whose compliance allowed his mother to reign supreme.

"Yes, I dare, and what's more, since there is no use for this discussion to continue, I'm going to change the subject. Why have you interfered with the intern program? I've informed HR and the head of the program to conduct a thorough investigation of the charges that you evidently encouraged both to make against a particular intern, but I'd like to know why you have done so."

"You may be finished with the discussion, but I assure you that I am not." Camilla all but spat out the words. She never did like it when Neo pushed back against one of her tantrums. "And if you refuse to take care of the situation, then I will be forced to do so without your help."

"Mother," he said warningly, getting slowly to his feet before facing her. "I realize that I have no one but myself to blame for the current situation that Pi is in, but that doesn't mean I'm foolish enough to let it get worse. You may consider a war with the other Papaioannous your hill to die on, but it is not mine. In fact, I believe that I will reach out to Dmitri and see if there is a way that Pi can work with his green branch."

"Neo!" Camilla's face grew so red with anger that for a few minutes he was genuinely worried that she might have a rage stroke. "You would not do anything so stupid! Tragically, ignorantly stupid! No son of mine could ever want anything to do with those people. They tried to ruin us! They refused to help when your father died! They did everything they could to discredit your uncle! And now you have the gall, the unadulterated spite, to tell me you will consort with our enemies?" She took a deep, shuddering breath before pronouncing, "I will die before I allow you to destroy your life in that manner!"

He wanted badly to give his mother a golf clap to indicate just how much he appreciated the dramatic scene, but along with being honest, he tried not to be deliberately rude, so merely said, "With respect to your feelings, Mother, I will do as I see fit. What did you do to the intern named Ziggy? Apparently, you have taken a personal interest in the situation. I'd like to know why."

For a few seconds, her gaze wavered; then she smiled a long, slow smile. "Darling, as you just pointed out with a brutal, vicious sensibility that can only have come from you living in the wilds amongst god knows what sort of primitive people, I am powerless, not even recognized officially. How could such a nonentity have any sort of an impact on an intern?"

Neo was not willing to throw the HR rep under the bus despite the fact that the woman had told him his mother was pressuring both them and the legal team to take action against Ziggy. "I said you held an unofficial role in the company. I did not imply you are a nonentity. Why have you taken an interest in the intern Ziggy?"

"I know of no one by such a foolish name," she answered with obvious dismissal. She glanced at the clock and turned to gesture at her husband. "We are late. Lancelot, my bag. As you are clearly feeling the effects of flying from South

America, Neo, I will allow you to regain your temper before we discuss the matter of the Sri Lanka situation. I'll see you in the morning."

"Bulldozer, thy name is Camilla," he murmured as she gathered up her bag, evening wrap, and husband before sashaying off to her party.

Chase entered the living room a minute later. "I take it the coast is clear?"

"Yes, thankfully." Neo gave the back of his head another rub and wiggled his shoulders to loosen them up. "I think, in light of the fact that I already have a stress headache, I'm going to bunk down in my boat rather than stay here."

Chase gave a little mock shudder. "You're welcome to it. I prefer to stay on land."

Neo laughed. "You're the only person I know who can get seasick while a boat is docked. Did you mean what you said about helping me?"

"Of course," Chase said, looking earnest. "What do you need?"

"Some work that an assistant should be doing, but I don't have one since I let the last one go."

Chase gave him a mock bow. "I live to serve. Let me know what you want help with, and I'll get my PA on it."

Neo thought for a moment. "I want to find out where Beam is staying. Er ... full name is Moonbeam Nakai. She has to be somewhere in the city, and yes, I know that hotels aren't going to be willing to tell you if she's staying there or not. I'm sure you'll figure out a way around that."

"Nothing is impossible if you grease the right palms," Chase agreed.

"I'm sure her niece Ziggy's information is with the intern department, but you might as well pull the details on her and let me have them. Next, I want some work done by the engineers. I gave them preliminary orders, but I want a more thorough look at what happened to the test server." He gave a series of instructions that were so detailed, he had to repeat them before Chase had them accurately.

"I'd order all those reports, but I won't be able to summarize or even interpret them for you," Chase said, still making notes on his phone. "You know how bad I am with coding."

"Yes, but you don't have to be. You just have to be a genius with finances," Neo answered, flipping through a few texts on his own phone. "And don't worry about interpreting the details of the reports. I'll look through them as soon as they're available."

"And about the situation with your cousins?" Chase asked, following when Neo went to his bedroom, a three-room suite that had the same view as his office.

He pulled out an old duffel bag and quickly sorted through the clothing that he left at home, and gathered up a few clean garments, stuffing them into the bag before glancing around the room. It had been so long since he'd last been home, it felt cold and impersonal, as if his mother's touch could be felt even here. "I've already dealt with that. Or started to. I've set up an appointment tomorrow to meet with Dmitri so I can get his side of the situation."

Chase gave a low whistle. "Your mother won't like that."

Neo shrugged. "That can't be helped. Besides, you wanted me more involved with the company. That's what I'm doing."

"There's involved, and then there's fouling your own nest," Chase said, taking the duffel bag when Neo collected his laptop case and the small suitcase that he'd brought with him from Peru. "I'm just pointing out that your mother isn't going to be happy if she finds out you are working against her. And speaking of that, I spent the last hour gathering up a little intel from our friendly board members. I'll get a summary of it to you in the morning. I think you'll find it interesting how your mother has been spinning Pi's involvement in a variety of interests that you might find counter to company policy."

Neo was less worried about the direction his company had moved in the last two years, since the few hours he'd spent before seeing his mother had reassured him that although a couple projects had been put into place that he would have no qualms squelching, the focus of Pi had not shifted beyond correction. It wouldn't take much but his time and attention to bring things back to what he wanted. "That's fine. Send me what you find about Beam and Ziggy as soon as you can. I'll be on the boat until sometime tomorrow."

"Aye, aye," Chase said, saluting, and depositing the duffel bag in the elevator when the doors slid open. "Bon voyage, and all that crap. Oh, what do you want me to tell your mother if she asks me why you're missing from Chez Camilla?"

"Tell her I've gone to hell," Neo answered with a grim sense of martyrdom just as the doors closed.

He had a horrible presentiment that his quip might be all too true.

SIX

"Hello? Yes, I'm still here, and I'm sorry that I still don't speak Greek, but there we are. Did you not find someone who can help me? I can speak a little French, and merely functional Spanish, although I don't know that my vocabulary is up to what's needed to hire a lawyer." I tried hard not to scream in frustration, glancing over to where Ziggy sat cross-legged on the bed. Although she had maintained a sunny attitude, I could see the lines of strain around her mouth, and knew she was more worried than she let on.

The thought that Neo and his mother were responsible for that state infuriated me. Pushing down my emotions, I took three deep breaths, and when the woman on the phone explained in tangled English and Greek that she could not help me, I slowly read the five sentences from the language app on my phone. "I would like to hire a lawyer," I said in what I hoped was understandable Greek. "My niece is threatened by a company in Athens. She is innocent. She is an international student at the University of Athens. Is there someone who can help us?"

The woman rattled off an answer in Greek. I had my phone held to the receiver in translate mode, and managed to get the gist of what she'd said. "We will meet with Mr. Panoush Friday at ten," I agreed, hoping that the translation was accurate as to the appointment time.

The woman spoke again.

"My apologies," I corrected myself, typing into the translation app to get my next couple of sentences. "We will meet with Mr. Panoush Adamos at ten on Friday. Thank you."

"Is it going to cost a lot to see a lawyer?" Ziggy asked when I clicked off the call and turned in the chair at the tiny desk to look at her. Her face was relaxed, but I disliked the air of uncertainty that seemed to cling to her.

"Not horribly so, no. Don't look so guilty, Zigs," I said with a smile that I hoped would reassure her. "I have money set aside. Sure, it was going to be yours when I kick the bucket, but eh. I figured you'd rather have use of it to hire this Panoush lawyer than to wait until I'm gone."

She scooted back on the bed so I could sit next to her. "It's not like—"

A loud brassy blast interrupted her.

"Oh no. They're back from their breakfast break," I said, slumping onto the bed. "Were you able to find any earplugs?"

"Sorry, no." She winced when another tinny sound emerged from the room to the left; then a bagpipe started up with "Flowers in the Forest" across the hall. "Did you ask the reception for some?"

"Yes. They pointed out that they told me when I booked the room that the hotel was filled with overflow for the marching band competition, so I didn't get a whole lot of sympathy."

"Maybe you should switch hotels?" Ziggy suggested.

"No, this one is OK. They don't play too late at night, and the hotel owner has three ginger cats who roam the hotel. You know how much I miss my kitty." I waited until the bagpiper ran out of steam before adding, "I take it you haven't heard anything more from the Pi people?"

"Nope. I'd tell you if I did." Ziggy gave me a long look. "Are we going to talk about what Mr. Papaioannou said, or are you continuing to pretend it didn't happen?"

I gave a groan and let myself fall back on the bed, my arms spread. "There's nothing to talk about. Neo is a lying creep."

"He accused you of all sorts of stuff."

"That's because his parents told him that shit, and he believed them rather than me." I turned my head to glare at her. "If someone told you I was a drug-pushing prostitute who stole stuff, would you believe them?"

"Of course not," she answered with a little waggle of her hand. "But I've known you my whole life. How long were you married to Mr. P.?"

"In total?" I stared at the ceiling. "Less than two months, but we'd been together for six months before that."

"When you were eighteen," she pointed out.

I pinched her knee. "You're only twenty, girlie. You do not speak from such lofty distance from that age."

"I'm just pointing out that maybe what you considered knowing each other super well wasn't really that at all. I mean, maybe it wasn't Mr. P.'s … Neo's … fault that he believed that bunch of lies about you."

I considered that fact, my face warming at the memory of the meeting with him the day before. "That doesn't excuse him for calling me deceitful and all the other things he said yesterday."

"No, but you did slap him, and he didn't get upset about that. That kind of says that maybe he felt like he deserved it."

"I doubt if any man thinks he deserves to get slapped," I said, raising my hands, then letting them fall. Everything seemed so hopeless. "Besides which, I don't condone violence. I should apologize for striking him."

"Yeah, but it was probably pretty satisfying," Ziggy said, pulling out her phone and popping in a pair of earbuds before starting to gather up her laptop and notebooks, obviously in preparation for returning to campus for her afternoon classes.

"Very," I agreed.

"Speaking from a purely impartial standpoint, Neo sounded pretty irate at you, like he felt you were the one at fault. He didn't seem guilty at all."

"And you are surprised about this how?" I asked, rolling over onto my side. "I told you that he believed his parents. Of course he had the worst view ever of me. What concerns me is that now that he knows our connection, he might join his mom's vendetta against you. Against me."

"My point is that you both have differing points of view, ones that aren't going to resolve until you talk them out. Tell him what his parents did to you. Then maybe he'll see the truth, and you'll find out what they told him."

"I know what they told him."

"Do you?" Ziggy asked, collecting her bag and getting to her feet, heading for the door. "Maybe what they told him was different than what they told you."

"That's not likely. The things he said fell right in line with the bullshit they manufactured about me."

"Mm-hmm. But you won't know for certain until you talk to him."

I scooted over until I had possession of the entire bed, and rolled onto my back again, lying spread-eagled to try to cool down. The room came with a tiny air conditioner attached near the ceiling, but it didn't do much more than make some gurgling wet sounds, and occasionally emit a cough that would do a five-pack-a-day smoker proud. "Have you been talking to my therapist? No, don't keep picking at me. My life isn't what's important here. Yours is."

"I'm just saying that you could do worse than to talk to Neo about what really happened," she said, opening the door, then squawked in surprise.

Neo stood outside the door, his hand raised to knock, looking momentarily startled.

"I agree," he said, looking first at Ziggy, then at me. "In fact, it's why I'm here. May I come in?"

I got off the bed, gently pushed Ziggy out past him, gave him a long, long look, then said, "No," before slamming the door in his face.

Immediately, guilt poked at me. I made a face at the door, my inner Real Housewife telling me that was rude beyond what Neo was due. I snarled a mental oath at her, and opened the door.

"—has strong feelings about what happened, which, given what your parents said about her, is totes understandable, don't you think? Psychologically speaking, that is. I mean, stuff like that is bound to haunt you, and Aunt Beam has been in therapy forever because of it," Ziggy was saying to Neo, who looked mildly confused. "I had a psych class last semester—oh hi. I was just telling Neo—"

"Yes, I heard what you were telling him," I said with a glare that I hoped she would take to heart. She just grinned at me and booped me on my nose. "Go away, you pestilential child. Attend the classes for which I have scrounged and saved and gone without so that you might be educated in a country that hates me."

"I can stay if you need help—" she started to say.

"Go!" I said firmly, pointing down the hallway.

She turned to Neo. "As an impartial bystander, I'd like to offer my services. If it would help you and Aunt Beam, I would be happy to act as your advocate."

"Ziggy!" I said, outraged. I gestured toward Neo. "He's the enemy! You're on my side. You can't go advocate for the enemy if you are the whole reason I'm here in the first place."

"I don't believe I'm the enemy," Neo said, frowning.

"I can advocate for both of you," Ziggy said at her most winsome.

I pointed again toward the stairs. "Go. No, we do not need the insight you bring from your Psych 101 class. I'll see you later this afternoon."

"OK, but you know where to find me if you need me," she said.

"That would have sounded better if you had said that to me, and not my mortal enemy," I said loudly as she hurried down the hallway.

"You keep bandying about words like 'enemy,' but—" Neo stopped. The trombones at the opposite end of the hall chose that moment to do a sound check, or whatever it is bands do to tune up. "What the hell?"

"There's some international band competition going on this week," I said, studying his face, telling my stomach to stop doing excited flip-flops. "Why are you really here? Is it to hit me with some sort of lawsuit documents? A subpoena? A warrant for my arrest?"

His gaze moved from where he was staring at the door of the room from which the trombones were now running scales, to me, studying me just as I had studied him. "If I told you that I never wanted anything ill to befall you despite what you did, would you believe me?"

I fought the urge to grind my teeth. "Those are door-slamming-in-your-face sort of words," I said, my hands itching to do just that.

He thought for a moment, then nodded his head. "If I revise the statement to say that I don't wish you ill, would you believe that?"

"At this moment?" I narrowed my eyes, my inner self swooning at the sight of him. Neo at eighteen was so handsome that all the women who came within twenty yards of him gravitated toward him, drawn by his face and body and general sense of dishiness. But Neo at forty-two was mind-stoppingly gorgeous, the sort of gorgeous that you achieved only by being in Hollywood or on the cover of a men's magazine. His hair was shorter than when we were together, cut with a slight angle at the back that reminded me of 1920s and '30s movies. There were a couple of strands of silver at his temples, which made me feel a whole lot better about the gray hairs that had been coming in since I was twenty-five. His face was familiar, and yet not … a strange dichotomy of memories that had faded over the years and a familiarity with every plane of his face, every line of his jaw, including the little cleft in his chin that always made me feel wobbly in the knees.

And here he was standing right in front of me, my Real Housewife voice telling me to stop stalling and let him in already so we could start the healing process, but I knew better. "I am not going to strip you naked and have my way with you," I informed Neo. "No matter how much my inner Housewife tells me I need to do it."

He blinked twice. "Inner … ?"

"Housewife." I made an impatient gesture. "You know, like the Real Housewives of Insert Your Favorite City Here? The narrative part of my brain is just like one of those snarky ladies, criticizing the choices I make in life, and offering copious amounts of bad advice."

"All right," he said after a few seconds of silence. "If I promise that I won't be upset that you don't wish to have sex with me, may I come in so we can talk?"

"I didn't say I don't want to have sex with you. I said that I'm not going to indulge in it. That aside, why?"

"Why do you want to have sex, but you won't?" He rubbed his chin. My inner Housewife squealed with delight. "Only you can answer that."

"Smart-ass. Why do you want to talk? You made it pretty clear yesterday what you thought of me," I answered, refusing to be charmed by him no matter what my brain wanted.

He glanced down the hallway as if he was uncomfortable speaking there, but I wasn't about to let him into the close space of my room until I was comfortable with that idea. "Life is short."

"It is. What does that have to do with you wanting to talk now?" I asked, waiting.

To my surprise, he bent forward like he was going to bow, parting his hair along the back left side of his head. "Do you see a scar there? I had a tumor removed five years ago. I went through a year of chemo after that. I've been cancer-free for three years now, and hopefully, will remain so. My oncologists said that they don't expect the cancer to return, but regardless, the whole experience drove home the point of just how fragile life can be. That is why I want to talk to you."

"Because you had cancer?" I asked, my breath tight in my lungs. I fought the urge to hug him when he straightened up, wanting badly to comfort him.

"Because I realized a few months ago that I have been too isolated, and I'd like to reestablish connections that I've lost over time."

"All right, you can come in, although I reserve the right to throw you out on your extremely attractive butt if you say any more mean things to me." I moved back so he could enter the room.

He came in saying, "Not that it matters, merely as a point of conversation, but how do you know what my ass looks like? It's not like you've seen it in person in twenty-four years, and I can assure you that asses change over time, mine included."

"I know because I saw it yesterday," I said, wondering when my life had turned into an absurdist comedy. How had it come that yesterday I was ready to punch Neo in the face, and now we were discussing his butt?

"You did not," he said, standing in the middle of the room, a familiar stubborn expression on his face.

I pointed at the expression. "Oh, I so do not need to see that."

"My face?" He took a step back as if I'd startled him with the gesture.

"No, your expression. I remember it well. You always got that same look on your face when you were unreasonably stubborn about something. And I did see your butt. You turned to talk to your boyfriend, and I could see it in profile. It was nice, very nice. Possibly nicer than when you were at Oxford. It looks like you still have all those swoopy bits, and your pants fit really nice around your butt cheeks. I used to love your butt cheeks."

"I remember that. I also liked yours."

We stared at each other for half a minute. Then I said, "Why are we talking about our butts?"

"Whimsy?" he asked, one eyebrow rising in a manner

that made my inner eighteen-year-old swoon right along-side the Housewife. "Also, it's better than discussing my tumor. Beam, yesterday we both said some things that perhaps were best left unsaid."

I thought about the text conversation I'd had with my therapist overnight. She'd encouraged me to try to meet with Neo again, in a neutral situation, so that we could speak without giving in to dramatic scenes. "Actually, I don't regret anything I said." I stared at him for a second, feeling tears rise despite my need to remain in control of my errant emotions. "How could you believe I lied to you? That I was a sex worker? That I sold drugs? How could you think that about me?"

Neo was silent for a moment, his gray eyes more serious than I'd ever seen them. There was a sense of weariness about them, as if he'd seen a lot in the last twenty years, and not much of it was good. Before he answered, he reached out and touched his fingertip to a tear that streaked down my face. "I saw the proof of your lies. My parents—"

"Wanted me out of your life," I said, trying to hide the sob that made my voice quaver. Angrily, I snatched up a couple of tissues from a travel pack and wiped my face and nose. "And they weren't above destroying my life to make sure that happened."

"Why would they go to so much trouble to do that? They apologized when I went home. They told me they were happy to welcome you to the family. But it was you who told them you'd leave if they paid you."

It was my turn to be silent as I watched him, my mind so full of despair and grief so deeply bound to me, it was etched into my soul. "That you can believe I would do such a thing tells me what I need to know."

Suddenly drained, I sat on the bed before my legs could give out, wanting to do nothing so much as cry out twenty-four years of pain and betrayal.

"You didn't ask them for money?" Neo asked, his voice flat and lifeless.

"No." The pain inside me was so deep, I didn't know how to cope with it. "They offered me money when I came to Athens to talk to you."

"What? When did you do that?" The bed dipped when he sat next to me, his brows pulled together again. "Why didn't you tell me you were here?"

"I did. I tried. I called you. I texted you. I even had your rugby buddies try to get ahold of you. They told me that you weren't interested in talking to me."

"That doesn't make any sense," he said, frowning down at the worn carpet that sat beneath our feet. "I never got any calls. Not from you, or from anyone. You were in Athens? You came here on your own?"

He turned to look at me then. I mopped up a few more spilled tears, shaking my head. "No, I had Autumn with me. She was so excited to be abroad. She got her passport when I got mine, because she was going to visit me after I'd been in England for a couple of years—" My voice broke with the memory of our trip out of Greece, me shamed almost to the point of all bearing, and Autumn disappointed and confused. "I saw your parents. Your dad was alive then. He showed me papers that he said a private detective gave him. The reports were all lies. I don't know where they got them, but they wouldn't listen to me." I glanced at him for a second, the hard lines of his jaw making me want to run away. "Any more than you would."

Neo said nothing, his profile as stark as my heart.

"I just want to know one thing, Neo. Just one thing, and then I'll be done with the whole thing. My therapist thinks it's important for me to ask this because it's keeping me from having any relationships, and given how much she's helped me over the last fifteen years, I believe her."

He didn't say anything, but did turn to meet my gaze.

"Why did you believe your parents over me?" I asked, fighting the sob that followed the words.

"I didn't," he said, his voice emotionless, his gaze skittering away to stare at a picture on the wall next to me. I had a feeling he wasn't really seeing it. "I didn't have to believe them because I found the proof of your … activities … myself." His gaze moved back to me, pain visible in his eyes. "My parents may have told you that they had a detective find those reports, but that wasn't the truth. I found them. They told me that they would accept you into the family, but they wanted to do a thorough background check on you. I told them I'd do it myself, because I didn't want you to feel like you were being hounded."

Anger rose hot and sticky in my belly. "You manufactured those lies?"

"No!" he said quickly, shaking his head. "I didn't have to. It was all there for me to see."

"Where?" I asked, wanting to shriek and scream and punch him in his perfect face. "Where could you find lies like that? I swear to you, Neo, I have never done any of the things your parents accused me of—you accused me of. I don't have a police record. I never have. I don't even have so much as a speeding ticket."

"You must," he said, then hesitated, his gaze searching mine. I prayed for my own sanity's sake that he could see the truth. "I saw the records."

"Where?" I asked again.

"Online. My father had me use his computer to do the search …" He stopped, his gaze dropping to my shoulder. "He had me use his computer."

I pulled out my phone. "Show me where those reports are. I want to see them for myself."

"My father …"

"Show me!" I insisted, shaking my phone at him, anger mingling with sorrow inside me until I felt like my head was going to explode. "Show me where you found those lying reports!"

"I used my father's computer," he repeated, his gaze on mine again. He twisted so he could grab both my arms. "He had me use his computer, his VPN, his access to the police databases."

"Show. Me," I ground out, pushing my phone in his face.

He released one arm to take my phone, but simply set it down on the bed next to us. "No, you don't understand, Beam. My things were still in England. My mother insisted I fly home immediately, the same day you left for the States. I thought I was just going to be there overnight, so I didn't bring any of my gear. None of it. So I had to use his computer, and he had me use his account to access the legal databases. That's where I found the information about you."

"I want to see—"

"No!" he thundered, competing with the noise coming from the various rooms around us as the band members practiced their various instruments. "You aren't going to see, because there is nothing to see. Oh, Christ, Beam." He ran one hand through his hair, his eyes stricken. "You were right. You were absolutely right. My parents lied. To you, to me, to everyone. They set me up to find those reports. They must have known how I'd react if they presented it to me themselves, but by making me find it, making it seem like I stumbled over the truth myself ... goddamn him. My father deliberately did this. He must have paid someone to doctor the databases and make false entries about you. How could he do that?"

"They hated me," I said, watching him, so exhausted I wanted to melt into a puddle on the bed. After twenty-four years, I felt justified in my pain ... and at the same time, guilt rose in me at the agony that twisted Neo's lips. I put a hand on his, the warmth of his fingers making me want to weep again, but when he spread his fingers so that mine were twined around his, I almost lost the thin thread of control that remained to me. "I'm sure in their minds it was all quite reasonable. They couldn't have you married to a poor, mixed-race American, so they did whatever it took to get rid of me. They made you believe everything you knew about me was false. It all served their purpose."

"I can't believe my father would do that. He said ... they both said that they had thought about it, and were happy to have you as a daughter-in-law—" His jaw flexed, cutting off the words. His fingers tightened around mine until I had to wiggle my own to let him know he was hurting me. Immediately, he relaxed his hold, but the face he turned to me was clearly ravaged by guilt. "They told me you tried to get money from them, saying you'd let me go if they paid you twenty thousand dollars. I suppose that was a lie, too?"

I just looked at him. I didn't think my heart could break any more than it had, but at his words, I felt like I'd taken a blow.

"No, no, no. What am I saying?" He ran his hand through his hair again, then, with an exclamation, got to his feet and paced to the window. "Forget I asked that, Beam. I know it's not true. That's the years of thinking ... of believing ..."

"That I was the same sort of bastard I thought you were," I said sadly, the broken pieces of my heart gently piecing back together. "I'm sorry, Neo. I did everything I could to reach you, but I see now that there was probably more I could have done. If I had stayed in Athens ... if I had tried harder to see you in person—"

"You are *not* to apologize to me," he snarled, turning to face me. His eyes were blazing with anger, his hands fisted. "You don't owe me a single word of apology. It's I who should be on my knees before you, begging your forgiveness. And I would, except I hurt my knee last week falling off a roof, and kneeling would be painful until the cartilage repairs itself. Can I sit next to you and beg, instead?"

Yes, my inner Housewife screamed. *Dear goddess, yes. And then let's kiss and make up.*

I laughed, unable to stop at the sheer inanity of my mind. Neo straightened up like I had insulted him.

"No, don't do that. I wasn't laughing at you," I said, holding out my hand for him. He took it, sitting next to me, his knee pressing into mine, which immediately had the Housewife planning all sorts of illicit acts. "It was my brain. It went from being so angry at you I could punch you in the gooch, to immediately wanting to kiss you all over your face. Jeezumcrow, Neo, how is it that you have become even more good-looking? Men in their forties shouldn't look better than their eighteen-year-old selves."

He kissed the fingers on my hand. "You must need glasses, because I assure you that I am a sorry example of mankind. Beam. I can't begin to tell you how sorry, how very sorry I am that I believed the worst in you. I know there's not much I can do to prove to you the depth of my shame that I was too stupid to see a trap when it was sprung on me, but I swear to you that from this moment on, I will spend every moment of my life regretting what I've done."

"That was a truly epic speech," I said, tears pricking the backs of my eyes again. "Dammit, you're going to make me cry, and it seems like that's all I've done since I saw you again."

"I've made you cry," he said, looking like he wanted to burst into tears, too. "Christ, I really am the monster you think I am."

"You're not a monster, although I admit that I wouldn't have said that yesterday," I told him, my heart hesitantly peeking out of the darkness where it had resided all those years. "I ... what do we do now? Part of me wants to tell you everything I've done since that horrible day when I left Athens, and the other part wants to cry over the lost years, while the Housewife just wants to get you naked."

He smiled at the last part, but his expression was serious as he considered the question. "I don't know. I've never been good with people. You know that."

"Not even all those girlfriends who had to ask permission to touch you?" The words were out even before I knew it.

Neo's eyebrows went up.

I blushed.

"That was a particularly good example of just what an ass—no, 'asshat' was your phrase—of just what an asshat I have become. I would like to apologize for the way I treated you yesterday, as well as all the other sins I've conducted against you."

I stared at him, wanting to ask him, but unable to gather the courage to do it.

"Four," he said, one corner of his mouth curling up in a wry smile. "None of them were … sticky."

"Sticky as in you didn't have satisfying sex?" I asked, wondering at the emotions that were twisting around inside me.

For a moment, intense anger fought with jealousy, but then reason caught up with them, and pointed out that he had every right to have relationships once our marriage had been destroyed.

"Sticky as in they didn't last more than a couple of weeks. One didn't even make it a whole week." He gave me an oddly unreadable look from the corner of his eyes. If I didn't know better, I would say he was bracing himself for a blow. "How about you?"

"How many boyfriends have I had?" I asked.

He gave a short nod, still wearing a wary expression.

I let him suffer for a few seconds, unsure if I wanted to bare my soul to him. Part of my brain, the bit that had been hurt so much, wasn't sure it trusted this 180-degree shift. My heart, on the other hand, was warming up nicely, and slowly solidifying from its formerly shattered state. "None," I finally admitted.

His eyebrows rose even higher.

"I'm not lying, if that's what you're thinking," I told the eyebrows.

He gave a twitch that I interpreted as a flinch. "After the last twenty-four hours, the last thing in the world I'd do is assume you were lying. I admit to being surprised that you haven't had sex since we parted. That seems like a very long time to be chaste."

I gave a little shrug. "I didn't say I was asexual. Far from it. I've had sex, lots of it, just none with any person other than you."

He actually looked confused by that. "You … er … utilized one of those Sybian devices for women?"

"I have no idea what that is. I just have plain old regular toys. And you can stop looking at me like I'm weird. I dated a few guys, but it never got serious, or past the stage of a couple of dinners out. I even went out twice with a woman, although I realized almost immediately that bisexuality might seem like a good idea, but it just wasn't for me. The woman in question, fortunately, understood, and she became a good friend until she got married and moved with her wife to California. Four women, Neo? In twenty-four years? That's one woman every six years. I find it hard to believe with someone who looks like you, with your chest and butt and that jaw that always drove me wild, wouldn't have women flinging themselves on you like flies on shit."

He laughed, obviously recognizing that I'd chosen an obnoxious simile on purpose. "Some do, yes. But they always did, even when we were together. It's just something that happens. It doesn't mean anything to us."

"There is no us," I felt obligated to point out, even though his thumb was now gently stroking over the back of my hand in a manner that made all my internal parts melt into hopeful puddles of goo.

"There wasn't, but now that everything has been cleared up, that doesn't mean that there can't be something again."

"You have got to be kidding me!" I stood up, pulling my hand from his, giving him a look that was filled with disbelief. I pointed at the door, saying, "Just ten minutes ago you walked into this room one hundred percent positive that I was the worst sort of lying, cheating, stealing person there is, and now you have the balls, the unmitigated balls, to think that just because you realize that I was telling the truth, we have a future together?"

"I don't think balls can be unmitigated," he said slowly, his face adorably puzzled. "Can they?"

"Don't you even think of being endearingly confused at me," I said, shaking a finger at him. "Because I am not eighteen, Neo. I am not falling for your adorable ways. You wronged me—for twenty-four years you wronged me."

"Yes, I did. And for that, I will be profoundly sorry until my last day on earth," he said, standing and taking both my hands in his.

Just the nearness of him caused me to sway toward him, my inner Housewife making a list of things she wanted me to do to him with my tongue.

"You broke my heart," I said, ignoring the Housewife.

"I did. I'm sorry. I was wrong to not know enough about the world to understand that you couldn't be what the evidence said you were."

"You ruined my life," I said, the heat of his chest when he pulled me gently forward an impossible lure. I leaned against him, my forehead on his shoulder as I breathed in his lemony scent. Dear goddess, how I missed that scent. No man had come close to smelling as good as Neo.

"I'm sorry," he said simply, his arms moving around me to hold me tight against him, his breath ruffling my hair. "There aren't enough words to tell you how sorry I am. I can only plead ignorance, stupidity, and naivety. I see now that my parents ensured that I didn't receive any messages or calls from you, and that should have been suspicious, but at the time, I believed them when they said you'd run off to greener pastures after they refused to pay you for an annulment. Believing them made it hurt less, or so I thought at the time."

I sighed, the mistruth bothering me enough that I had to push myself out of the delightful comfort of being held. "You didn't ruin my life. I did that. Or rather, you weren't responsible for my life—I was. Am. That's one of the many things I learned in therapy, so I apologize for dumping that on you. The rest of it, though—"

He touched my lips, instantly causing fires to burn in deep, intimate parts. "The rest of your accusations are absolutely justified. Beam, what are we going to do?"

"About Ziggy?" I asked, wondering what he'd do if I flung myself at him and kissed the breath right out of his lungs.

"No. Well, yes, but that's a different matter. What are we going to do about us? You said there's no us now, but ... would you be willing to see if there isn't something we could salvage?"

I searched his beautiful eyes, but there was no animosity in them. Just wariness, with a tinge of pain. "I don't know," I said with all honesty. "Twenty-four years is a long time, Neo. We're not the same people we were then."

A spasm of pain passed over his face. "Thankfully, we aren't. I was an idiot in the past. I'd like to think that at least one of the benefits of being older and wiser is that I can see what I did wrong, and make sure I don't repeat those mistakes."

I wanted him. That thought both startled me and made perfect sense. Of course I still wanted him. I never stopped wanting him, even in the worst moments of pain and despair. No one could ever live up to his memory, not that I ever tried to move past it. "By the goddess, she was right," I said, a revelation striking me with the force of a meteor hitting the earth.

"Ziggy?" Neo asked, looking adorably confused again. I wanted to chastise him for that, because at best, I looked vapid when I was confused by something.

"No, my therapist. She said all along that the reason I couldn't do more than last a date or two was because I clung to the memory of what we had, and I would not—could not—give it up. She is a genius, Neo, a genius. It's almost scary how well she knows me."

"Does that mean there's hope for us?" he asked, going to pull me to him again, but I stepped back. I felt like the only way I could think was if I had a bit of distance from him. "Are you willing to forgive me?"

"Forgiveness doesn't happen at a snap of the fingers," I said, even though my own heart had decided that it was ready to do just that. "It takes time."

"I understand," he said, his arm dropping, leaving me feeling bereft. I yelled at myself for falling so quickly back into a state where he was everything to me. The deeply wounded part of my psyche was still waiting for the other shoe to drop, half-expecting him to turn on me again. That hurt, I knew, would take a while to heal. "You need to be courted. You want me to prove myself to you. I accept your terms."

I laughed, shaking my head at him. "You always were so literal. I don't need to be courted, Neo. I'm not sure we—both of us—can come back from the past, and all the time that has passed since then, but I'm willing to …" I stopped, unsure how to put into words my feelings.

Jump his bones, my inner Housewife urged. *Fall madly in love with him again. Live happily ever after.*

"Try?" he suggested, his eyes watchful.

"Yes," I said after a moment of soul-searching. "I'm willing to get to know you, the you who is Neo now, and let you find out what there is to know about me. If it turns out we're just not meant to have a romantic relationship, then we'll have learned that, and we can both move on."

My Housewife laughed insanely at that last thought.

He shook my hand before lifting it to his mouth. "I agree. We can start by—damn." He released my hand to pull out his phone, which was giving a pulsing beep. "I have to go. I'm late for a meeting."

Before I could say anything, he was out the door. I stared in confusion after him, about to comment on his rudeness when his arm extended through the partially open door. "Come with me?"

"Go where?" I asked, taking his hand without thinking.

He pulled me up against his side as he hustled me down the hallway toward the stairs. "A meeting with my cousins. I've never met them before, and I'd appreciate having a friend on my side, since the situation might well be filled with hostility and acrimony."

"You really know how to woo a woman," I told him, suddenly filled with joy so sweet that once again it brought tears to my eyes.

I might not have the future with Neo that I had always hoped for, but at least, with him acknowledging the truth of our past, I felt like we'd started down a path to friendship.

My Housewife warned that wasn't going to be enough, but I ignored her. It might be all I was given. It would have to do.

SEVEN

"I don't remember you mentioning cousins."

Neo felt alternately an anger so deep it seemed to boil his blood, and guilt that seared his soul. There was also a fair dollop of shame in the mix, enough to make him call himself any number of names for being so gullible in the past, but he couldn't focus on that now.

"You were your parents' only child, right? I don't think I ever heard you mention your uncle with the water name having kids."

That he could so wrong Beam, lovely, innocent Beam, spoke a lot to the folly of man. No, he corrected himself, the folly in question was his alone. He had been responsible for hurting Beam, not anyone else. Not even his parents. He could have stopped them. He could have sought out Beam to confront her, to learn the truth, to let her tell her story, but he hadn't.

And he'd carry the weight of that guilt for the rest of his life.

"Neo?"

"Hmm?"

"You're the one who dragged me out of my perfectly nice, if noisy, hotel room. If you wanted to ignore me, why did you make me leave when I could have lain on the bed naked, applying damp cloths in an attempt to cool down?"

He'd make it up to her, he swore to himself. He didn't care what it took; he'd prove to her that he was a changed man. He'd make her understand that he wouldn't be happy without her at his side.

"I mean, seriously. How do you cope with this heat? Not that I'm unused to high temps. New Mexico can get hot. Very dry and hot. But we have air-conditioning. It doesn't seem as prevalent here as I'd expect."

He didn't even wonder at the knowledge that Beam was necessary to his happiness. He had a niggling feeling that the truth had always been there, buried under layers of recrimination and pain, anger, and a sense of betrayal that now he was ashamed of ever having felt. "Your therapist is a genius."

Beam stared at him. "I mean, she is, but why would you say that?"

"Because what she said about you applies to me, too."

"You have an unnatural aversion to spiders, as well?"

He gave her a long look.

She giggled. It was normally a sound that made him feel slightly itchy, but a giggle as performed by Beam was unlike any other woman's giggle. Hers was delightful, indicating a sense of humor that he had always loved. "Sorry, I couldn't help that. I assume you mean she was right about our past relationship making it difficult to have romantic connections with other people?"

"Yes." Her words penetrated the miasma of guilt and self-recrimination that surrounded him. "You want to get naked?"

"Well, not here," she said, looking scandalized, casting a worried glance toward the driver. "And I really only said that to see if you were listening to me. You weren't, by the way."

"I was, I was just busy mentally lashing myself," he said, his mind now full of images of Beam lying on the bed on his boat, her hair splayed across his chest and belly. He wondered if she liked sailing, and one thing led to another until he was picturing her on a hammock with her long, luscious legs wrapped around him while he plunged into her again and again.

She said nothing for half a minute, then put her hand on his, giving it a little squeeze. "You don't have to do that, you know."

"Have a hammock put in my bedroom?" he asked, trying to decide where in the cabin to put a small hammock that would double as a sex swing. "It will fit, I think, if it is put in the corner where an unused armoire sits. There should be enough room in that corner for you to sit in the hammock, and allow me to rock you in ways that should give immense pleasure."

Slowly, she turned to look at him, her eyes wide, her pupils dilating even as he twined his finger through hers before resting their joined hands on his thigh. "You have a sex swing in your bedroom? I thought you said you didn't have a lot of girlfriends? Why do you have a sex swing if you don't have sexual partners? Wait, did you try bisexuality, too? Have you had boyfriends? Is that why there's only been four girlfriends in twenty-four years?"

"Yes, I tried it, but that was the summer before I went to Oxford," he admitted, not even surprised that he would tell Beam something so intimate. "The psychologist my parents sent me to explained that it was merely an experimental stage common to young men and women in their teens. Like you, I decided that it wasn't something that I wanted to pursue. And for the record, I do not have a sex swing. I was thinking about a hammock that could double as one, but it could also be used to simply sit in, or even lie down if it's big enough. The swaying might be nice."

"I think I'm just going to move past this part of the conversation, and tell you that you don't have to martyr yourself."

"I wasn't aware that I was," he said, unhappy when she pulled her hand from his to check her phone, which had pinged.

"Neo, I know you feel guilty about what happened. But I wouldn't be honest if I didn't point out that although I would like to believe I'm the blameless victim, the reality is that after I visited Athens, I gave up trying to contact you. That was stupid of me. I should have kept trying until I reached you. And before you say what you look like you want to say, don't. We're both to blame. I think until we reach the point where we can both accept that, we're not going to be able to put the past behind us."

"And you're willing to do that?" he asked, hope blooming deep in his chest.

"I would not be sitting here in this fancy car with you if I didn't think it was worth seeing if we can move forward. Tell me about this cousin we're meeting."

He cherished the feeling of blossoming warmth in what he'd thought of as the cold, dead parts of his soul. Only Beam could bring light to them, light and hope. He wasn't certain whether he could do as she asked and share the blame for the past, when it was clear to him that he was solely at fault, but if that's what it took to bring her peace, then he'd try. "There are three cousins on that branch of the family. I've never met any of the cousins due to a family disagreement that happened years ago, when I was young. My father and Uncle Okeanos were twins, you know, and they always backed each other against the rest of the family. The cousins' fathers had some sort of an agreement to go into business with my father and uncle, but then they stole my father's investment, and kicked him and Okeanos out of the company, leaving them to start over from scratch."

"Wow, that's pretty evil for family to do to each other," Beam commented, looking up from her phone. "Sorry, I wasn't ignoring you. I just had to tell Ziggy that I haven't killed you, and I'm not bonking your brains out—her words, by the way—either of which she apparently expected to happen after she went to class. Why are you meeting with the cousins if they did your family a nasty?"

Neo was distracted a moment by the brush of Beam's hair against his arm. He breathed deeply, just catching the scent of a sun-warmed woman, something he hadn't considered even remotely arousing until that moment. He felt himself becoming hard, and shifted slightly, telling himself that he would be damned if he marched into a meeting with his hostile cousins sporting a raging erection. "As I said earlier, life is short. My mother is bent on stirring up a vendetta against the cousins; I don't think she has any grounds to do so. Instead of arguing with her, I've decided to meet with them and get their side of the situation. Also, I'd like to meet them. They are family, even if that side is estranged from mine."

"I've never had family other than Mom and Autumn, my cousin, and Ziggy," Beam said, sadness tingeing her voice. "I can't imagine what it's like to have three cousins that you've never even met."

"Oh, I have more than three cousins." He tried to count, but his parents' isolation from the rest of the elder Papaioannou brothers gave him a hazy idea as to the total number of relatives. "There were seven brothers who had children. I think there are ten or twelve cousins, but I'd have to ask my mother to be sure."

He didn't miss the face that Beam made in response to the mention of his mother, but he pushed aside the thought of the lengthy conversation he would need to have with Camilla. Although his father had been the one pushing him to look for information on Beam, the words she'd thrown at him the day before indicated that his mother was complicit, as well.

"Are you sure you want me to be at this meeting? If it's going to be so dicey, maybe I should just wait for you, and bolster your sagging spirits afterward?"

"On the contrary, I'd much rather have you bolstering before all the sagging begins."

"But what about your cousins? Won't they be annoyed if you march in with a stranger?" she asked, looking genuinely distressed.

"I'm just as much a stranger to them as you are. Would it make you uncomfortable to be there?" he asked, concerned that he was being selfish and asking too much of her too quickly.

"No," she said slowly after a moment's thought. "I just don't want to be responsible for screwing anything up if you are trying to mend fences with your family."

"You couldn't possibly do anything to upset anyone, and as I said, I'd appreciate having someone in my corner there. I don't have an assistant anymore, and Chase—a friend who's also CFO at Pi—is busy working on other things for me." He stopped, a thought striking him. "That's one of the reasons why I wanted to see you today."

"Your friend?" Beam asked, tucking away her phone.

"No, what he's looking into for me."

"And here I thought you wanted to work out the issues of the past," she said in a light tone that sounded oddly strained.

Neo studied her face, his heart warming at the sight of her bright, interested eyes. He almost couldn't believe she was there, next to him, but his body was all too aware of her nearness. "I did. But I also ran across something last night when I was poking around in the backup server. Do you remember Beowulf?"

Her gaze, which had skittered away, snapped back to his, those glorious eyebrows pulling ever so slightly together. "Beowulf? Your four-month anniversary present? I remember I gave it to you, but I couldn't tell you what the code was."

"I can. It demonstrated how businesses were losing potentially vast sums of money because they stopped calculating money at three decimal points. Your program took the fact that so many transactions have fractions that reconciliation programs ignore, and diverted those fractions and dumped them into a reserve account."

"Oh, now I remember," she said, a slow smile making the delicious line of her lower lip curve. "We figured out that if we could just run that program on a bank or somewhere, we could be millionaires. What made you think of that?"

"I saw a mention of it last night," he said, his mind busy

trying to sort the facts that had been slowly cycling through his head since he had studied the backup server earlier that morning. "It was in a deletion log. I wondered why the code would be on there, since I haven't seen it in a long time. A modified version of it was integrated into the Pi accounting code, of course, but I handled that myself eighteen years ago when I was writing the core programs. No one else had access to the code. I've kept it off-line, on a drive that's locked in a safe."

"Does it have something to do with Ziggy?" Beam asked, looking worried.

"No. I can't see how it could. According to what I saw last night, she was working on a program to facilitate the creation and deployment of interactive software providing health apps for vulnerable girls and women in third world locations."

"She said she was working on something that would help teen girls who were denied education when they had their periods, which is why I thought it was so strange that your mother should claim she was doing something to harm your company. I thought Ziggy's project was the sort of thing Pi did."

"It is. It should be." He slotted a few more thoughts into the compartments that made up his mind. "I haven't been watching it as closely as I should. When I got the news that the cancer was gone, I decided that I wouldn't risk getting sick again before I accomplished what I wanted to do. So I went off to South America and tackled two educational infrastructures there."

"That sounds very worth your time," she said, her expression unreadable.

"It was. But it meant that I dumped the running of Pi on the board, who admittedly I handpicked just for that purpose, but still. Chase is right that I should have been keeping a better eye on things. Ah. It looks like we're here." He assessed her expression, wishing that either he was better at reading her face or she would tell him everything she felt, as she did when they were younger. "Are you sure you're willing to join me?"

"Yes," she said with a dismissive shrug of one shoulder, taking the hand he held for her once they emerged from the car. "As long as you're sure my presence won't ruin any negotiations, I'll be happy to tag along. To be honest, I'm kind of curious to see these nefarious cousins. Will they yell, do you think? Normally, I don't like it when people get shouty, but a few years ago I had an obnoxious neighbor who had some serious anger management issues, so Ziggy and I took a self-defense class just in case he got physical. I'm not saying I could stop an outright fight between you and your cousins, but I can flip a two-hundred-pound man over my hip. Ziggy was better than me, but she was sixteen at the time, and you know how kids are at that age—walking bags of hormonal rage."

"I very much want to hear about the class, as well as how you ended up with your niece, but that aside, I won't require you to be my bodyguard. I did some martial arts training in my midtwenties, and will happily flip any and all attacking cousins over my own hips." He tucked her hand firmly in the crook of his arm and squared his shoulders, mentally girding his loins, and reminding himself that he wasn't alone. Beam was with him, and just the warmth of her body next to his gave him a comfort he hadn't felt for decades.

"I have to admit, I'd kind of like to see that. Not that I want your cousins to get all pissy with you, but seeing you defend yourself would be fun. Wait, that came out wrong. I didn't mean I want you to get beat up ... Oh, never mind."

He laughed and gave her fingers another squeeze, just because he loved her long, sensitive fingers. "I know what you mean, don't worry." He stopped at a security desk and gave his name, explaining that Beam was accompanying him. They accepted their visitors' badges and proceeded through the metal detector.

It took him three times before he made it through without setting off the alarm.

"Do you, like, have some sort of gentlemen's personal equipment piercing?" Beam asked, staring pointedly at his fly.

"No, and if you keep staring, you're going to make it difficult for me to walk. Yes, that is all the metal I have." He patted down his pockets to make sure he hadn't missed anything. "Other than a few titanium fillings in my teeth, I don't have any metal attached to my body."

The security officer used a handheld wand to go over him, but it gave off the same indicator that he was carrying a weapon.

"Oh dear. Is it strip search time?" Beam asked, clearly fighting a smile.

Neo sighed and held his arms wide again as the officer went over him again with the wand. "I trust it won't come to that. I have a tendency to set off metal detectors. I swear they have something against me. Even the one in Pi Tower that's specially calibrated to allow me a few seconds to get through still sometimes goes off if I linger too long."

"Is there a problem?" a young man asked, stopping in front of them. He looked to be in his late twenties and spoke in Greek.

"Just my personal body chemistry creating havoc, as usual," he answered in English. "I'm Neo Papaioannou, and this is Beam Nakai … er …" He glanced at Beam. "Did you keep my name?"

Her shoulders squared as she sucked in an indignant breath. "Of course not! You *annulled* me. I wasn't going to use your name after that."

"I didn't annul you. Or rather, I did, but only because my parents …" He became aware that the young man in front of them was watching with interest. "Let's leave that discussion for another time when I'm not at risk of being escorted to a back room for a cavity search."

The young man laughed, and switched to English, as well. "I don't think it will go quite that far. I'm Alexis Condos, a junior broker for Papaioannou Green. Dmitri sent me down to bring you to the meeting. Hello, Beam. That's an interesting name. I'm sorry you were annulled. I think you can stop, Arsenio," he said to the security guard, who was determinedly running the wand over Neo's body, *tsk*ing every time the alarm went off. "I think we'll risk Mr. Papaioannou smuggling in an arsenal. If you'd please come this way."

Alexis and Beam chatted about Athens as they rode the elevator to the top floor, Neo finding great pleasure in the fact that when they entered what was obviously a conference room, Beam took his hand with a firm squeeze that he knew was an expression of support.

The fact that she would do so warmed yet another part of his cold, dead heart, bringing it back to life. He couldn't remember the last time someone tried to provide him with comfort and support.

He stopped right at the door, spinning around and putting his hands on her upper arms, ignoring the three men who had been clustered together at the far end of the room. He looked down into her startled eyes and said in a voice pitched for her ears only, "Did you ever imagine that this would happen?"

She leaned out to look around him at the others before straightening up and whispering, "That you would meet your cousins?"

"No, that you and I would be here, together. Supporting one another. Here for each other. Friends again."

"Neo, is this really the time for a relationship discussion? Because we've been friends for about an hour now, and I'm not sure this is the point where we should be reevaluating what we have or don't have together. In fact, the phrase *insanely, intensely premature* comes almost immediately to mind."

He kissed the tip of her nose, making her eyes cross as he did so. "It was a thought that just occurred to me. Ready?"

"Are you on any sort of medication I should know about?" she asked him, her face scrunching up in a manner that delighted him to no end. "And if so, did you take all of it this morning? No, Neo, don't answer. Just stop stalling. I won't let them do anything mean to you, OK?"

He fought the urge to kiss her properly, his spirits soaring for the first time in decades. How had he ever been so idiotic as to let her go? "Eighteen is an exceptionally stupid age, and especially so when it came to me," he told her, and, without waiting for her to reply, spun around and with one hand on Beam's arm strode forward, his free hand outstretched. "Good afternoon. I am Neo, and this is Beam, my ex-wife. She's American, and doesn't speak Greek. You must be my cousins. I'm sorry it's taken so long for us to get to know each other."

"We are," the tallest of the trio said. Neo was very aware that the cousins had presented a solid front, their expressions not forbidding but not very welcoming, either. At a nod from one of the other men, Alexis left the room with a murmur about doing some work elsewhere. "I am Iakovos. This is my brother, Theo, and our cousin Dmitri. Er ... your ex-wife?"

Neo shook hands with all three cousins, noting that although the two brothers had a vague similarity, neither man looked like Dmitri or himself. "Yes. It's a long story, and one that's a bit touchy right now, but Beam has thankfully returned to my life. These are my cousins, Beam."

"So I gathered," she said, shaking their hands with a polite smile, but he couldn't help be pleased that she remained close to his side. "It's a pleasure to meet all of you."

The three cousins shared a glance amongst themselves before turning back to Neo. "It would appear that we have something more in common than just family," Dmitri said, his expression guarded. "I'm told that you have been in contact with a broker in Sri Lanka about a piece of land we acquired."

"Ah. Straight to the point," Neo said, nodding. "Are you neurodivergent, too?"

Dmitri's eyes widened a little. "Not that I know of," he said after a moment's silence.

"Are you?" Theo asked, his eyebrows rising.

"I've been told I am. I don't see it, myself, but I wondered if it was a family trait." He glanced around the room, then asked, "Would it be possible to get some water? Beam has only been in Athens for a day, and I neglected to ask her if she was fully hydrated given the temperatures we've been having this summer."

"Would you excuse us just a minute?" Beam asked, taking him by the arm and pulling him after her to the far side of the room. Once she got him there, she asked in a furious whisper, "What the hell are you doing?"

"Asking for water? I thought you might want some. You look dehydrated."

She pinched his wrist. "I do not! Why are you being so weird around your cousins?"

He rubbed his face, trying to balance the need to sing and dance about Beam being there with him, and the knowledge that he had to fix whatever was wrong between him and his estranged family. "I don't like conflict?"

"Don't give me that shit," she said with a knowing glance. "You love to debate."

He leaned close and said softly in her ear, "I'm uncomfortable. I say things like that when I'm uncomfortable."

Her pupils flared at his nearness, and he knew she was feeling the same pull of attraction that he did. "Since when?" she asked.

"The last twelve or so years," he said after a moment's thought. "It's gotten worse with time. It's one reason why I'm normally by myself. If no one else is around me, then it doesn't matter what I say."

The look she gave him was long and searching. Then she made a quick nod, and turned him around, giving a little push toward the group of cousins, who had now moved halfway down the table. "You're not alone now. Go dig out that charm that used to drop all the female students at twenty paces, and make peace with your family. I'll be right here with you."

"One moment," he told the cousins' expectant faces, then spun around, pulled Beam into his arms, and kissed her with all the joy, gratitude, and warmth that had awoken inside him. "I'm going to fall in love with you again," he told her, then turned again and returned to the clutch of cousins. "My apologies. I'm nervous, and I say things that many people find awkward when I'm nervous, but as Beam has reminded me, you are family."

To his surprise, Iakovos, the most intimidating of the cousins, gave a slight smile, then tipped his head in acknowledgment. "Relations between our respective sides of the family have been strained, so I believe we can overlook any awkwardness this meeting triggers. Please, take a seat, both of you. We will be happy to provide Beam with whatever beverage she desires."

"See?" Neo said, escorting Beam to a chair and pulling it out for her. "Even Iakovos thinks you look dehydrated."

Beam burst into laughter, making his formerly stone heart stir.

He had a feeling, a very strong feeling, that his life wasn't ever going to be the same since she'd come back into it. He just hoped that was a good change, and not a harbinger of doom.

EIGHT

"Stop looking so smug," I told Neo a half hour later, when I'd drunk three glasses of deliciously cold iced lemon water. "Athens isn't any hotter than New Mexico. You guys just have fewer buildings with air-conditioning."

He smiled at me, the laughter reaching his eyes in a way that had my inner Housewife making a list of smutty things to do to him, then turned back to his cousin Dmitri as the two men discussed just what Neo's mother and uncle had tried to do.

I studied the three men, trying to find a family resemblance to Neo, but found none. Oh, it was true they were all fairly tall, were handsome, and had manners that, once they unbent, were charming, but none of them touched Neo's drop-dead gorgeous face, too-sexy-for-his-own-good body, and delightfully quirky personality.

A warm glow of happiness continued to beam inside of me as I cherished the words he'd spoken, but more, the fact that he obviously wanted me there with him. I wondered what sort of life he'd lived since we'd parted. He said he'd had relationships, and although he had a smooth, polished manner when he wanted to exude it, underneath it I could sense a solitary being that called to me.

"—I will admit to being grateful that you will stop any further actions conducted by your mother," Dmitri was saying when the double doors behind me opened. "Not that she had any grounds since we legally purchased the land—ah. Here they are."

I glanced over my shoulder to see three laughing women enter the room, the leader with brownish-blond hair that flowed around her in a tangle of waves. The second was a shorter woman with round glasses, and a braid that wrapped around her head, and the third an elegant slender woman with straight auburn hair.

"May I present my wife, Her Serene Highness Juliane, the Crown Princess of Beck. To her right is Harry, Iakovos's wife, and on the left is Kiera, Theo's wife. Ladies, this is our cousin Neo Papaioannou, and his ex-wife, Beam."

The short woman with glasses made a face, then turned to eye both Neo and me with interest. For a horrible moment, I thought I should bow or something, but stood frozen, instead. "Ex-wife?" she asked, just like Neo's cousins had done. She held out her hand, shaking first mine, then Neo's, adding, "Please, ignore the title, and call me Thyra. Dmitri likes to use it to see whether he can get people to curtsy."

The woman named Harry laughed and moved over to greet us, as well, giving Neo a long look before shaking his hand. "The men make such a big deal about it. Not that it isn't incredibly cool that we have a princess in the family, but Thyra isn't like any other royalty, so don't feel like you have to stand at attention or anything around her."

"OK," I said, wanting to laugh but deciding that it might be interpreted as rude. "I won't curtsy or do a Beefeater impression."

"Oh, are you British? You sound American," Kiera said, shaking hands, as well. I noticed that after the introductions were made, the men drifted over to their respective wives.

"I am. Born on the Navajo Nation, educated—for a short time—in England, as well as the US, so sometimes a few Briticisms slip out."

"I'm sorry, this has to be me getting old, but did Neo say your name was Bean?" Harry asked as she leaned into her husband, who immediately put an arm around her waist.

"You're not old, sweetheart," he said immediately. "You're just … ripe."

"No more children!" she said, elbowing his ribs.

Everyone laughed except Neo and me.

"Sorry, that was exclusionary, wasn't it? We have five kids, you see, and the last one was definitely the last of the bunch, especially since Yacky got resnipped just so we wouldn't change our minds again," Harry told me.

"Yacky?" Neo asked at the same time I said, "Resnipped?"

Iakovos sighed dramatically, pulling his wife over to a chair before retaking his seat. "If we could just go one day without you telling everyone about my vasectomies, I would be delirious with joy."

"Oh, you're delirious," Harry told him, waggling her eyebrows. "You get to have wild, unbridled sex without worries of birth control."

"This is true," he allowed, then turned to me. "Harry likes to pretend she can't say my name, Beam. And because turnabout is fair play, I will mention that her real name is Eglantine, a fact she detests."

"I mean, seriously," Harry said, appealing to everyone. "Who could love a name like that? It's not fun, like Bean."

"It's Beam, actually," Neo said before Iakovos could correct her. "Short for Moonbeam."

Everyone looked at me, speculation rife in their respective eyes.

I glared at Neo for two seconds before telling everyone, "My mother was firmly entrenched in the hippie movement of the early 1970s, so I completely understand your feelings, Harry."

"Welcome to the weird-name group," Thyra said with a glance toward Kiera, who nodded quickly.

"It's like having a slightly odd name is a requirement to be married to a Papaioannou … oh. Er …" She glanced at me. "Are you guys … that is, you said you were exes? You're not … uh …"

"We're reacquainting ourselves," Neo said with great dignity. "With each other, that is. We haven't seen each other for a long time. When we were eighteen—"

"No," I said, interrupting him, putting a restraining hand on his forearm.

He looked down first at the hand, then at me, one eyebrow cocking. "No?"

"We don't need to bare our dirty laundry to everyone. I know you want to be fully honest with these new-to-you relations, and I know you are nervous, but you don't need to tell everyone about what happened twenty-four years ago."

"You've been apart for twenty-four years?" Kiera asked me, her eyes wide. "And you're still friends?"

"As Neo said, we're in the process of learning about each other again," I said simply, then glanced around the table, puzzled by the behavior of everyone. "Don't you guys … that is, aren't you all supposed to be talking serious business stuff like why you haven't talked to Neo before, and why his mom is evidently trying to steal a bit of land from you, and all that?"

"Eh," Harry said, gesturing such ideas away. "We hashed all that out this morning, when Dmitri and Thyra rolled into town. Neo's parents stole a bunch of money from Iakovos's and Theo's dad, and then ghosted him. I gather that was before Neo's time, so no one really blames him for being caught up in a family feud. We're much more interested in who Neo is, and by extension who you are."

"Wait … my father stole money from yours?" Neo was frowning now and shaking his head as he tapped lightly on the table. I suspected it was a nervous habit he wasn't aware he was doing. "That's not right. It was my family—my parents and my uncle Okeanos—who were robbed of the business all the brothers joined."

Neo's cousins exchanged pregnant looks, before all looking back at him. The air suddenly felt very hostile. "That is not what happened," Iakovos said slowly, obviously taking up the mantle of leader. "I don't know what you were told, but my father's business was destroyed by yours. If you like, I can provide the legal documents showing my father's lawsuits attempting to regain funds stolen, as well as the loss of the company itself."

"Oh dear," I said softly, watching Neo. His jaw worked a few times, his fingers now stilled. I had a feeling he was looking inward, sorting through what his cousin had said, and trying to justify it with his image of the past.

"You knew nothing of this?" Dmitri asked, pulling out a tablet and typing on it. "Most of the documents are archived, but here's a copy of the original papers the lawyers drew up, and the subsequent statement by the accountant acknowledging Aris Papaioannou's removal of all company funds."

Neo stared at the tablet that Dmitri slid his way, not moving to take it. It was as if he had turned to stone.

"Neo?" I said softly, leaning in close to him, touching him on his leg. "Breathe."

He remained frozen for another few seconds before taking in a deep breath, and half turning toward me. Pain was clearly evident in his eyes, so sharp that it made me want to take him in my arms and hold him tight against it. "They lied to me."

"They seem to have made a habit of doing that," I said slowly, not wanting to rub salt in the wound, but aware that my own scars needed to be acknowledged, as well.

"I have a feeling we just pulled the rug out from under you two," Harry said, glancing at her husband, who gave a nod. "And since that is never a good feeling, how about we give you a little time to process? Let's see. … Tonight we have a function at the archaeology museum, but we're having a family dinner tomorrow night to celebrate Thyra and Dmitri's return to Greece for a few months—why don't you join us? We're blissfully child-free, since we left everyone back home with our nanny for a few days, although Thyra's cat is with her, since he gets fussy without them. You guys aren't allergic?"

"No," I told her after another ten seconds of Neo staring blankly at the tablet. "I'm not, and Neo never used to be."

"Dinner would be fine," Neo said suddenly, snapping back to life. He gave a brief grimace. "My apologies, that came out rude. What I should have said is that we would be pleased to attend a family dinner with you all, child-free or not. And I like cats. Beam?"

"They get a thumbs-up from me, but much though I appreciate you including me in the invitation, I'm afraid I can't. I promised Ziggy we'd do dinners together while I'm in Athens, and since I don't get to see her while she's doing her year here, I'd kind of hate to miss one."

"Ziggy is her niece," Neo explained, taking my hand in his in a way that told me he wanted me to accept. I was torn, part of me wanting to give him the comfort he obviously needed, while the other part warned me against rushing into another relationship with him.

The Housewife, on the other hand, was wondering how long was polite before asking a man to marry you for the second time.

No, I told her with a firmness that I hoped would quell such errant thoughts. *We were impetuous once. We don't need to go through hell again.*

"Naturally, we'd love for your niece come with you," Harry said with a genuine smile. "Seven sound good? Excellent. Come along, you world's sexiest bachelor, you. Let's go to your office and make out."

Iakovos gave another faux sigh, but he was on his feet and following his wife with an alacrity that bespoke a man in love. "We'll see you tomorrow night. It was a pleasure to meet you both."

"Ooh, necking in your office," Kiera said, batting her lashes at Theo.

"World's sexiest bachelor?" I said aloud to no one in particular.

Theo, who was hustling his wife to the door, tipped his head toward Thyra. "Ask her about it. I'm surprised Neo isn't on the list, to be honest. They seem to work their way through all the Papaioannous."

"Actually …" Thyra and Dmitri exchanged looks; then Thyra suddenly smiled. "My editor wanted me to interview Neo last year, but since he was from the bad side of Dmitri's family, I declined."

"Editor? What editor? What list?" I asked, confused even more when Dmitri and Thyra followed the others out of the conference room, clearly heading off to have some private time for themselves.

"It's nothing," Neo said, staring at the tablet that Dmitri had left. "Just a list of available bachelors in Europe. It doesn't mean anything."

I stared at him. "You're on it, aren't you?"

He tapped at the tablet, magnifying one of the documents. "This looks legitimate."

"You're on a world's most rich and eligible bachelor list, aren't you?"

"My parents lied to me, Beam."

I breathed heavily out my nose a few times just to let him know how I was feeling. "A list. Of bachelors. And you are on it. How many bachelors, Neo?"

He sighed the same sort of sigh that Iakovos had heaved a few minutes before. "Ten. And before you ask, I'm number two. I don't care about it, and I refused to be interviewed by the magazine that makes the list. I had no idea that Dmitri's princess conducted the interviews. Don't you think it's interesting that she's a princess? A real princess?"

"You," I said, ignoring his attempt at a diversion. I stood up so I could point a finger at him more effectively. "You are a number two world's most eligible bachelor, and you have only had four girlfriends in twenty-four years? How is this possible?"

He stood up slowly, tipping his head to the side in the way that always used to make my body turn to melted Beam. It threatened to do so now. "I'm selective?"

"I'm going back to my hotel now," I told him, then

walked out of the conference room.

He followed. "Dinner tonight? You and Ziggy, naturally."

I fought with my inner Housewife for a good twenty seconds before inclining my head. "Fine. But it had better be someplace that is cool. And I don't mean in a hipster way."

"I'll pick you up at seven," he called after me as I walked with determination to the elevator, still fighting with my inner self.

"I am not jealous, I am not jealous," I told myself as I took the elevator to the ground floor, then had one of the reception people help find me a taxi to take me back to the hotel.

I'd be damned if I was jealous of something that had no meaning for me anymore.

Number two. The bastard.

NINE

"So, what do you think of Athens?"

I ran my finger around the rim of the water glass and studied the man who sat opposite me in a restaurant open to the harbor town of Piraeus. "I haven't seen much of it, but it seems pretty. I like the red roofs, and Ziggy is going to take me to the Acropolis tomorrow. How exactly did you meet Neo?"

Chase, Neo's friend who had picked up Ziggy and me at my hotel and driven us the short distance to Piraeus, didn't appear in the least bit offended by my abrupt question. He looked to be in his late thirties, with dark blond curly hair, a goatee, and a friendly smile that reminded me of a particularly happy golden retriever. "We met in college, actually. He was a grad student and assisting in a class I had. I was horrible at coding, but needed a STEM class, and fortunately, he took pity on me and helped me pass it. After that, we remained in touch. When he said he needed help, I decided that working for a new start-up was going to be infinitely better than trying to find a mindless job for a big corporation, so I joined the Pi team."

"What was Neo like then?" Ziggy asked, leaning her chin on her palm, staring intently at Chase. "Does he always brush his dates off on you to transport, or is he just being rude to Aunt Beam? Who was his last girlfriend? When did he break up with her? How come his mom is such a—" She managed to censor herself, but only after I had started sending her wild signals via eyebrow semaphore. "—harridan?" she finished, waggling her brows back at me.

Chase had been taking a sip of a cocktail, but set it down now and offered Ziggy a basket of flatbread. Considering she'd eaten several pieces already, as well as half a bowl of olives and marinated feta, I decided it was a gesture intended on limiting her seemingly endless questions. "That's a lot of questions. Let's see if I can take them in order. I don't think Neo has ever brushed off a date, and in fact, I offered to pick up both your aunt and you, since he was delayed. I'm sure no rudeness was intended for either of you." He shot me a particularly brilliant smile. "As for his last girlfriend … I'm not entirely comfortable discussing his personal life without permission. I'm sure you understand."

"Not in the least," Ziggy said, tearing off a bit of flatbread and dipping it into the olive oil and lemon marinade used on the feta. "But since you don't want to tell us, I'll ask Neo. What bee got up his mom's ass?"

Chase looked confused. "I'm sorry, I don't know what you mean."

"Ziggy was notified right before you picked us up that her internship was canceled. A second time. Neo said he'd fixed things with the intern office while he was looking into what happened, but then she got a message an hour ago that she was out of the program." I glanced at the clock on my phone, feeling antsy. I wished Neo were there so I could pin him back about what was going on with Ziggy. I wanted to make sure he was all right after the shock that his parents had lied to him again. And most of all, I just wanted him there next to me, thinking and saying the things that only he could think and say, and smelling delicious, with his sexy jaw and chest and hands.

I wanted him, pure and simple.

Really? I asked my Housewife. *Are you so quick to forget those twenty-four years of hell?*

My mental self gave me the same sort of look my therapist used in response to me trying to shift blame and responsibility away from myself. I gave a mental sigh and retracted my statement, acknowledging that although I had been hurt and treated badly by Neo and his family, I didn't do much to help myself.

"Aunt Beam?" Ziggy asked, giving me an odd look that had me realizing either she or Chase had asked me a question while I was in my introspection zone.

"Sorry, what was that?"

"I asked if you had talked to Neo about the message sent to Ziggy," Chase asked, his phone in hand, clearly about to send a text.

"No, I figured we'd do that at dinner. Is he going to be here soon?" I tried to keep the acid note from my voice, figuring that my issues with Neo weren't his fault.

"He should be," Chase answered, checking his phone. "When I picked you and Ziggy up, he said he was just going to do a little work, then take a shower and meet us here."

"We could have eaten in Athens, if that was more convenient," I said politely, quelling my irritation at having been palmed off on Chase.

"Neo's not in Athens." He looked from me to Ziggy, then smiled at us both. "Didn't he tell you about his boat? He has one here. It's on the pier to the left. If you look past that big gold monstrosity that is taking up most of the pier, you'll see Neo's navy blue boat."

We both looked. Just beyond what must have been a superyacht, I could see a few feet of the rear end of a boat in dark blue, with a white gangplank stretching down to the dock. "Why does he stay on a boat when he has an apartment on the top of his building?" Ziggy asked.

I pursed my lips, wondering if his boat was where he had been considering placing a hammock, and understood now why he thought it would be effective. The rocking of the boat would definitely enhance its use. Hmm.

Chase gave another friendly-puppy smile. "He isn't in

Greece much, but he prefers to be somewhere quiet, where he can do as he pleases without having to answer to his mother and stepfather, who live in the penthouse at Pi Tower."

"Ugh. Can't fault him there," Ziggy said, pushing away the remainder of marinaded feta.

I shifted my attention from thoughts of wave action on lovemaking, and eyed her. She appeared as careless as ever, but I saw the tension in her fingers, and the occasional tight set of her lips. She was more upset than she let on, which made me resolve to tackle Neo about the issue. I wanted answers, and I wasn't going to let him distract me with his seductive self, or needy emotional state.

Chase chatted for another fifteen minutes, telling me about Piraeus, what Neo had been doing in South America for the last few years, and how he much he admired what Pi stood for, and how it was helping people in communities that had restricted access to everything the Internet could provide, specifically education for marginalized peoples.

"Cool," Ziggy said at the end of the latest glorification of all things Neo, then met my gaze and said, "Would you mind if I took off early?"

"I'm sure Neo will be here at any time—" Chase started to say.

"Why?" I asked her, searching her face for a sign that she was in distress. I was prepared to go into full enraged-aunt mode if that's what was needed.

"I'm tired," she said frankly, then stifled a yawn. "Didn't get much sleep last night, and I have a project due on Friday that I am a bit behind on."

"I thought you'd want to talk to Neo about what's going on at Pi," I told her, ignoring Chase when he started murmuring that Neo was sure to regret missing seeing her.

She gave me a slow smile. "Yeah, but I think you'll do the job just as well. Maybe better. Do you mind if I dip out?"

"Of course not," I said, getting to my feet. "We can get a taxi back to Athens—"

"I'm sure Neo will be here—" Chase said.

"Nuh-uh," Ziggy said, gathering up her big, oversized bag that she took everywhere. "You have to stay and beard the dangerous and sexy Neo in his den."

"Ziggy—" I said, wondering if she wasn't trying to manipulate me into spending time alone with Neo. I wouldn't put it past her, since she'd made a few coy references to the fact that he'd taken me with him to see his cousins.

She held up her hand to stop me. "Dude. I just meant that I'm counting on you to tell him what happened, and see what he thinks. If he really doesn't want me in the intern program, then I suppose I'll survive, but I'd like to know why the intern office keeps doing one-eighties. Talk to you in the morning."

"Do you need any money—" I stopped when she shook her head.

"I'll take the express bus. Later, tater!"

Worried despite her apparent desire to leave, I watched her wind her way through the tables of the restaurant. Was she so upset she didn't want to see Neo, or was this part of a plot to get Neo and me to hook up again?

I had a suspicion it was the latter, especially since my own brain was avidly working toward that goal, despite the sane part of my mind telling me that I needed to take things slow, and rebuild a relationship—if there was to be one—without throwing my heart at Neo and leaping after it.

Chase chatted for another five minutes about Neo's boat, and how he—Chase—got seasick even when the boat was docked, but my mind wasn't on being overly polite. I was too busy fighting with my inner self. After Chase's anecdotes ran down, I stood up and announced, "That's it, I'm through waiting. I'm going to go find Neo. What's the name of his ship?"

"Boat," he corrected. "It's *Athena Rising*, but—"

"Thanks," I said, and, after popping a piece of feta in my mouth—that stuff was addictive—slapped down a few euros on the table for what Ziggy and I had eaten, and marched off to the sounds of Chase's protests that he didn't need the money, and also, Neo was sure to be there in the next few minutes.

Even at night, the docks where the big sailing boats and yachts were parked were anything but empty. People hurried hither and yon, some who obviously worked as crew members bringing shopping and food, while others were dressed in glittery club wear or shiny suits, obviously on their way to hit the Athens nightlife.

As I came around the hindquarters of the big gold megayacht, I stumbled to a halt. I don't know why I had envisioned Neo's boat as something likea big cabin cruiser that I had seen in San Diego, but the sleek, curved lines of the boat that bore the name *Athena Rising* were definitely not that. A long swooping arch ran from the bow to the stern, holding an upper deck that appeared to have not only couches, lounges, and a full dining table, but also a Jacuzzi. A narrow white gangplank ran down to the dock, but I just stood at the foot of it and stared, my mind trying to process what I was seeing.

"This isn't a boat. It's a freakin' luxury yacht," I said to no one in particular, noting lights glowing from wide double doors immediately beyond the outside dining room. Above it all rose a canopy that duplicated the midlevel arch. It was sleek and gorgeous, and reeked of affluence. "Right. I don't know what the protocol is, but let's hope Neo doesn't get his knickers in a twist," I murmured as a group of partygoers pushed past me toward the street. Without looking at the black water below the narrow ramp, I hurried up it, hesitating at the double doors before opening one a crack and saying loudly, "Neo? You in here?"

For a moment, there was silence; then a door clicked. "Beam?"

"Yes." I stepped into the lounge area of the boat, and goggled for a few seconds. "Holy shitsnacks, Neo. This is incredible. Is that a bar? You have a bar in a living room on a boat?"

The living area was dominated by a U-shaped couch in taupe, with scattered navy and taupe pillows, behind which ran a bank of windows. On the other side, a low credenza stretched, obviously housing some sort of electronic equipment. At the far end of the room was a wet bar with four tall barstools and, across from it, two deep comfy leather chairs.

Neo's head emerged from the floor, making me blink for a moment before I realized there was a spiral staircase that led down to the deck below. "Of course I have a bar. Why wouldn't I? What are you doing here? Oh shit!" He had glanced at his wrist as he spoke, then back at me, swearing profanely in Greek. "I'm sorry, Beam, I lost track of time. I was looking into the situation with Beowulf, since I had a few minutes before Chase brought you out here, and … well …"

"You got involved and forgot me," I said, walking toward him, still trying to take in all the gleaming brass and polished oak of the fittings. "This is a seriously pretty boat. Yacht. Ship. Which is it?"

"Technically a yacht, but I just call it a boat, because that's what it is. Tell me you forgive me," he said, coming forward to press a kiss to my hand.

"Nope," I said, gathering my wits, remembering how irritated I was with him. "You don't get to tell me what to do. You also don't get to make me feel bad because you didn't pay attention to the time."

"Where's Ziggy?" he asked, ignoring my comments. "I was going to bring you both here after dinner."

"She went back to her room to study. Which reminds me, I need to talk to you about that." I bit my lip, wondering for a few seconds if he was playing me, or if he truly did not know what was going on with his own company.

"Her studying? Is there something I can help with?" he asked.

"Yes." Distracted for a moment, I asked, "What were you doing with Beowulf?"

The look he gave me was odd—it started as annoyance,

then softened to what looked to me like resignation. "I don't know. That's the problem. I don't know what I'm doing with it. I can't access part of the code—it's encrypted, and although I've tried the best programs I know to break it, I can't." He looked at me.

I looked back at him.

His eyes widened with a plea.

"No," I told him.

"Please."

"I couldn't."

"You can. You were always so good with encryptions. It's why you wrote Beowulf."

"Don't tell me what I did. I was there. I know what I did, and why I did it," I said, my irritability audible with each word.

Neo held both my hands, his fingers warm and solid and filling me with a sense of comfort that I hadn't realized was missing from my life. "You wrote it because you wanted me to have a secure future. You know this code, Beam. You can dig into it where the encryption programs can't. You can figure out how it's been integrated into Pi's source file, and get to the bottom of what it's doing."

"I haven't seen that code in twenty-four years, and besides, computers are light-years away now from when I wrote that old bit of code. Surely there must be some program that can crack it wide open." I leaned forward, unable to resist the lure of him.

He gently pulled me against him, his lips brushing mine. "I've tried, Beam. You did your job too well with it. The encryption might be able to be broken, but it will take time, and I want to know what it's doing, and who put it there."

I bit his lower lip, making him take a step back in surprise. His arms cartwheeled as I lunged forward, grabbing him at the same time he caught himself on the brass rail that curved around the spiral stairs.

"I'm so sorry! Are you OK? I didn't realize you were standing right on the top step," I apologized, damning myself for ruining what was promising to be a humdinger of a kiss.

He gave a rusty chuckle, then, taking my hand, turned and proceeded down the stairs. "I'm fine, but I believe we'll have that kiss down here, where it won't knock me off my feet."

"This is really so amazing," I said when we stopped at the bottom of the stairs. This deck clearly held the cabins, since it consisted of a narrow hallway paneled in oak so polished I could see my reflection. A door at the far end was open, revealing a glimpse of a big bed.

"I like it. Would you like the tour? There are four cabins altogether, and one office off my cabin. Hardwood floors throughout, and the doors are inlaid satinwood copying an ancient design I saw in a local museum." He pulled me after him as we stepped into a cabin that ran the width of the boat. A huge bed sat facing a bank of curved bow windows, under which was a window seat, which held a few scattered items of clothing, clearly garments Neo had tossed there after changing. "My bathroom has marble veneer—marble itself would be too heavy, so I had to go with a lighter veneer—and a jetted tub."

I gawked at the tub, marble walls, and counters, and looked pointedly at the shower, which looked big enough to hold a pony. It also had a teak bench along one side that made my inner Housewife start calculating who could do what to whom in a hot, steamy shower.

"Each cabin has its own en suite, and there's Wi-Fi, naturally."

"Naturally," I said, my mind a bit squirrelly by now after taking in all the nautical opulence.

"And my office is there," he said, gesturing to a door that led off the main cabin. "Would you like to look at the code now, or should I make love to you as I've wanted to do ever since you walked out of my life?"

"Your family pushed me out of your life, and … hey!" I put a hand on his chest when he tried to scoop me in his arms again. "Stop distracting me with your Greek bachelor number two self. I have a couple of things I want to say to you, first."

"Then we'll have sex?" he said, hope filling his voice and eyes.

"No. Maybe. Possibly. I'm not sure I want to have sex with a man who tells a woman he'll fix whatever's going on with her niece, and then reneges on his word." I tried to adopt a haughty tone, but somehow found myself sitting on the big bed, more or less draped over Neo as he kissed a spot on my neck.

He stopped kissing. I turned my head and bumped noses with him.

"What are you talking about? I told the head of the intern program to remove the objections to Ziggy's program, since it was obvious that she had done nothing wrong, and it was our server safeguards that were at fault."

"You may have told the people that, but someone isn't listening very closely." I placed a hand on his cheek, my heart singing at the sight of his face. Dear goddess, how I had missed him. I didn't realize until that moment just how empty I'd felt without him bumbling around in my life. "They've not only kicked Ziggy out of the intern program altogether—she got a notice from a lawyer that legal action is going to be taken against her for all the damage she supposedly did. What's going on, Neo? Who is doing this to her? Is it your mom?"

"I don't know," he said, his eyes searching mine. He hesitated, clearly wanting to say something but struggling for the words. "Have you ever felt that there was something going on around you that was obvious to everyone else, but no matter how hard you tried to see it, you couldn't?"

"That sounds like common paranoia," I said, then gently kissed one corner of his mouth. "And yes. Sometimes I feel just like that. What are we going to do?" I hadn't meant to ask that last sentence, but it slipped out. Damn that Housewife and her attempts to get Neo back into my life.

"Do you trust me?" he asked, surprising me.

I touched the thin lines that fanned out from the edges of his eyes. I'd never thought of crow's-feet being particularly sexy, or even attractive, but I liked the way they added character to Neo's perfect face. My fingers stroked down to his cheek where the day's growth of whiskers made my fingertips tingle. I thought about what he asked, really thought about it. I didn't see any deception in his eyes, but that didn't mean much—I never was good at reading people's faces. But my heart knew things. It had suffered, been fractured into a million pieces, and slowly rebuilt itself over the years, finding love with family and a handful of friends.

Neo was different. He filled my mind just as he filled my soul. "For better or worse, I trust you," I finally said.

His eyes seemed to warm up, the hint of a smile flirting with the corners of his mouth. "If I told you that I like the fact that it took you a while to answer, would you understand?"

"No, but that's OK, because relearning what makes you tick is something I look forward to. Make love to me, Neo."

"Thank all the gods, goddesses, and any other deities who I can't think of at this moment," he said, his lips moving over mine. His mouth was both strange and new, and triggered a hundred memories that had faded over the years. I let his tongue push mine around for a bit before I decided fair play was in order.

I straddled his legs, my knees around his hips as I kissed him with a passion that surprised me, my tongue dabbing at his while I struggled to peel his shirt off.

His hands were busy on my back, yanking down the zipper on the one nice dress I'd brought with me for any fancy restaurants that Ziggy and I might visit.

"You're awfully good at kissing for a man who's only had four girlfriends," I told him a minute later, coming up for air. "Is that how you got to number two?"

"Christ, I don't know. I didn't ask," he said, hoisting me upward for a moment to whip my dress off over my head. I used the time to pick off his cuff links, and pushed his shirt off his chest, immediately taking possession of his delicious pectorals. "It's more likely that I'm inspired by you. Don't they say men peak sexually at eighteen, while women wait until they are in their forties? I need to prove to you that I'm worthy of your peak time. Up."

"Up to you, too … oh." I moved off his lap so he could shuck his pants, wondering if I should strip myself naked, but then decided that allowing him to remove my bra and undies might constitute a form of striptease, so instead waited until he had everything removed. He turned toward me, and I just stood there and ogled him.

"What are you doing?" he asked, a little line between his brows.

"Ogling you. Damn, Neo."

His hands fluttered in a mild gesture of discomfort. "I'm a bit out of shape. I used to run, but got out of the habit after my surgery. I was going to take up an exercise-bike routine once I got back in Athens, but there hasn't been time to get one ordered."

"Stop it," I said, putting my hands on his stomach. "You don't even have a tiny bit of a belly. And your chest! Hoo! It makes me go hot just looking at it. No, not hot, steaming. You're stupidly gorgeous, Neo. Like, how do you have an almost six-pack if you haven't exercised? That's just wrong! If I miss even a week of water aerobics, I immediately swell like a puffer fish at full bloat. You, sir, are very much number two hunky Greek bachelor."

He looked pleased at my compliment, his gaze dropping to my breasts. "I don't see even the slightest hint of puffer fish about you. Far from it—you make my mouth water with your delectable, sleek flesh."

"I am hardly sleek," I said, looking down at myself, then, with an annoyed *tsk* at myself, dropped my hands where they were hiding my stomach. "I should lose twenty pounds. My hips are too big, and I can't go braless without having floppy boobs. And my thighs are gigantic. We won't go into what my butt looks like. No, don't look! It'll traumatize you. I'm not the lithe, supple eighteen-year-old you remember. Oh, hell. Why are we doing this? I'm a middle-aged woman with a spread because I spend so much time in front of the computer, and you're going to be nothing but disappointed."

His grin had a wolfish tinge to it as he took possession of my breasts, my nipples immediately hardening against the fabric of my bra. "Sunshine, you may think that a lush body makes you unattractive, but it most definitely is not the case. You are a goddess come to life, with soft, enticing flesh, and curves that make me want to touch you. All of you. You are Aphrodite personified, and the thought of your body makes me harder than I've ever been in my entire life, and that includes the time we spent together in my idiot youth."

I melted at his use of his old pet name for me, my hands dancing down the planes of his chest and flanks before sweeping upward on his back, gently dragging my nails in a way that I remembered made him shiver.

He quivered, reeled back for a moment, his eyes hot with passion, his hair ruffled even though I hadn't run my hands in it, and his penis ready to rumble. "You do not play fair!"

"No, I don't. I have a whole lot of years to make up for." He froze, a flash of pain in his eyes at my words. I realized that he had misinterpreted, and leaned forward to lick one of his nipples. "That wasn't a dig at what happened in the past. I simply meant that I have twenty-four years of Neo fantasies built up, and I'm very much anticipating exploring them."

"Fantasies," he said thoughtfully, his expression softening as I reassured him. "I like the sound of that. I have a great many stored, as well."

"Really?" I had kicked off my shoes and was about to remove my bra, but I paused, wondering what sort of things he was into now. "Like what?"

He eyed me, his lips pursed. "Right now? A striptease."

"I'm not much of a dancer, but maybe I could do a little something along that line," I said, wondering at my daring spirit. I'd never in my life thought about doing a striptease, not even for Neo. "But we don't have any music."

"Pi?" he said, turning his head slightly to the side while keeping his gaze firmly locked on me. "Play something seductive."

"You have your own voice-activated thingie?" I said with a laugh when a slow, sultry song started.

"Of course I do." He stood watching me with an avidity that both pleased and slightly disconcerted me. "Do you not like this song? We can pick something different."

"No," I said, letting go of my doubts and inhibitions. "This'll work. Let's see. ... I guess I just move around? Does this do anything for you?"

I did a little belly roll that I vaguely remembered from a long-ago belly dancing keep-fit class, accompanied by a slow hip move while I dropped first one bra strap, then the other.

"Christ, yes," Neo said, his big chest moving in a way that made me think that he, too, was finding his cabin a bit short on oxygen. "Do it again."

"I think I can do better than a bra strap drop," I said, then shimmied my way out of my bra, making sure to slide my hands first along my breasts, then along my hips.

Neo's eyes were huge, his hands fisted.

"I sure hope you meant what you said about my abundance, because ... well, this is what I am. I've pretty much made my peace with my body," I said, doing another slow hip roll as I slid my hands lower to the top of my underwear, mentally thanking my Housewife for encouraging me to put on my best lace-edged undies that morning.

"Your body is meant to be worshipped," Neo said, his voice taking on a hoarse tinge. "And I fully intend on doing so the second you are done torturing me."

"You're the one who wanted the striptease," I said, peeling off my underwear and, in a moment of sheer frivolity, tossing it at him.

He caught it with one hand, never taking his eyes off me, his gaze moving from my breasts, to hips, to face, and then cycling through the points of interest again. "Thank you. I'll treasure them."

"I'll need those back," I said with a little laugh and a hip shake before spreading my hands. "Thus ends the striptease. What did you think?"

He flung the underwear to the side, moving forward with an avid light in his eyes.

"Neo—" The word turned into a squeal when he picked me up and tossed me onto the bed, immediately following me down.

"I think you have been made to drive me almost to the point where I can't bear it any longer. I think you're sensual, and desirable, and so very, very hot. I think you're my sunshine, and if I wasn't too busy thanking every god in the pantheon for your return to my life, I'd be on my knees in gratitude."

His mouth was hot on my breasts, my belly, my hips. I squirmed beneath him, the feel of him touching and tasting and teasing me driving me into trying to do the same to him.

"You taste salty," I said, kissing his shoulder before nipping it carefully. "You taste like the Neo I remember, only a bit more …"

"Old?" he asked, rubbing the stubble of his cheeks on the undersides of my breasts.

I arched back. "No. More. Just more. More Neo. More sexy bachelor number two. More …" *My love,* my mind whispered, but there was no way I was about to acknowledge the words, let alone speak them out loud.

"I have no idea what that means, but since it seems to please you, I'll go with it. Foreplay or not?" he asked, pulling back so that my body mourned the removal of his against it.

"Didn't we just do foreplay?" I asked on a moan, my fingers digging into the blanket beneath me.

"Perhaps. How about we do this, first?"

"Dear goddess, yes, let's do this," I said on a half gasp when he shifted downward in order to rub his cheeks on my inner thighs. My body came alive like it had never done with my toys, his mouth doing things to me that I had no idea were possible. He touched, he probed, his tongue swirled and dipped in a delightful tango against my intimate parts, winding me up tighter and tighter.

"Like that, do you?" he asked, sliding a finger into me. My intimate muscles cramped trying to grasp him.

I slid my fingers into his hair and tugged. "Yes … yes, I like that. Do it again, and again, and again, and then do it again some more," I demanded. He shifted a little, adjusted his angle, and gently bit my thigh as a second finger joined the first, curling into me.

The orgasm ramped up, my muscles tightening even as he moved up, sliding into me just as heat washed up my belly. My body both welcomed him and gave way before the orgasm to end all orgasms. The Housewife set off a bunch of fireworks before collapsing in a sated heap.

"Thank god you were close," he said, a groan slipping from him as my muscles continued to contract, little after-shocks of pleasure making them grab him as he thrust faster into me, the short, hard movements making me see stars. "I don't think I can … Christ, Beam, don't move!"

I wrapped my legs around his hips, and tightened everything I could around him, my body wanting to just melt into a puddle of goo.

He went wild, bucking against me a couple of times before he cried my name, his hips flexing a few more times before he collapsed on me, his chest heaving, his breath harsh in my ears.

"OK," I said a few minutes later, when I managed to get enough air into my lungs to speak. "That was amazing. Spectacular. Life changing. Don't let anyone ever tell you that you're over your sexual prime, because it's just not true, and I had the orgasm to prove it."

He moaned as he slid out of me, and rolled over onto his back, staring up at the ceiling, one hand on his chest as he continued to breathe heavily, his chest damp with sweat. "You killed me. I can't believe you killed me with sex, but I couldn't possibly have survived that. I'm a ghost now, aren't I?"

I smiled as I rolled onto my side, trailing my fingers down his chest to his belly. "You feel awfully alive to me. Oh, hell!"

"Me?" he asked, a little worry flashing in his eyes.

"No. Well, yes. But me, too. We didn't use a condom."

"Oh," he said, relaxing back into the sheets, pulling me up against his side. "That's OK. I don't have any diseases, and it's been since before my surgery that I had a lover. Oh, wait, you … er …"

"IUD," I said, allowing myself to snuggle into him.

I could feel the curious look he shot me.

"Periods," I told him.

"What about them?"

"You don't have as many with an IUD. And I always had bad cramps, if you remember, so when my doctor recommended I get one even though I wasn't sexually active, I got one. This one was going to be my last, but I still have a few years on it, so we don't have anything to worry about there for a while."

"Good," he said, heaving a big sigh. "Not that I object to the idea of children, but I just found you again. I really don't want to share you with anyone but your niece. Are you hungry? I'm hungry."

"That's because you didn't show up for dinner," I said, watching with approval when he got out of bed and stretched. "Damn, Neo. Your butt is even better than when I saw it yesterday."

He tried to look over his shoulder at his rear, causing the muscles to flex. I gave a little mental swoon, wondering what he'd do if I bit one of those tempting butt cheeks. "I'm glad you approve, but I will admit that I haven't done much to deserve such praise. Do you like omelets?"

"Yes," I said, somewhat bewildered when he strolled out of the cabin buck naked.

"It's one of the few things I can cook well," I heard him call back. "I think there's some smoked salmon left. I'll make us a salmon omelet."

"He is naked," I told the room, then decided that I didn't want to miss the sight of a naked Neo making me food, and, after pausing to slip into his shirt, which barely hit me at midthigh, hustled out after him.

I found him on the deck below, in a narrow galley, clad in only an apron as he pulled out a variety of food from one of three refrigerators.

"Er … " I said, glancing at the windows that lined one side of the galley. "Do you want me to pull the blinds?"

"If you do that, I won't be able to see the lights of the harbor," he said, examining a couple of mushrooms before tossing them in a bamboo basket that sat in the sink, along with peppers, onions, and a clump of herbs.

"Yeah, but your apron doesn't cover your backside, and much though I like to watch the muscles of it when you move—oh, do that lean to the left again—I'm not sure you really want to entertain everyone who happens to pass by."

"The windows are tinted. No one can see in the lower decks," he said, his back to me as he washed veggies before chopping them with quick, efficient moves.

"Oh. Good."

He paused to glance over his shoulder at me. "Could that be a note of possessiveness?"

"No," I said, giving him a frown that faded the second he turned around. "Of course not. I am not a jealous person. I never have been. I mean, if I wasn't jealous about the fact that I've had exactly zero lovers, while you've gone through a third of a dozen, then I think it's safe to say that I'm not the possessive sort."

My inner Housewife had a good, long laugh about that. I ignored her, as I so often am forced to do.

"I'm glad to hear that. I, on the other hand, am very jealous." He moved over to the stove, whisking together several eggs in a bowl before dumping them into some browning butter.

"Since when?" I asked, casting my mind back to our time together.

"I've always been that way." He added the veggies and cheese, stretching to reach for seasoning.

My eyes widened at what that stretch did to his back. How on earth was I getting turned on when I'd just had the orgasm of a lifetime?

His butt muscles flexed when he stepped to the side to dump the dirty dishes into the sink. My breath hitched in my throat, and I decided that orgasm or not, I'd have to be dead a good year before I stopped appreciating the view of a naked Neo.

"I never noticed you being jealous," I said, wondering if time had robbed me of some of my memories.

"That's because I was careful not to let you see it. Toast?"

"Sure, I feel like we earned a few carbs. Where's the bread?" I asked, moving over to where he nodded. I pulled out from a drawer a loaf of French bread, and cut off some slices before popping them into a fancy toaster. I couldn't help but add, "I never gave you any reason to be jealous, you know."

"I know, but you didn't have to. It's just something that I live with." He served up the omelet, retrieving a bowl of chopped fruit from the fridge, setting everything on the table. I joined him with several slices of toast, taking the chair he held out for me before taking his own seat. "Did you want some wine? I haven't had alcohol since my surgery, but I can open a bottle for you."

"I'm not a big drinker, either," I said, accepting a glass with several slices of lemon in bubbly water. "Neo, I have to talk to you. I don't like doing it while we're both still afterglowing, but since hunger made pillow talk moot, I'll have to do it now."

"About Beowulf?" he said, nodding as he chewed, sliding the bowl of fruit toward me. "It's bothering me, too. That's why I'm asking for your help."

"And I appreciate the fact that you think I'm some coding wunderkind despite the fact that I haven't even looked at a program since I returned home with Autumn, but that's not what I was talking about. Ziggy needs help. Your help. I won't let her career be ruined like mine was. And before you get all stiff and awkward, I'm not blaming you. Not any longer. Your mother, however, is another matter."

"You keep mentioning her, but it was my father who set up false information about you to find," Neo said, biting into a piece of toast loaded with a bit of omelet and smoked salmon. "My mother liked you. She told me that she wouldn't have a problem with us being married."

I stared at him, a forkful of eggs halfway to my mouth. "Are you insane? Don't you remember that phone call when you told them we were married? Your mother had to be frothing at the mouth to say the things she said."

He waved that away with a small clump of grapes. "We took them by surprise. Later, once she had a chance to process the information, she had come around to the idea, and was more than happy to have you as my wife."

I didn't for one single second believe that, but I didn't want to argue with him, the postcoital glow being what it was. "The fact remains that someone has put pressure on the intern people to dump Ziggy, not to mention ordering your legal people to go after her for malicious software. I realize you don't know Ziggy like I do, but I can assure you that she's the least malicious person in the world. She's a sunny, happy, bright girl, and I won't let your mother—or whoever has their sights set on her—take her down."

"I don't know why you think I'm lying to you," Neo said, setting down his fork, his gray eyes now stormy. "But I told you that I took care of the situation with Ziggy, who, for the record, I do not believe did anything intentionally malicious. She may have written a bit of code that got out of hand, but I am confident that she wasn't trying to bring down Pi."

My hackles went up at several things he said, but I pounced on the most important. "I didn't say you were lying—I said that the situation has not been taken care of. Or maybe it was, but it's back. Regardless, the whole reason I'm here is to help Ziggy." I ignored a twinge from my conscience that pointed out I'd also intended on meeting with Neo. "I'll do whatever it takes to help her."

"If there is an issue, I'll take care of it," Neo said, his expression darkening. "But I don't see why you are obviously so stressed about this. It's my company. No one can do anything without my approval."

"She's already been kicked out of the intern program," I pointed out, wanting to yell, but knowing that wouldn't help.

"I doubt that. I made my wishes explicit with regards to her," he insisted. "Even if somehow wires were crossed and she was removed from the intern pool, it's not a big deal. Not now that you're here."

I pushed my mostly eaten plate of food aside, saying slowly, "Now that I'm here?" Could he be saying what I thought he was saying?

"Yes." He waved a hand toward my torso. "Now that we're back together."

"Neo, we aren't together," I said, my ire rising. "Not in the sense that I think you mean. We just met again."

"We had sex," he said, his eyes narrowing on me. "You enjoyed it. We both did!"

"I'm not denying that, but the best sex in the world—and we came damned close to that standard—doesn't make a relationship. Not one that lasts."

His knuckles went white on the hand holding his fork. "Are you saying you don't want to be with me? You were just using me? Taking a trip down memory lane?"

I sighed, wondering why it always fell to women to be the rational ones. "I'm not saying any of that," I said, putting my hand on his until he released his death grip on his fork. "I'm not a soothsayer, Neo. I don't know what the future is going to be, and that includes whether or not we'll be together. I agreed to stay on for a bit so we could reacquaint ourselves, but that doesn't automatically come with a guaranteed happily ever after."

"I want one," he said, a familiar stubborn note entering his voice. "With you."

"And I appreciate that. But I'm not ready to commit myself. For the love of all that's holy, Neo, yesterday I was ready to punch you in your nose, and you thought I was evil personified. Besides, you said you were going to woo me. One round of the sheet tango does not a wooing make."

He thought about that for a few minutes, obviously not liking the fact that I wasn't ready to fling myself headlong into a relationship with him. "You weren't like this before," he finally said.

"No." I couldn't help but smile at that as I gave his hand a little squeeze. "I was a naive eighteen-year-old who fell in love with a handsome, if geeky, Greek boy with a delicious English accent and an even more delicious body. Now I'm older and wiser, and I've been through a lot since then. Besides, you can't honestly say that you're suddenly head over heels in love with me after just a few hours together."

"Of course I can," he said, getting up and clearing the table, putting the dishes in a dishwasher. "Papaioannou men always know the woman they will marry right away. My father did the first time he met my mother. My uncle was the same way. I knew when I saw you sitting by yourself that you were going to be the perfect fit for me."

He stopped, staring at a bowl in his hands for a few seconds before shaking his head and placing it into the dishwasher.

"Stop beating yourself up," I said, weariness claiming me. I wasn't sure if it was a remainder of jet lag, or the effect of lovemaking, but my limbs felt like they were cast out of lead. "We've moved past that, remember?"

"Yes," he said, then turned around and caught sight of my expression. "What?"

"You cook, you clean up after yourself, you have a bitable butt—no wonder you're number two on that bachelor list."

An indescribable emotion flitted across his face. "You want to bite my ass?"

"Yes," I said a bit defiantly. "Gently, not hard. I also want to squish your butt cheeks together, and maybe tickle your balls, but that's nothing so shocking that you should be star-ing at me like I'm out of some deviant porn movie."

"I'm not staring at you like that. I'm staring at you in the sudden realization of just how much I want to bite your ass. In fact, it's moved up to the top of my Beam-related fantasy list. I don't suppose you're multiorgasmic?"

"Not that I know of, and don't you even think of trying to seduce me back into your bed, because we have serious stuff to talk about," I warned him, leaping out of my chair and backing up when he started toward me, a lustful glint in his eyes.

"We do?" He stopped, sighed, then gave a sharp nod. "We do. Very well, we'll proceed on a businesslike status since you are in the middle of being wooed, and aren't yet ready to acknowledge the fact that we're meant to be togeth-er. How much will you charge to look at the Beowulf code?"

It was my turn to stare at him, and stare I did. Then I walked forward the three steps it took to get to him, made a fist, and punched him in his fatless belly. Not hard enough to do any damage, but enough that it took him by surprise.

I was in his cabin and had jerked on my dress and un-derwear, my bra stuffed into my bag, before he appeared in the doorway. "What the hell, Beam?"

"What the hell, indeed, Neo." I pushed past him, so an-gry I had to keep from shouting at him, reminding myself that his brain always had worked a little differently from other people's, and what seemed perfectly normal to him was anything but. I made it to the living room before I de-cided that was bullshit, and spun around as he emerged up the steps from the lower decks, still clad only in the apron. "How dare you put my help on a monetary basis? How dare you!"

"You seem to want to keep our relationship on an im-personal level—" he started to say, but I marched forward and slapped both hands on his chest, glaring straight into his eyes.

"I don't have impersonal relationships with men I sleep with."

"You've only slept with me—"

"Gah!" I yelled, spinning on my heel and storming off his boat.

"Beam?" he called after me, at the back of the boat when I carefully made my way down the narrow gangplank.

I ignored the fact that he was giving a passing couple an eyeful, and yelled back, "What?"

"Do you want me to pick you up tomorrow morning? We can work in my office at Pi Tower and look at the Beowulf code together."

"You can go to hell," I yelled, then realized that I was cutting off my nose to spite myself. "Fine, I'll help you. I'll be at your office at nine, but not one minute earlier!"

You're so falling in love with him again, my inner Housewife commented from where she was lying on a fainting couch, buffing her nails.

"And you can shut the fuck up, too," I told her, angry at the part of me that wanted more than anything to welcome Neo back to my life. "We're doing this on my terms. And that does not include him paying me. The nerve. The absolute nerve of him!"

Definitely falling in love again, my annoying brain said.

I had a horrible feeling she was right.

TEN

"Darling, I don't know why you insist on hiding. People want to see you. You're the head of the company. It's important for you to be seen to be in control. You should be here with us."

The voice echoed throughout the bathroom. Neo adjusted the volume of the Bluetooth speaker before rubbing a towel over his head and eyeing himself in the steamy mirror. "Good morning to you, too, Mother." He tried to see himself through Beam's eyes.

It was true that all the time in Peru had kept him relatively fit, but he didn't see the sort of definition in his chest and arms that Chase had. Maybe he should take up a weight-lifting regime. Something to give him a bit more of an impressive physique.

"Your yacht is, of course, very nice, and speaking of that, Lancelot and I would like to take it to Italy next month, with a few friends for a little cruise. You'll have to hire a crew, but I'm sure the people you had when we took our anniversary cruise around the Mediterranean last year would be perfect. Also, do rent some of those Jet Skis. You know how Lancelot loves those."

He looked at the few strands of gray that were starting to show up at his temples. Definitely he would start lifting weights.

"Now, about dinner tonight—we're having a small party to welcome you back. Just an intimate gathering, friends who will be happy to see you again and, of course, a few ladies who are dying to meet such an eligible bachelor. Number two, did you see? You remained at that spot for the latest list, although everyone else fell down a spot. Except for that Italian actor, but he doesn't count."

He rubbed his chest, where his heart beat away like nothing had happened to it. And yet, for the first time in twenty-four years, he felt like a person, a living, breathing man who had a purpose in life. He felt like a man who had a woman.

The trick was to get Beam to come to that same conclusion.

"It'll be quite informal, so no need to go to the length of black tie, although a nice suit is always appropriate."

His mother's voice, emerging from the speaker attached to the wall, suddenly filtered through his thoughts. "What is informal?"

"Neo! Weren't you listening? Your welcome-home party, of course. It'll start at seven, so be sure to be here a little early. I'll want you to greet your guests rather than leaving it to me to do."

"I can't come to your party tonight," he answered, fully aware that any event his mother arranged was for her own purposes, rather than his. "I have a prior engagement."

"Then you must cancel. This is important," Camilla said, a note of steel entering her voice.

Bulldozing to commence in three, two, one … , he thought. "Much as I appreciate you feeling like I need a party to see your friends, I have made other plans, and no, I won't cancel. I'm sure your party will be a great success without me."

"Darling," she drawled, giving the word a razor edge. Neo was always mildly amused at her attempt to be affectionate when she really wanted to yell at him. "I can't have this. What will people think? You can move your event. Is it a date? Who are you seeing? Is it anyone I know?"

It was on the tip of his tongue to tell her he was going to meet with his cousins, but he had too many things to get done over the course of the day to put up with the temper tantrum that was sure to follow that news. "Make my apologies to everyone, and blame pressing matters at Pi. It's the truth, by the way. If that's all, I need to shave."

"No, it is not all. Neo, I would have thought you'd acknowledge what I have done for you by acquiescing to one simple request. This party—"

"Can't talk and shave," he interrupted. "I'll be in the office later today, so no doubt I'll see you then."

He hung up before she could do more than sputter a few harsh comments about sons who disrespected their mothers, quickly shaving before pulling on a favorite pair of white pants and a navy shirt. It was a little stereotypically nautical, but the pants were tighter than what he normally wore, and he remembered that Beam had always liked him in dark colors, saying it brought out the silver lights in his eyes.

An hour later, a voice heralded the arrival of a visitor.

"Neo, I hate to be the bearer of bad news, but there are a couple of things that I think you should be aware of."

"That doesn't sound like anything I want to hear," Neo responded, flipping through several screens of an internal organizational system that dealt with the Pi servers. It was odd how every trail he followed regarding Beowulf faded into nothing. He found one reference to the source being added some thirteen years before, but that was a single line in a backup log, and since the file name was encrypted, he had to trust that his software had decrypted the information correctly.

Thirteen years ago. He was in New Guinea then, working with an international medical group, helping them set up a network that stretched to all the hospitals and many clinics in the area. Somehow, during that time someone had uploaded and integrated Beam's Beowulf into the core software running Pi.

"I'm sure you won't like it, but I wouldn't be doing my job if I didn't warn you what was going on," Chase said, grimacing as he took a seat next to Neo, casting a disparaging glance out the window. A ship was passing nearby, making the boat rock a little in the wake.

"Can't you deal with it?" Neo asked, giving up on another lead that ended abruptly, as if its history had been erased from the root. "I've got my hands full with that Beowulf code I told you about."

"Actually, I have a feeling it's related to that."

Neo stopped a tracer program and looked over at his old friend. "You know something about it?"

"No." Chase made a face, a faint line of perspiration dotting his forehead. "God, why is it always so rough in the harbor? Are you going to keep working here this morning?"

"For another hour, yes. What is the bad news related to Beowulf?"

"It's not so much the code itself, it's … er … look, I'm just going to come right out and tell you what I've found out. I won't blame you for wanting to shoot the messenger, but just remember that I've always been on your side, and I wouldn't want to do this unless it was necessary." He took a deep breath, then said quickly, "I thought I'd check into Beam, because I knew you wouldn't. And it's my job to protect you even when you don't think it's necessary. Well, I'm glad I did."

"I really wish people would stop taking it upon themselves to try to protect me from Beam," Neo said, itching to get back to hunting down clues as to what was going on with his core programming. "She's done nothing wrong. Quite the contrary, in fact."

Chase held up a hand. "I hate to dump this on you now, when you're trying to rebuild a relationship with her, but I thought you should know what's happening out of your sight. She's not in a good position right now, Neo. She recently lost her job with a firm of CPAs who she'd been with for fifteen years. She is freelancing now, but from what our people could find out, she's pretty deeply in debt. She's paying for her niece's education, and there seems to be some situation with the CPA firm that I couldn't get to the bottom of, but it smells like some form of ethical issues. It's pretty clear that she decided that you were her ticket out of the trouble she's in. I can't prove it yet, but it wouldn't surprise me at all to find out that she and Ziggy cooked up a plan to get Beam back into your life so she can have access to Pi."

Anger like nothing Neo had experienced rose within him, making him literally see red for a second as he stared at Chase, his mind whirling.

"There's one last thing," Chase said after half a minute of silence, during which Neo struggled for control over his emotions. "I took a look at the Beowulf code. I'm sure you noticed that it's siphoning off fractions of currency and channeling it into a special account."

"Yes," Neo finally managed to say, his voice sounding as rough as cement.

Chase took another deep breath. "Well, I had the boys in security work on it, and they managed to catch a transaction in the process of being moved to another account. One in the US. I don't know where yet, but … well, it will look bad for Beam if it turns out to be an account she has access to."

Neo flinched, just as if the words were a physical blow. Slowly, he turned his head back to look at the computer screen.

"I'm sorry, Neo, really sorry," Chase told him, patting him awkwardly on his arm. "But you can see why I thought you should know. If she's using you for her own purposes … well, forewarned is forearmed, and all that."

"I'm glad you told me," Neo said, his jaw so tight that the words were almost ground between his teeth.

"I'm off to the office," Chase said with another glance at the window. "Do you want me to do anything there? I can have security bar Beam's access to you—"

"No. Just the opposite," he said, flexing his fingers, which were stiff and cold. "I very much want to see her."

"I understand," Chase said, giving him one last sympathetic pat before leaving.

Neo continued to face the screen, his vision turned inward, the sense of betrayal so strong, he felt as if the world had shifted somehow. Everything he thought he knew was wrong, so wrong. Even his affection and trust were somehow tainted now.

He didn't know how long he sat staring blankly, but once he realized he was doing so, he made three phone calls, sent two texts, and gathered up his laptop, all the while thinking of the night before.

His heart wept.

ELEVEN

"Wow. This is an office?" I stopped at the entrance to the room that had floor-to-ceiling windows, light filling the vast amount of space between a small conference table and chairs to the left, a couch and couple of matching armchairs on the right, and, straight ahead, a sleek glass and chrome desk. I took a step forward, then squinted at the raised section of landscape visible through the massive windows. "Is that the Acropolis? Neo has a view of the actual Acropolis from his office?"

"Yes. The same view is visible in the penthouse," the woman who'd escorted me to Neo's office informed me. I gathered she was a general secretary, since Neo had said he had no assistant. She gestured toward the chairs and couch, adding, "Mr. Adams said that he expected Mr. Papaioannou in shortly, and that you were to make yourself comfortable. Can I bring you something to drink? Coffee? Tea? Wine?"

"Thank you, but I try to stay away from boozing it up at nine in the morning," I said, moving over to gaze with wonder out of the window. "Who's Mr. Adams?"

"Mr. Chase Adams is the chief financial officer of Pi," she answered, and, after making sure I didn't need anything else, left the office, the door closing with a soft little whoosh.

"I knew you were doing well, Neo, but damn. Why would

you stay on that boat when you have this sort of view?" I asked the scenery. Ahead of me was a sea of white buildings—the business section of town—while to the right lay the older part of the city, where for the most part the buildings were made from a mellow cream stone topped with red tile roofs. Above it all, the steep flanks of the Acropolis plateau rose, crowned with the impressive buildings that made up the complex. I stared at the Parthenon, wondering if I could convince Neo to take Ziggy and me there, before remembering that I was still mildly annoyed that he thought I was so mercenary that I'd charge him for my help.

"Right." I sat down at his chair, and tapped on the laptop keyboard that sat before me. A screen popped up asking for a password. I mused on that for a moment, then with a twisted smile entered my name.

The computer beeped at me and informed me the password was incorrect.

"Yeah, well, I didn't think it would be that." I thought for a few minutes, trying to remember what he used as the basis for his passwords. I knew it had its source in a favorite childhood pet, but he had some complicated method of appending a number to it. "Not his birth year," I mused, then hesitantly typed in the dog's name and the year we were at Oxford.

Welcome, Neo, the screen read before clearing to reveal a number of icons arranged in tidy squares in the four corners of the screen. His computer wallpaper, I was interested to note, was a picture of Neo about eight years old, his arms around a shaggy black-and-white dog. I'd never seen the picture, and couldn't help but wonder what sort of a child he was.

How had so much time passed without me making an effort to contact him? What would our lives have been if I had found him earlier, and we'd realized that neither was the monster we'd thought? Would we have had children? A happy life together? Would he have taken me with him to South America to help the people there?

A noise audible from beyond his office door reminded me where I was, and I shook off the introspection. "It does no good, not now," I said with the wisdom of many years of Daria's help under my belt. "Right. Let's go see what is going on with Beowulf."

An hour later, I was elbow deep in the code, Neo's laptop screen littered with a number of text snippets of code that I'd isolated and copied to dig into further. He had encryption software that listed its release date as later that year, so I gathered it was a beta version that he was allowed to use ahead of others. I ran it through its paces on a bit of code to see how it worked, making notes on a tablet of paper that I'd discovered in a drawer.

The door whooshed as I was whipping up a quick and dirty decryption code via one of the test server's sandboxes where developers had access to various coding languages.

"—don't forget the board is meeting at three, and you promised Mrs. Zola you'd be there."

I glanced up to see Neo entering the room, Chase on his heels. My stomach seemed to do a leap, waking up my dozing Housewife, who immediately noticed that Neo had shaved off all those wonderful whiskers that sent shivers of delight just from my remembering how they had felt on my inner thighs. His eyes were on me, an odd, flat gray.

He wore a pair of white pants that held my attention for far longer than was polite, the fabric skimming his body in a way that immediately made me want to run my hands along its contours.

"Beam," Neo said, nodding at me, his gaze shifting to the laptop in front of me. He hesitated for a few seconds, his brows pulling together. "You're using my computer."

"Of course I am. I can't very well help you if I don't," I told him, my happiness at seeing him starting to fade with the odd stiffness of his manner.

"Indeed," Chase said, apropos of nothing. When I glanced toward him, he gave a little cough and, with a look at Neo that I felt was far too fraught with meaning for my comfort, added, "I'll be in my office."

I waited until he closed the door behind him before asking Neo, "What got up his butt? For that matter, what's wrong with you?"

"Why do you imagine something is wrong with me?" he asked, setting a laptop bag on his desk before moving around to stand next to me.

"For one, you act surprised that I'm using your laptop. Did I hallucinate you asking me to look at Beowulf? Because if I didn't, then I'm at a loss how I'm supposed to do so without some sort of access to your servers."

"I was just a little taken aback that you were so easily able to break my password," he said in a neutral tone that left me feeling uncomfortably prickly.

"Neo," I said, holding up a hand and raising an eyebrow at him. I ticked off my fingers. "One, you always use your dog Hydra as the basis of your password. Two, you told me never to use a birth date, but instead pick a year that had a meaning to you that you'd not forget. Three, you and I were both traumatized by our year at Oxford. It wasn't that hard to guess."

He looked thoughtful for a moment, then released a breath like he'd been holding it in. "I should have known you would figure it out. You were always so good remembering passwords, where I had to write every one down. So?"

"So?" I repeated, wondering why he'd suddenly come to life. Had he really suspected me of snooping on his computer?

"What did you find?" He pulled a chair around to my side of the table, sitting close enough next to me that his leg pressed against mine. I told the Housewife she did not have the right to encourage me to run my hands along his clearly defined thighs, and instead addressed my worry.

"Are you upset I guessed your password? If you are, I'm sorry. I suppose I should have waited for you to get here to give me access, but it seemed like a perfect opportunity to see what the code is doing."

His gaze met mine, his eyes warming from the cold silver ice that had greeted me a few minutes ago, to the lovely gray that made me feel like the temperature in the room had risen ten degrees.

"I don't have anything to hide, Beam, so no, I'm not upset you took the initiative to dive into the code. Will you show me what you've found?"

"Of course." I turned the laptop so he could see the screen, and spent the next forty-five minutes walking him through my discoveries and suppositions.

"I saw a mention of it in the log dated thirteen years ago," he said when I was done, flipping through the notes I'd made on the paper. "But I didn't realize that it had been split apart and hidden in existing code."

"Those are only the tendrils of it that I've found," I said, looking back at the laptop.

"Tendrils. That's a good word for it. So it's not the root program itself; it's the tendrils that we have to worry about." Neo looked both thoughtful and angry, an oddly endearing mix of emotions.

I couldn't help myself. I put a hand on his thigh, giving his leg a little squeeze. "Do you have any idea who could have done this?"

"No. It had to be someone who has extensive knowledge of coding, encryption, and the proprietary language we use for Pi." He was silent for a few minutes. "There are only a handful of people who have the sort of access needed, although if someone was that savvy, I suppose it wouldn't take much to grant access that they shouldn't have."

I wanted badly to ask if his mother or uncle had that access, but before I could do so, he looked at me, his pupils flaring. Beneath my hand, his thigh tensed.

"Beam," he said, a throb in his voice that instantly pushed my body into full arousal mode.

"I know," I said, finding it difficult to breathe. "You smell so good."

"You make my senses swim."

We stared at each other for a second; then we were on our feet, my mouth on his even as we struggled to pull clothing off each other.

"Door!" I said, sanity returning to me for a moment when I kicked off my shoes so I could remove my linen palazzo pants.

"What about—oh!" He hopped on one foot over to the door, one leg of his white pants hanging free while he yanked off the other before he flipped the lock on the door. "Floor? Couch? Desk?"

"Wall?" I asked, flinging myself on him, making him stumble back two steps until he hit the door, my mouth and hands touching and tasting everything I could reach.

"I'm not sure—I've never tried standing—oh, Christ, yes, wall, it is," he moaned into my mouth when I slid my hands down his belly, pushing his underwear off, and filling my hands with him.

I did a little dance when he tried unsuccessfully to remove my undies, until I stopped caressing him and yanked them off before kicking them aside, returning to his body to move my hips against him in a way that had my inner Housewife cheering. "You feel so good, Neo. I never realized just how good you felt until this exact moment. I like your chest. And your arms. And neck, and belly, and butt. And all your other bits."

His hands were all over me, touching first my breasts, then my butt, and my back, finally holding onto my hips while I wiggled against him. "Sunshine, I know you want to do this here, but I'm not sure that it's going to work. For one, I think you have to be against the wall, and for another—there's a couple of secretaries right outside the door, and I think they'll notice if we pound rhythmically against it."

I giggled into his collarbone, then gave a little purr when he swung me up into his arms and carried me over to the couch. "You're right, I couldn't face them if they knew what we were up to. No, Neo, not the fingers. You'll make me mindless, and it's my turn to do that to you. …"

He had laid me down onto the couch, his fingers already dancing around in my intimate parts, but my desire for him was too much to remain passive. "It's my office; thus, I decree what happens here," he said in a tone that I could tell strove for lofty indifference, but nonetheless allowed me to push him onto his back.

"It may be your office, but now you're my prisoner," I said, growing bold with the desire that raged through me like an inferno. I straddled one of his legs, bending down to swirl my tongue around his nipple. "And I get to be the boss of you. Are you still ticklish here?"

He bucked beneath me when I dragged my fingernails up his inner thigh, almost dislodging me. "Christ, yes! Don't do that again. Wait, do it one more time with the other leg, then stop."

"Not having the vast experience that you've had with numerous sexual partners, I don't know if your sensitivity is normal, but I do like how responsive you are. Ready? Leg number two incoming." He squirmed, his toes curling when I repeated my action to the leg that was off the couch due to lack of space.

"Four, Beam. I've had four lovers in twenty-four years," he said, groaning when I scooted down a bit, nibbling my way up his sensitive thighs. "How many toys do you have?"

"A hell of a lot more than four," I said, eyeing his penis. He was already pretty aroused, but I thought we could do better. "I have a memory of making you wild. Shall we see if I can duplicate the past?"

Neo looked down the length of his body, his eyes wide with hope. "If you have any mercy in you, yes. Er … that is, only if you want to. I realize that I'm much hairier than you are down there."

"That's because women are expected to prune, while most men feel like doing the same is emasculating."

"Beam …"

"And yes, you have body hair, but that's all right, because your blond mother gave you some very good hair genes. I remember your father being fairly hirsute, but you're just moderately hairy."

"Beam, we have limited time before someone comes looking for me."

"Your door is locked. Besides, body dysmorphia is rampant in our culture, and I won't allow it to get hold of me. I was thinking of letting my leg hair go wild. Do you have thoughts on that?"

"Yes," he said, his leg tensing as his hopeful look turned to a mild glare. "I don't give a damn what you do with your leg hair. Keep it or shave it or even braid it. But if you continue to touch me like that, there are going to be repercussions, and they won't bode well for me being able to make love to you as I want to do."

I looked down, a little surprised to find that while I was talking, I'd taken him in both hands, and was evidently stroking him to a hardness that I very much wanted to romp on. "Oh, sorry. That was my inner Housewife. She loves your penis."

I dipped my head down to lick the underside of his shaft, spending a little extra time on what I remembered were sensitive spots.

His answer was unintelligible, a noise that was half groan, half a prayer for me to never stop. "No, I changed my mind," he said four seconds later, his hands on my shoulders as I really got down to business. He pulled me off him with an audible popping noise. "Stop or I really won't be able to last."

"OK, but this is supposed to be my turn to make you— Neo!"

I don't know how he did it—gymnastic ability, basic physics, or pure magic—but somehow, he managed to get out from under me without getting off the couch, while at the same time shifting me so I lay facedown on the couch, my legs splayed, while he slid an arm under my belly, pulling me upward at the same time he stuffed one of the throw pillows that had fallen to the floor under my abdomen.

"There's only so much I can stand, and you, madam, have pushed me well past that point. You forfeit the rest of your turn to be bossy because of your cruelty in insisting on making me insane. Now, I believe you mentioned two fingers …"

"Neo!" I squawked, the words ending in a moan when his fingers danced around in flesh that was hot and almost throbbing with need. "This is a new position! We never did this before. I'm not sure—my butt is right there where you can see it. That can't be pleasant viewing."

I could feel him looking at my behind. "On the contrary, it's a delightful ass, round and pink. I like it. I will bite it another time, but right now, if you are ready—"

"I've been ready since you walked into the room," I said, trying to roll onto my back, but Neo drove all thoughts of missionary position out of my head by lifting my hips and thrusting forward.

"I think you missed," I said, feeling him along the crease of my thigh. "Don't … uh … I'm not into back-door action, if you get my drift."

"I'm delighted to hear that, since it's not something that I wish to explore. Right. This should work." He tipped me ever so slightly to the left, and again tried to thrust into me.

"Nope. That was my other leg. Did you put lube on or something? You feel kind of sticky." I tried to prop myself up with one hand so I could reach back and help him with the other, but it was a difficult position.

"I would be with the way you were licking me. Also, I'm a bit anticipatory, and that means there is a certain amount of stickiness to share. Stop squirming, and let me aim properly."

"OK, how about this? We do this the normal way, and you won't have to use my butt crack as a guide," I said when he did just that, fortunately skipping over the off-limit parts to head for my party zone.

"There is nothing abnormal about this," he said, sounding like the words were ground out as he made a couple of wild stabs. "It's perfectly normal. It's just that the couch doesn't allow for full extension of your legs, but I've been told this is an extremely pleasurable position for women, and dammit, I want you to feel extreme pleasure."

"Almost," I said, laughter building in me as he very nearly hit the right spot, but skittered off toward my pubic bone. "No, left. Your other left. Just a smidgen to the right—argh!"

Neo snarled something obscene under his breath at the same time he hoisted me upward until I was on my knees, and managed to guide himself to my intimate welcoming embrace.

"There!" he said, full of triumph, the word melting into a groan of pure pleasure when he took a few strokes.

"Doggy-style?" I said, simultaneously thrilled and shocked. "I didn't know you were a doggy-style person, Neo! This is different. It's … it's so very different. What are you seeing? Just my big ass? I'm not sure I approve of this. I liked it better when you were at least lying on my back, because then you couldn't see my butt rising like a full moon."

He started laughing, the movement causing him to pull out, leaving me feeling bereft on many levels. Before I could protest, he pulled me into his arms, the pair of us sitting naked on the couch, unfulfilled, sticky, and, in my case, red-faced. "For the record, I couldn't see your ass at all, just your back. But that aside, I forgot how much I love the way you say whatever you're thinking. Would it make you happier to have us face-to-face?"

"Yes," I said, momentarily wallowing in embarrassment until I realized just how ridiculous the situation was. I gave a couple of hiccuping laughs, and leaned forward to kiss the tears of hilarity that leaked from his eyes. "I'm sorry to be such a prude, but honestly, Neo, butt first is not how I want you to think of me."

He adjusted us until he was leaning back on the couch, with my knees straddling his hips. "I'm sorry, sunshine. I never want to make you feel uncomfortable. I just thought it would bring you pleasure."

"*You* bring me pleasure," I said, my mouth lingering on his. "Let's try this again, but this time, I'll drive."

He gave one last laugh that turned to a moan when I positioned him, then slid down him with exquisite slowness, feeling every inch of him as he pushed his way into all my intimate muscles.

But it was more than that, I realized as I rose and fell on him, his hands on my hips, his mouth nibbling and kissing along my neck and shoulders. The familiar coiling tightness began to build inside me as I acknowledged the fact that this was more than merely a sexual encounter.

Being with Neo had shifted my determination to lay the ghosts of my past to something more positive. I didn't know if we could overcome the events of the past or all the years of separation, but at that moment, as we both raced toward our climaxes, I knew that this time, I would fight for him.

For us.

For a future together.

I clung to him, smothering his face in my breasts as my body shook with the orgasm, tears pricking my eyes at the emotions that burst into glorious being. "I love you," I told him, clutching his head even as he thrust upward wildly, clearly riding his own pleasure. "I loved you before, I loved you even while I hated you, but now I love you again. Goddess help me, Neo, you had better not break my heart again, because this time, I'm not going to take it."

He mumbled something, but the words were unintelligible until I realized I was still smothering him in my boobs. I pulled back, and he took a long, gasping breath, his face red, his hair standing on end where I had clutched it.

"What was that?" I asked, my body humming like a plucked harp string.

"I said that I love your breasts, even when I can't breathe because of them," he said, taking both of them into his hands, and kissing them.

I stared at him for a second, disbelief chasing horror, followed by anger. I grabbed his hair with both hands, tugging in a less gentle manner than I might have had I not just had the epiphany to end all my epiphanies. "You love my boobs?"

He tipped his head up, his eyes delightfully crinkled, as he carefully pulled my hands from his hair. "I do. They are perfect. You may not think so, but they are everything I could desire. They are plump and warm and perfectly fit my hands and mouth."

"Neo," I said in what was very nearly a growl.

He laughed, the bastard. The number two world's most wanted bachelor bastard.

"I love you, too, sunshine. If I didn't love it when your eyes get all sparky with anger, I would chastise you for not knowing just how much I love you."

"Are you sure?" I asked, narrowing my eyes on him. "It's not just girlfriend-number-five lust?"

"Beam, my adorable contrary, infuriating, intriguing, and endlessly fascinating Moonbeam, you are the only woman I've ever wanted. There's a reason why those former girlfriends lasted a week or less. None of them held a match to you. Every time I was with them, it drove home that I had lost the love of my life, and no one would be able to fill that empty hole in my life."

I kissed both corners of his lips, his face between my hands as I said, "You didn't try to find me."

"No." Sadness leached the humor from his eyes, and I felt as if a cloud had blotted out the sun. "I didn't. And I will regret that to the end of my days. I should have. I should have known that my father was manipulating us. I should have seen through the lies. I should have trusted in your character instead of believing that my parents were right."

Something inside me shifted at that moment, the cloud dissipating as a pain I hadn't realized I'd carried eased, and slowly evaporated. "I forgive you," I said, tears once again burning my eyes. "I don't know if you are ready to forgive me for not fighting for us—"

"There's nothing to forgive. The fault was on my side," he interrupted, shifting us so that I was no longer impaled on him, but sitting across his lap, our bodies damp and sticky, but pressed together in a way that filled my soul with joy.

I wanted to force him into forgiving my part in our broken relationship, but years of Daria had brought me some insight, and part of that was that the choice was his, and I had no say in it. "Some, yes, but I've been through too much therapy to lie to myself. I'm sorry that I didn't have enough trust in you to try to reach you."

"We were both so young," he said. "The manipulation of my father aside, I think you're correct that we're going to have to move past what we should have done, and accept it for what it was. Because what we have now is far more important."

I kissed his cheek. "You always were so much more eloquent than me. It's one of the things that—"

The doorknob rattled at that point, causing me to stare in horror at it for a moment.

"It's locked," Neo said as I got off his lap and looked around for my pants and top. He did likewise. "You don't have to worry—"

Voices could be heard faintly through the wood of the door. Neo tipped his head like he was listening intently, then leaped up and flung a soft lap blanket that had been draped over one arm of the couch at me just as the door lock clicked open, and the door was thrown back with force.

"I thought you said he had come into the office—Neo!" A woman strode into the room, followed by three other people, one of whom was Chase. "You're nude! What in heaven's name do you think you're doing?"

Quickly, I wrapped the lap blanket around myself, and stared with growing worry at the pair of my underwear that dangled from a standing lamp next to the door, slightly behind the group of interlopers.

That's when I realized that everyone was getting an eyeful of Neo, including the secretary, who was staring at him with wide, dazzled eyes.

"Out!" Neo demanded in a near shout, pointing at the door.

"Darling, this is—"

"OUT!" he repeated in a roar. "You can return in a few minutes."

To my surprise, everyone piled out of the room, although I caught the secretary casting a highly admiring gaze at him before she left.

"Right. I'm going to die of embarrassment now," I said, gathering up my clothing and hurriedly putting it on.

"It's what I get for letting security have a key to my office," he muttered as he, too, pulled on his clothes. "I'm sorry, Beam. I wouldn't have exposed you that way for the world."

"It's not your fault. You wanted us to pick up the pace, and I insisted on being a chatty Cathy," I said, enjoying the embrace he pulled me into.

"That's only because you were nervous. I understood. Ready?"

I nodded, and kissed the visible spot on his neck. "As much as I'll ever be."

He opened the door, and gestured in the people who were clustered together, obviously discussing what they'd seen.

"Mother, I've told you before that I don't appreciate you barging into my office when the door is locked," Neo said, his arms crossed over his beautiful chest.

"I am your mother!" Camilla said, for indeed, it was the woman I'd seen so many years before. I had to admit, she wore the twenty-four years well, her hair carefully coiffed, not one hint of gray in the expensively shaded blond hair. Her face was unlined, and she had the bronzed glow of women who spend a lot of time and money looking like they live an active outdoor life.

Then her gaze turned onto me, and I had to brace myself to keep from hiding behind Neo. I clutched the back of his shirt and tried to keep the quaver out of my voice when I said, "Hello, Mrs. Zola." I struggled with my need to balance politeness with truth, then decided a little kindness was never out of place, and added, "It's a pleasure to see you again."

"Again?" Her gaze raked me, a faint pucker between her perfectly groomed brows.

I could tell the moment when she recognized me, because her eyes went flinty, and her fingers flexed a few times, like she wanted to punch something.

"You! You dare to come here with your lies and treachery? I knew that there must be a reason that your bastard child tried to infiltrate my beloved Pi, but I never imagined that you'd have the bad manners to push yourself where you're not wanted. Chase, darling, call security. Have this … person … removed from the building. If she tries to return, have her arrested for trespassing."

"Chase will do no such thing," Neo said, sighing, putting his arm around me in a way that had me leaning into him. "I've told security that Beam is to be given full access to any and all of the offices. As for your personal comments about her …" He made a gesture toward the group behind Camilla. "I will speak with you privately."

Chase raised his eyebrows and sent Neo a sympathetic look before herding the secretary out before him. Camilla and a man with curly red hair remained, the latter looking mildly interested.

"While I appreciate your willingness to hide what has obviously been a gross lack of your common sense, I will not have you consorting with this thief, this liar, again. That goes for her bastard."

"OK, first of all, I don't have a child. If you are referring to Ziggy, she's my niece, my sister's child. She's also a sweet girl, funny, smart, and if you say so much as one mean thing about her, I'm seriously going to punch you." I took an aggressive step forward, my hands fisted.

"Beam," Neo said in obvious warning, pulling me back, one arm around me as he tugged me up tight against his body.

"I'm not going to let her pick on Ziggy," I told him, righteous indignation making me heedless of caution and common politeness. "She's blameless!"

"She is," he agreed, pulling up one of my fists and kissing it before turning back to his mother. "And my mother will apologize for her hasty and unfounded assumptions."

Camilla's nostrils flared in a dramatic manner that I thought made her look a bit like a horse. "I have never apologized for speaking the truth, and I have no intention of doing so now!"

"Beam has done nothing wrong," Neo interrupted her. My heart gave a little cheer, my Housewife swooning with how wonderful he was. "And I'll thank you to stop saying things about her and Ziggy that aren't true. I realize that you may have been as fooled as I was by the false information that Dad manufactured against her, and arranged for me to discover"—he made little air quotes about the last word—"but that is very far from the truth."

"Your father didn't have to manufacture things against her—" Camilla started to say, but once again, Neo stepped up to the bat.

"Bullshit," he snapped. "You only have to know her to realize how unreal the claims were that he made against her. I'm just ashamed that I was so naive and trusting that I believed you over my own knowledge of her personality."

"Her *personality*," Camilla sneered, shooting me a look of pure venom that had my gut suddenly feeling as if it were filled with oatmeal. Cold, clammy oatmeal. "Her personality is one of deceit and manipulation, and I won't allow her to try to turn you from us again! I won't let her influence ruin you!"

"The only thing Beam's influence has done is to make me feel loved, and like I'm no longer alone in the world. I realize now that in the time we were apart, I was hollow inside, not truly living, just getting by, so really, you ought to be singing her praises for making me happy at last."

"Happy!" Camilla's lip curled. "You poor thing, she's confused you just like she did before. It's quite evident that she's reached you the only way women of her ilk do so—via her body—but that should be a warning to you, not an act that deserves praise. Far from it. If I didn't know about her true character from that unfortunate incident in the past, I would certainly not be in doubt after hearing the information Chase has found out. Tell me, Neo, did your precious lost love tell you how she hired a private detective to find you?"

The oatmeal turned to cement. I froze, my breath caught in my throat.

"Did she tell you that she searched for you first in Peru, and then here? Did she tell you how she verified the flight you were taking home? That she booked one to arrive just before you, so that she'd be here when you arrived?"

Beside me, I felt Neo withdraw. Not physically, but emotionally. I took a step to the side so I could face him, wanting to explain, but my cheeks flamed at the thought of baring my soul in front of Camilla, and the man who I assumed was Neo's stepdad.

Neo didn't look at me, but I could see a muscle in his jaw flex. "More lies," he finally said, the words sounding like they were forced out through clenched teeth.

"Ask her," Camilla crowed, making a grand gesture that expressed nothing but contempt and triumph. "Ask her about the private detective she hired in New Mexico, and who spilled everything when our security—the security that I myself ensured was in place to protect you from just this sort of abuse—tracked him down and forced the truth from him. Ask her why she, a woman who is unemployed, fired from a job because she knowingly falsified documents for one of her former firm's clients, would be so desperate to be here just when you arrived home."

I tried to get breath into my lungs, but they were having none of it.

"Ask her how she arranged for her niece to be here, conveniently able to corrupt the servers with her malicious program. And then you might ask yourself a question—why would she be here now, destitute, without a job, to see a man she loudly proclaimed broke her heart? Because I don't know about you, but I can only think of one reason for such a woman to be pursuing you. Go ahead, darling. Since you know her so well, ask her all these things. See what she says. I'm very interested to hear her answers."

I kept my gaze on Neo, wanting to simultaneously cry, scream, and run away so I could lick my wounds in private. But even as I thought of excusing myself, Neo turned his head toward me, and I saw the pain in his eyes.

"It's not like that," I finally managed to say.

"You hired a detective to find me?" His voice was as rough as gravel, his face so stark of emotion that I wanted to weep for him. "You arranged to meet me? It wasn't an accident that you were in the office just as I arrived?"

I wanted badly to lie, but I couldn't. Not to him. Not to the man who had always held my heart. "I knew you were coming home," I admitted. "But I didn't know we'd meet."

"Why?" he asked, just the one word, but it was filled with a whole universe of pain.

I took a step forward in response, reaching for him, tears filling my eyes when he stiffened at the approach of my hand. "I ... I told you before ... there were things ... Ziggy ..."

"No," he said, the word stabbing at my heart. "Not Ziggy. Don't bring her into it. Why did *you* hunt me, Beam? Why, if you believed I was at fault for everything that happened in the past, did you want to see me so badly that you'd hire a detective to find me?"

It was my worst nightmare come to life, I thought absently as my gaze flickered to Camilla's smug expression, to the wide eyes of the man behind her, and finally back to Neo, who radiated a cold fury that made me feel alternately hot and freezing cold. I wanted to vomit. I wanted to scream. I wanted to cling to him and sob out my heart.

"I ..." I swallowed back a big lump of tears, my face hot with the mortification of having to tell him how I'd wanted to get over him by confronting him in person. I couldn't do it. Not with his mother there, ready to mock me and point out to Neo just how wrong I was for him.

"You can't tell me? You can't give me even one answer?" he asked, his voice as frigid as my soul. I met his gaze, seeing only anger.

"Not now. Not here," I said, gesturing toward his mother.

His jaw worked again. "I see." He turned to look at his mother, who had started to smirk at him, but the expression faded with his next words. "I think it's time you find an interest other than Pi, Mother. I will inform the board that you will no longer be attending any future meetings. You will also retire from acting as a contact point for any other in-company interests you have, effective immediately."

Neo was through the door before either Camilla or the silent redheaded man or I could respond. I stared at his back as he strode out of the room, scattering orders as he went. Without waiting to see what Camilla would do—beyond the squawk of protest that she made in response to his directive—I hurried after him, needing desperately to explain myself, to make him understand why I had wanted to see him in person after avoiding it for so long.

How could the day have gone from so wonderful, to a nightmarish hell?

I caught up to Neo when he stopped next to the open door of an office, his profile one of a vengeful god come to life, terrible in its beauty. "Chase, pack up your things. You're fired."

"Is this a joke?" Chase half rose from behind the desk, his expression as stunned as I knew mine must be. "Or are you drunk?"

"Neither." Neo seemed unaware of me as I stood just at his shoulder, wanting badly to say something, but my inner Housewife told me that I'd done enough to ruin our blossoming relationship.

"Neo, I demand an explanation." Camilla stormed toward us, her face red, her eyes filled with spite. "Your actions are those of a madman. Come back and let us talk sensibly, away from this … bad influence."

Chase had gotten to his feet and moved around the desk by now. "Is that it? Your friend there has said things about me? Neo, you know me. We've been together for almost twenty years. I have only Pi's best interests at heart. Your best interests. Whatever she told you I did, it's not true."

I felt battered and bruised, as if I were surrounded by whirlwinds that kept buffeting me from different angles. I could ignore Camilla's spite, knowing its source, but that Neo's friend would jump onto the trash-Beam bandwagon left me hurt and wanting to escape. If I could just get Neo alone, and explain everything to him …

"I'd find it interesting that you immediately blamed Beam for my decision, but I don't care what you think anymore." He turned to a small group of people who'd popped out of the offices that made up this floor. "I want security here in the next three minutes escorting this man out. Then they can help my mother and her husband pack up their things."

He spun on his heel and was off before I realized it.

"What did you say to him?" Chase asked, looking as hurt and shocked as I felt. "Why do you hate me so much? What have I ever done to you?"

"Nothing, I swear I've said nothing," I protested, ignoring Camilla when she demanded that security be called to remove me, alternating with shrieking at Neo.

"You must have said something," Chase said. "Why else would he do this? I don't understand."

"I don't either," I said, then ran after Neo, dodging more people as they emerged from their offices, no doubt drawn by Camilla's increasingly vocal demands for explanations. "Neo, what's going on?"

He ignored me, yanking open the door to the stairwell and disappearing into it.

I glanced back behind me, seeing Chase and Camilla standing together, Chase holding her back while her hands waved wildly. I raced down two flights of stairs, catching a door just as it was closing, emerging into a vast open room filled with cubicles, plants, and people. Neo walked down a center aisle, calling out what I realized were people's names.

"Danielos. Katopodis. Mikos. Papadiamantopoulos. Vasila-kis. Roman. Pappas. Schmidt. Scala. Konstantine."

People emerged from various offices that lined two sides of the massive room. Several heads popped up from the cubicles, everyone watching with surprise as Neo leaped up onto a table. "If I called your name, get your things, and leave. As of this moment, you're fired."

"What the hell are you doing?" I asked, half-scared, half-worried that he was having some sort of a mental health episode. When he jumped off the table and started to brush past me, I stopped him, grabbing his arm. The room was dead silent as everyone stared in shock. "Neo, what are you doing?"

He spun around and faced me, his eyes as liquid as mercury. "Do you want to tell me why you wanted to find me so badly?"

I glanced around. The entire room of about sixty people watched us. "I want to explain, yes, but not here—"

"Then leave me alone. I have things to do." He jerked his arm from my hold, heading back toward the stairs.

"What things?" I yelled, slapping my hands on my legs. "Why are you firing everyone just because you're mad at me?"

His expression was one of such fierceness that I had a feeling I'd just roused a lion, and now I had to face the consequences. "I'm doing what I should have done years ago. I'm cleaning house. I'm getting rid of anyone who isn't contributing to Pi in a meaningful manner."

"But if these people are innocent—" I said, following him to the stairwell when he marched off.

"They're not," he said, shooting me a potent glare over his shoulder. "Any more than you are."

"How can you say that?" I asked, yanking open the door when it closed in my face. "I've never lied to you, Neo. Never!"

"You can't tell me the truth, either," he snapped back, his footsteps echoing as he thundered down the metal stairs.

I stood there for a moment, my whole world crashing and burning around me. *How can he believe the worst in me?* my wounded Housewife asked. *Why is it that whenever he's presented with something that makes me look bad, he always believes it? Why does he never believe me?*

Tears of pity and shame burned down my face as I ran down the remainder of the stairs, somehow making it back to my hotel room, where I lay on the bed and indulged in the biggest pity party of my life.

"How could things go so wrong so quickly?" I asked Ziggy two hours later, when she arrived to find out why I wasn't answering my texts. I'd given her a quick update as to the morning's events, minus the lovemaking, too miserable to care that she knew how pathetic I'd become. "How could he be so loving one moment, and assuming I'm the worst person ever in the next? How can he support his mother against me? Again?"

"You said he more or less told her to keep her nose out of Pi," Ziggy said, sitting on the end of my bed, resting her chin on her knees. "That doesn't sound like a man who's supporting her. Kind of the opposite, don't you think?"

I mopped up my eyes, and tried to discreetly blow my nose. "I suppose so. Maybe. But he clearly doesn't trust me. It's all well and fine for us to have incredibly hot sex, but when it comes to trust, I'm no better than a stranger to him."

"Right, because he'd ask a complete stranger to help him figure out what's going on with that code you wrote him eons ago," she said with a knowing glance before pulling out her phone.

I scooted myself up so that I was sitting on the bed with my back to the headboard, gathering up the mound of sodden tissues that I'd used while indulging in the pity party, and sweeping them into a trash bin. "That's different. He needs me to look at the code because I wrote it."

She cocked her head at me, lowering her phone for a moment. "Aunt Beam, I love you, but damn, son. You're delusional if you think that's true. I mean, I may not have known him as long as you have, but it's obvious he's been doing everything he can to get you back in his life."

"He more or less called me a liar—" I started to protest, but she lifted a hand and stopped me.

"I repeat: damn, son. Look at what he's done—he came here to talk to you after the first time you saw him, when you were so mad."

"Well … he … uh …"

"Instead of arguing, he admitted he was stupid when you guys were younger, and then went on to drag you off to see his family." She gave me a pitying look that those under thirty have perfected so well to people they deem too old to understand. "You don't do that to someone you don't trust, Auntie."

"Maybe not, but what he said today … and now that I think of it, he was definitely upset when he came in and found me on his computer. He probably thought I was trying to do something nefarious."

"Uh-huh. Because he couldn't have found probably at least a dozen other people to do what he asked you to do."

"I told you—I wrote the code, so I'm the only one who can pick through it." I stopped, the words ringing warning bells in my brain.

"Do you really think that Neo, head of one of the best-known philanthropic tech companies around, would not have on tap any number of people who could dig out a bit of code? Do you honestly think it's realistic to believe that *only you* can understand what's going on with the code you wrote twenty-four years ago?" She shook her head and returned her attention to her phone. "I get that your feelings are hurt, but you're not thinking straight. It's probably because you're in love, and it's messing with your common sense."

My gaze dropped to the box of tissues, where it lay on its side on the floor next to the bed.

Dammit, she was right. What sort of egotistical mind trip had I been on to believe that I was the only one who could detangle the code situation with Beowulf? "But why would he say that I was the one who had to work on the code?" I asked aloud.

"He was clearly looking for excuses to keep you around, probably because he was worried that you'd run away again."

The "again" was followed by a stab of guilt. "It wasn't like that. I didn't run away the first time. We both left the relationship."

"Uh-huh. Regardless, Neo is obviously trying to keep you involved in his life. Why else would he take you to meet the cousins he didn't know? Speaking of that, can I wear your gauze sundress to the party? I didn't have a chance to do laundry, and I assume you'll wear your good dress tonight."

I blinked at her a few times, unable to get my brain to do more than spin around the things she'd pointed out, slowly trying to make them fit into my new worldview. "Tonight? What—you don't honestly think I'm going to go to Neo's estranged-family party, do you? After what he did to me today?"

She didn't lower her phone this time, just did the head tip, and asked, "What exactly did he do other than ask you to explain something that clearly hurt his feelings?"

"He ... he believed his mother—"

"Aunt Beam," she said, the words dripping with disbelief.

"Fine," I said, slumping against the headboard, feeling mired in misery. "Have it your way. Be reasonable. But dammit, Ziggy, we can't go. *I* can't go. Not after the way he looked at me. I'd die of embarrassment."

"Ugh, old-people romance!" she said, getting to her feet. "You'd think you'd have your shit together by now."

"Ziggy!" I said, a little hurt at her words.

"Aunt Beam, I love you more than anyone, but you really need to get over yourself. No, not yourself ... your past self. Because if you don't stop dwelling on all the stuff you went through before, you're going to ruin what you have now."

"I'm not dwelling," I protested, realizing I was in fact doing exactly that.

"Not only are you dwelling—you're reveling in the pain of the past. And you know why? Because you're scared."

"I'm not scared. I just don't want to go through what I did before, and now Neo … if you could see the way he looked at me …" I put my hands to my cheeks, feeling another blush.

"You know what's wrong with you?" she asked, stuffing her things into her backpack and slinging it over one shoulder. "You're so worried about being embarrassed, you're missing the whole point of what Neo did. We're supposed to be there at seven, right? I'll meet you here at six thirty, OK?"

"Neo isn't going to want to see me …" The sentence faded away into a puddle of indecision and reluctance to admit that Ziggy was right. "You mean what he did in that he didn't throw me out? Or yell at me? Or tell his mom that she was right?"

"Bingo," she answered, pausing at the door, obviously waiting for me to respond.

I wanted to argue more, but I couldn't lie. Not to her, not to myself. "Dammit, have you been talking to Daria? Because you're getting way too good at dissecting my emotions and making me realize when I've been an ass. I have been, haven't I?"

"Dunno, because I was in my virtual environments and simulation class while you guys were having your blowout, but even I can see that you've really only got a couple of choices. You can either hold on to your pain, or you can have the man you love. You just need to make the decision about which you want more," she said, blowing me a kiss as she left, closing the door softly behind her.

I thought about the scene earlier in the day with Neo and his mother as a witness.

Was I wrong in interpreting his actions as being furious with me? He hadn't told me to leave. He hadn't said anything cutting to me other than what was true—I hadn't explained myself, even when he asked me point-blank to do so.

I'd let my pride rule me. Again.

"Dammit, everyone is right but me," I said, kicking the tissue box across the room. "I don't want to spend the rest of my life miserable because I couldn't handle a little scorn. Neo is what's important here." I thought of him facing his estranged family on his own, and sat up, straightening my back, and glaring at my reflection in a small mirror next to a sink. I looked like hell, my hair every which way, my eyes red, cheeks blotchy. "I may not be a prize, but Neo loves me. He said so. And I'll be damned if I leave him to face his family on his own."

My reflection gave a little nod when I made the decision, and smiled when I picked up the phone and asked the front desk if they could recommend a hairstylist who could fit me in at the last minute.

I hadn't been strong enough to face Neo's family twenty-four years before, but that was the past, and didn't matter now. What did matter was making my own happiness.

Neo had just better get with the program.

TWELVE

Neo strode into the penthouse apartment of his cousin Iakovos alternately irritated, amused, and hurt. The fact that he kept cycling through all three emotions also made him a bit annoyed because he couldn't just settle down to the normal placid calm that he liked to think was his métier, but ever since Beam had reentered his life, he'd been a complicated mix of emotions.

"Is my ex-wife here?" he asked the woman answering the door of the apartment. "I'm Neo Papaioannou."

"Kyria Beam? Yes, she's here," the woman said, her expression blank, but Neo wasn't fooled. Her sharp black eyes were busily assessing and judging him. He gathered he passed her examination when she unbent enough to nod toward a vast open space, clearly a living room that led to an expansive outdoor area. "She is with the others."

There was a tiny little hint of censure in her voice that had Neo saying, "I called for her at her hotel, but she'd already left."

"Ah," the woman said, but Neo felt a slight warming in her basilisk stare, and after mentally girding his loins for the upcoming meeting with his cousins, he strode across the living room to where he could see figures outside the big windows.

The patio area was huge, almost as big as the living space, with a nice view of the city and the harbor beyond, but Neo did not more than glance at it before his gaze snapped to where Beam stood laughing with his cousin's wife, Harry, and the other two women. Ziggy sat on the ground, petting a large orange cat with a black splotch on his head, while the male cousins were clustered together around a bar, their expressions all pleasant.

Neo wasn't fooled when their collective attention swiveled his way. They were judging him just as the woman at the door had, and this time, he was found lacking. "Good evening," he said, greeting his hostess. "You have a lovely apartment. Is that your cat? It seems to like Ziggy. Beam." He turned to face the woman who filled his mind and soul and every morsel of being, and took a deep breath. "Might I have a word in your ear?"

"Sure," she said, and seemed to brace herself. Her chin rose a little, and her eyes were filled with those delightful sparks that he swore boded well for a lifetime of never being bored. Not with her. Never with her. "Hit me with your best shot."

"Er …" Harry glanced between the two of them before sliding a look toward the other two women, both of whom were watching them with almost identical wary expressions. "Maybe we should give you two a little space?"

"No, that's not necessary," Beam said before Neo could respond. She kept her gaze firmly on his, the eye sparks increasing. "As my niece pointed out, I can't actually die of embarrassment. I might feel like I can, but the reality is that I didn't die of it twenty-four years ago, and I'm not going to now. So go ahead, Neo. Tell me what you think of me. I can take it."

He was very aware that everyone in the room was watching him. "I have no objections if you're certain you don't mind. What I have to say won't take long."

Beam took a long, somewhat shaky breath. "These people are your family, and although I don't know them very well, I like them better than your mother. So say whatever it is you want to say in front of them."

"Very well," he said after a moment's indecision. He got down onto one knee, took her hands in his, and said briskly, "Beam, would you marry me? Again? This time for good, without an annulment? Also, I don't have a ring, but I thought we could pick one out together. I was thinking a ruby."

Behind him, Ziggy whooped. Harry clapped her hands together and made a similar whooping noise. Kiera looked like she wanted to laugh, and the princess pulled a small notebook out of a pocket and started making notes.

"What?" Beam asked him, staring in what very much appeared to be utter and complete disbelief. She looked around at all the others, person by person, as if seeking enlightenment before returning to Neo. "What?" she repeated.

"It seems we are forever doomed to have unromantic proposals," he said, then winced. "Would you mind if I got up? My knee has never been the same since an ACL tear a few years ago."

"What did he say?" Beam weaved a little as she turned to Thyra.

"He asked you to marry him," she answered, pausing as she wrote, and adjusted her glasses. "You don't mind if I make a few notes, do you? I was going to take down a few facts for Neo's interview, since now I know he's not evil, and my editor really wants me to interview him, but if you're marrying him—"

"Again," Neo pointed out, then got to his feet because he felt he'd be a less effective lover if he limped visibly due to his bad knee.

"Again," Thyra agreed. "Maybe the magazine would be interested in how you two fell in love and got engaged. But do tell me if you want me to mind my own business."

"No one would ever say such a thing to you," Dmitri said, strolling over to put his arm around his wife, giving her a look that Neo wanted to give Beam, but one glance at the stunned expression still plastered on her adorable face warned him that now was not the moment for her to receive the full brunt of his smoldering intensity. "I'm sure Beam and Neo know you are simply doing your job as part of the *Noblesse International* staff. Although I admit to being a bit on tenterhooks as to whether or not we're going to have a new cousin-in-law."

"What?" Beam said for the third time. Neo sighed to himself, wanting to simultaneously laugh, kiss her, and sing to the skies about the woman who might not be perfect but was made just for him.

"Sunshine, I asked you to marry me. I don't want to pressure you, but given our activities earlier today, as well as the way you told me how much you loved me, if you wanted to accept me now, everyone would probably stop waiting for your response." He kissed her on the tip of her delightful nose.

"Marry you?" she asked, just like she couldn't believe it; then suddenly, the sparks were back. She punched him on the chest. "Marry you? But you said … no, you didn't say anything bad, you just stormed off, but your mother said I'm a liar and deceiver and a cheat and … and … dammit, I can't remember what else she said about me. But how can you ask me to marry you when I haven't even explained to you about the investigator I hired?"

Her hands were fisted, and she looked mad enough to punch him several more times. "Why do you care what my mother said about you? I don't."

"You do, too," she said, this time slapping the flat of her hand on his chest. "You ran away from me because you couldn't stand to look at me."

"I did not run from you. I had things to do. I did them. And as for you hiring a private detective to find me, I assumed you would explain that in private."

"Oooh," Harry said, her gaze swiveling between Beam and Neo. "OK, I didn't see that coming. Private eye, huh?"

"Sweetheart, I think you're right and it would be better to give Neo and Beam a bit of room," Iakovos said, clearly trying to herd his wife inside, but to Neo's surprise, Beam stopped them.

"No, you don't have to leave on my account." She gave a little toss of her head that had her hair, which was glossy and gleamed in the fading daylight, sending ripples of desire down his spine. He loved her hair. He especially liked it when it touched his naked self. "I made a mistake earlier, when you asked me to explain and I didn't. I let my pride get the better of me, but you are infinitely more valuable to me than that. So unless you object, I'll tell you what happened now."

"Beam, you don't have to do anything you don't want to do," he said softly. "We can do this later."

"It's all right. It's not really anything horrible or shocking," she told him. "The reason I wanted to see you again is because I was tired of fighting. For my whole life, everything has been a fight. My mother had to work three jobs to support my sister and me. I had to fight for everything, every step of the way. You don't go from a rural New Mexico town with a crappy school system that doesn't care for anyone who isn't white to Oxford without struggle, and I had that in spades. Then I met you, and I thought that at last I'd have someone to fight with me. For me."

To Neo's horror, Beam's eyes were shiny with tears. He wanted to stop her, to beg her forgiveness again, to take her away from all the people watching her bare her soul, but then she slapped his chest again.

"Then things went bad, and I was back to fighting everyone and everything. But this time I was alone with a fifteen-year-old sister who I had to struggle to keep from being sent into the foster system. With time and a whole lot of therapy, I realized a lot of things, but the most important was how wrong I was to thrust the burden of my expectations on you."

"Me?" Neo shook his head, confused. Was she saying she didn't love him anymore? Had his mother poisoned their love, as his father had done so long ago? "You weren't wrong, sunshine. I was."

"You were just as young as I was," she said, her eyes still shiny, but filled with an emotion he couldn't read. Sorrow?

Regret? Sincerity? "And we didn't know each other that well, not really. We were both just children, and were unprepared to be adults dealing with adult situations."

"I didn't fight for you," he said, aware of the others around them, but uncaring. If Beam could speak with such honesty in front of the others, then he could only do like-wise. "I believed what I was told without pushing back."

"Because you were young, too. I wanted you to be my protector, my savior. And you wanted me to be an unrealistic ideal woman who was wise and strong and patient."

"You are wise and strong and patient," he said, feeling at a loss as to what he could say to make her understand the depths of his emotions.

"Now I'm wiser, and stronger, and maybe have a smid-gen more patience, but back then?" She shook her head, her hair moving like a ripple of silk in a breeze. "I was none of those things. Which is why, when Ziggy asked for my help a few weeks ago, I decided it was a sign from the universe that I needed to make my peace with you, and what we'd lost twenty-four years ago."

"She didn't want to come to Athens, you know," Ziggy said softly, holding the orange cat. Her face twisted into a wry smile. "I had to fight like hell to get her out here."

"My therapist thought it was the only way I could lay the ghost of our relationship," Beam told him, her hand still on his chest, the heat of it seeping through his shirt to pierce his heart. "So I paid a detective to find you. I wanted to tell you that I was sorry. I wanted to tell you that even though I spent the bulk of my adult life feeling like you were a mon-ster for believing your parents over me, you weren't responsi-ble for my actions. Or my lack of them. I wanted to tell you that to your face because …" She blinked quickly, obviously fighting tears.

He couldn't stop himself. He pulled her gently to him, relaxing when her body fit so perfectly against his. He forgot the others, forgot everything but the woman who so com-pletely filled his life.

"I wanted to tell you in person because I just wanted to see you again. And to know it was truly over," she finally finished, the words thick and choked, and slightly muffled because she spoke them into his neck.

"You love me," he told her, wanting so badly to scoop her up and take her away where he could prove his love to her, one part of his mind started working on formulating an excuse to tell the others.

"I do. Goddess help me, I do."

"Don't cry, sunshine. I am not going to let you slip away from me again. I'm sorry that I wasn't the man you needed before, but I swear I'll change. You won't have to fight the world on your own anymore."

"Now you really are being an idiot," Beam said, pushing back enough to pinch his arm. "I don't want you to change, Neo. I love who you are now. I love your quirky mind. I love that you are the most literal person I know, and you don't like attention, and you are geeky and weird and utterly adorable. I don't want you to change at all."

"But I have," he said, breathing deeply of her scent, that same slightly floral sun-warmed scent that went straight to his blood. "At least so far as making me realize where my life has gone wrong, and that I'll do anything to keep from repeating past mistakes. I'll start with my mother. I'll tell her to move out of the apartment. You wouldn't like her being there. She has three houses she can live in here in Greece, and two in Scotland."

Beam laughed, charming and surprising him before she extricated herself from his hold. "While I appreciate the intention behind such a drastic act as kicking out your mom, why don't we start with setting some boundaries first, then see how it goes?"

"If you like. But I won't tolerate her abusing you any more than I will Chase doing the same." He looked over Beam's head to where Dmitri stood with his wife, who was sniffling into a tissue. "You can tell your magazine that they'll have to find someone else for the number two spot, because I have a feeling that Beam won't let me be on it anymore."

Beam gave another wet gurgle of laughter even as Thyra, with another sniffle, dabbed at her eyes and nodded. "I'll do that. Also, can I say congratulations? And welcome to the family, Beam."

"Again," Neo added.

"Wait, number two?" Harry, who had plucked a handkerchief from Iakovos's suit pocket and was wiping her own eyes, gave her husband a pointed look. "He was higher on the list than you? How is that possible? You are so insanely handsome women fall down on the street when they see you."

"Hardly, and frankly, I don't care about the list. I never have, which you know full well," Iakovos told her, clearly pinching her ass because she gave a little squeak and a jump.

"Theo was only number ten," Kiera said, smiling at her husband, who grinned back at her and waggled his eyebrows.

"And I was never so happy as to be kicked off it," he told her.

"Clearly Theo let the team down," Dmitri said, then frowned and asked Thyra, "What number was I going to be before you rescued me from actually hitting that damned bachelor list?"

She gave him a wide smile. "Eight, but I was willing to bet you could have moved up a few spots by the time I was done with your interview."

"Does every man in your family end up on this list?" Beam asked, giving Neo a smile that grew less watery with every passing second. "You don't own the magazine, do you? Is it some sort of way for your mother to hunt women for you?"

"Christ, I hope not," he said, wondering just what his mother had been up to the last few years.

"It's owned by a conglomeration based out of Paris, so I don't think so," Thyra said, glancing at Dmitri, who shook his head.

"I haven't heard that any of the family had concerns with that publication. Well. It seems we definitely have a reason to celebrate. Er …" He cast a glance at Iakovos, who was whispering something in Harry's ear.

"Hrm? Ah. Yes, just so," Iakovos said, shooting his wife a look when her hand slid around to his back.

"I like your new family," Ziggy announced, moving over to stand next to Beam. "Everyone is pinching everyone else's butt. I don't suppose you have any other cousins? Younger ones? Like … oh, about twenty-two? Male or female. I'm good with either."

"There are several of us cousins, actually," Neo told her. "But I don't know many of them. My father kept our side of the family isolated after the theft of the company."

"And we're back to that," Theo said, making a face, then tipping a head toward his brother. "Do we want to have the business discussion first, or after we celebrate the newest Mrs. Papaioannou?"

Iakovos's gaze flitted between his brother and Dmitri before settling on Neo. "Which would you prefer?" he asked, obviously leaving it to Neo to set the tone.

"Now, if you don't mind. Not that I want to step on your family celebration to welcome Dmitri and the princess back to Greece, but I very much want to take Ziggy home, so that then I might sweep Beam off her feet and do all the things to her that she even now is thinking about."

Beam gave a little jerk, her face flushing as she shot Neo a look that filled him with love and satisfaction. "I was not thinking smutty things about your chest and thighs and truly magnificent butt, so stop putting words in my mouth."

"Do you want us for this business talk or not?" Harry asked Neo. "We won't intrude if you men want to have bonding time."

"Burping and scratching yourself in unmentionable places," Kiera said, nodding.

"Not to mention speaking in Greek, so we can't understand their off-color stories," Thyra added, winking at Dmitri.

"I always translate my off-color stories for you," he protested.

"A wedding," Harry suddenly said, looking speculatively at Beam. "Are you a full-blown wedding sort of person, or a married-at-home sort of person?"

"Or at a registry office," Kiera said.

Thyra, who was leaning in obviously to kiss Dmitri, straightened up and added, "Or on top of a mountain. There's a very nice one here in Athens that we can recommend, assuming you can keep the paparazzi at bay."

"Ugh. Paps," Harry said. "They tend to follow Thyra around, Beam, but don't let that worry you. We'll get you on top of that mountain if you and Neo want to get married there. And this time, I swear I won't go into labor during the middle of the ceremony."

"That sounds like a very interesting story," Beam said, but her eyes were on Neo. He read concern in her face and, after a moment's thought, gave her hand a little squeeze.

"Do you want to stay or mingle?" he asked her softly, while Ziggy was asking Thyra of what country she was a princess.

She hesitated. "Will you be all right without me? I don't want to leave you to your cousins if you're still nervous."

"Nervous? Why would I be nervous? They are family."

She gave him a look that should by rights have stripped a few hairs from his head. "You made me go with you because you said you were nervous and anxious about meeting them."

"Beam," he said, pulling her hand to his lips, allowing them to caress her fingers until her pupils flared, and her eyes went soft with passion. "I would have said anything to keep you by my side. Go and get to know your new family. Send Ziggy for me if you need rescuing."

"I'm going to have a few things to say to you when we are alone, former husband," she said, her eyes sparking just enough to let him know she loved him as much as he loved her.

A strange sense of peace settled over him as the women took up seats on the patio, while Iakovos escorted the men into the living space. He didn't know what, exactly, his life was going to be with Beam, but he was satisfied that, at last, he was whole again.

THIRTEEN

"What were they saying?" Harry asked when Ziggy, who'd gone inside to use the bathroom, reemerged onto the patio.

"My Greek isn't good enough to follow how fast they were speaking," she said, sitting next to me and accepting the glass of wine Harry had topped up. "But I thought Dmitri said something about getting an expensive house for a hat, and then Theo made a comment about how he made a mistake fighting with someone during a race, and Iakovos got a bit indignant about swimming lessons. I think. Like I said, they talk very fast."

To my surprise, the other three ladies shared a look before bursting into laughter.

"I think we'd better explain before Ziggy and Beam think we're insane," Harry said. "Papaioannou men are ... well, kind of different."

"Handsome," Kiera said, leaning forward so she could look through one of the folding glass doors to see where the men were arranged on three couches. "So, so very handsome."

"As the day is long," Harry agreed.

"But genuine," Thyra insisted. "And although they may have had their heads turned in the past by man-grabbers—"

"Ethereal little twits who look like underwear models,"

Harry interrupted, narrowing her eyes at the interior of the apartment.

Thyra pointed at her. "Those, too. But even given their bad taste in the past, they can overlook what's shallow and superficial, and appreciate real-sized women who don't look like they belong on the cover of a magazine. No slur intended, by the way."

"None taken," Harry said, sipping at her wine.

"Definitely not," Kiera agreed, pouring out the last of the wine and making a face at the glass. "I can't hold a candle to any of Theo's past women. Peter's birth mom was outstanding. Especially her fake boobs. But fortunately, Theo doesn't care that I'm not in the least bit underwear-model worthy."

"Peter?" I couldn't help but ask.

"That's our oldest," she explained. "Theo and I got custody of him when he was ten months. He's mine now, since Nastia let me adopt him, and then earlier this year we adopted Channing, our daughter. She's sixteen months, and already has Theo wrapped around her fingers."

"Do you all have children?" I asked, unable to keep from patting Ziggy on the arm when she shifted on the lounge, sitting in a yoga pose that would make my knees hurt after five minutes.

"Just the two," Kiera said.

"We don't have human children, but we do have two cows, seven chickens, and two sheep who used to live in our house, along with Valentino." Thyra listed slightly as she spoke.

Harry suddenly rose and made her way over to the bar, taking a bit of a zigzag path to get there. "We have millions of kids," she said, grabbing three bottles of wine, which she brought back to the table.

The other two ladies laughed.

"Well, maybe not millions," Harry corrected, deftly using a corkscrew to open two of the three bottles, and handing them around while she worked on the third. "We have five. Monsters, all of them, but adorable and sweet and perfect except for when they are being awful. How long have you and Ziggy been together?"

I held out my glass when Harry waggled the new bottle at me. "My sister died in a car accident when Zigs was four, so I've been her guardian since then."

"Guardian," Ziggy said with a little roll of her eyes, then held out her glass for more wine. "You've been a mom. A second mom. Don't get me wrong, I love my first mom, but I really don't remember her, and Beam has been the bestest mother who could ever be. She even let me come here when I knew she hated the place because of what happened."

Maternal tears of love burned behind my eyes again, but I told myself that I'd done enough crying for the day, and blinked them away.

"Awww," Kiera said, smiling at us. "That's really sweet that you have each other. And now you have Neo."

"Has anyone hit on him in front of you yet?" Thyra asked, her lean increasing. She kept glancing around until I realized she was looking for her cat, who had disappeared into the house when the men decamped there. "Because that's a special sort of something." She waved a hand around vaguely. "What's the word? I can't think of it."

"You've had too much wine," Harry told her, then turned to me to explain. "Thyra doesn't normally like booze—"

"Tastes like rubbing alcohol," Thyra said, nodding five times and sliding down in her chair until she was half-reclined.

"—but then we found the wine we're drinking now, and it turns out it's the only kind she likes. So we always have it when Thyra rolls into town." Harry took a slurping sip. "Also, it is a special sort of something when the ethereal twits almost wearing dresses hit on your particular Papamaumau. I like stepping on their tiny little toes."

"I find plastering yourself on the front of him from knees to neck works well, too," Kiera said, then pointed at Thyra and went into a paroxysm of laughter.

"I just put my hands on Dmitri's butt," Thyra said from where she'd slid down to the floor, leaning back against the chair with her legs straight out in front of her. "And make eye contact with the woman who's trying to get grabby with Dmitri while squeezing cheek. Works every time." She hiccuped, then gave a little giggle.

I thought about what I'd do if some woman believed she had the right to just walk up and touch Neo. "I'd punch first, and ask questions later," I decided, feeling unusually aggressive. It had to be the wine. Alcohol always made me a bit militant.

Harry nodded, and slurped again. "I like that. Direct. To the point. Doesn't leave room for any gray-area misunderstanding."

"No." I had a better thought. "Hand on crotch. That sends an unmissable statement, don't you think?"

"Yes," Kiera said thoughtfully. "But if you are in public, it could get you in trouble."

"Good point." I pursed my lips at the problem. "And I'd want to make sure that Neo is on board with that first. I wouldn't want to embarrass him."

Harry saluted me with her glass. "Good plan. Welp. That takes care of that situation. What were we talking about?"

"Underwear models," Kiera said, curling up in her chair and closing her eyes. "And how we aren't them."

It might have been the wine or it might have been the realization that Neo truly loved me that made me feel as light as a feather, and full of bonhomie. "I just have to say—not that I want to argue with my new almost cousins-in-law—"

"Again," Ziggy said, having now scooted onto her side in a fetal position. She pulled the shawl that I'd worn to cover my bare arms over her head.

"—but you, all four of you, my slightly squiffy niece included, are gorgeous. I could absolutely see each and every one of you in underwear catalogs. The fancy kind, with lace thongs that get stuck between your butt cheeks if you so much as sneeze."

"Thongs suck donkey balls," Ziggy pronounced from under the shawl.

"Your butt is young," I told her. "Your butt is at its prime. You could be prancing around wearing the hell out of thongs if you wanted to do so."

"Meh," she said, one arm emerging from under the shawl to wave in my direction. "Comfy beats cute."

"She's an old soul in a young body," I told the others.

"I hate thongs for just the reason you mentioned," Harry said. "I'm willing to wear a lot of things to make Yacky happy, but I draw the line at butt-sucking thongs."

Thyra giggled into her glass of wine, paused, then giggled again and blew a few bubbles in it. "Right there with you, sister."

"Cousin," Harry corrected, pursed her lips, and then smiled broadly. "Sister-cousin."

"The sisterhood of cousins," Kiera said, flinging out her arms. "I love my sisterhood! You're all my best friends, next to Theo, who is my bestie best-best friend."

"Sisterhood of the Traveling Papaioannous," I said sagely, absently noting that of all the women there, I was clearly the one who could handle her booze the best. I kicked off my sandal and, to demonstrate just how much more capable I was while under the influence, used my toes to pick up a wine bottle by the neck. "That's a book, isn't it?"

"Should be if it isn't." Harry watched me carefully swing my foot toward me until I could grab the bottle and pour the remainder of the wine into my glass. I ferried the now-empty bottle back onto the table the same way it came to me. "Are we being overly nosy if we ask you about what Neo's mother said to you? Feel free to tell us we are. I don't want to pry, but I am a writer, and I do love good gossip. Not that Neo's mom picking on you is good, but I'm sure you understand."

"I don't mind. You're going to be family," I told her.

"Again," the three women said in unison, followed by a little snore from under my shawl.

"I'll have to go back twenty-four years," I said, taking a deep pull from my wineglass, then spent the next fifteen minutes telling the three women everything that I had been through, including the abuse from Neo's parents.

"OK, that's just criminal what they did," Harry said. Her chair was tipped back, and she had removed her shoes, her bare feet propped up on a low coffee table.

Thyra was flat out on her back, a pillow from the couch under her feet, and three half-drunk glasses of wine surrounding her head like a halo. She lifted a hand and said, "You should press charges. That was utter and complete bullshit. My brother is a cop. I'll have him arrest Neo's parents."

"His dad is dead," I told her, suddenly a bit sad that I'd never be able to tell him off.

"Eh. Chris has mad skills. He'll find a way," Thyra answered.

I tried to puzzle out that statement, but midway through it I got distracted by a memory of Neo's ass, and lost the train of thought.

"Theo and I have some security peeps that we use when we go anywhere he thinks is dangerous," Kiera said. She was now seated sideways on her chair, her feet resting in a small planter holding a dwarf lemon tree. "Their names are George, Paul, and John, but don't ask about Ringo."

"Never ask about Ringo," Harry said, leaning backward in her chair while twisting around, clearly trying to see the bar behind her. The chair wobbled for a minute, then fell backward with a whomp. Harry's legs kicked in the air, but she didn't seem to be hurt, because she said, "Ringos are always trouble, I find. What were we talking about?"

"The Beatles. I like the Rolling Stones," Thyra said, knocking over one of the wineglasses when she began to make snow angles on the floor. "'Paint It Black' is the best song ever."

"We were talking about Neo's parents, and how I will never be able to tell his dad off. But his mom is still alive. And she has a redheaded guy who hovers behind her, but never actually speaks. Oh!" I clapped a hand over my mouth, suddenly horrified at a thought. "Maybe he can't talk, and I'm being insensitive! I need to ask Neo."

"You do that," Harry's voice came from where she was still on the tipped-over chair, her feet now bobbing merrily as Thyra softly sang "Paint It Black" to herself.

"Right. I'll report back," I told the women, and, after rocking back and forth a few times to get some momentum, managed to get to my feet. I adjusted my dress, which had ridden up while my foot was showing the others how sober I was by lifting bottles, and made my way over to the big glass doors that led to the interior.

I pushed aside one of the doors, and stepped inside the relative coolness, noticing three things immediately. The first was that all the men had taken off their respective suit coats and loosened their ties. The second was that all but Theo held tumblers filled with an amber liquid, probably whiskey. And the third was that although Neo's cousins were all nice to look at, none of them could hold a candle to him.

"You're such a number two," I announced, striking a pose to point at him, feeling that the others needed to appreciate just how wonderful Neo was.

Dmitri, who was in midsip, choked and sputtered liquid all over Iakovos, who was sitting next to him, leaning forward as he made some point or other. Theo burst into laughter. Iakovos stared first in horror at his side, which was now splattered with damp spots, then at me.

Neo set down his glass when I walked over, carefully stepping over Theo's long legs to straddle Neo's thighs, seating myself on him. I took his face in my hands, and gently kissed first his upper, then his lower lip. "Hi. I missed you. Did you miss me?"

"I did," he said gravely, then made a couple of sniffing noises like he was smelling my perfume. "Er ... have you been ... er ..."

"Oh Christ," Iakovos said, getting up and approaching where I'd left one of the doors open. "It looks like a meteor hit. The women are scattered all over the patio."

"The others are a bit snockered," I told Neo. "But not me. My toes are as agile as ever."

"I have no doubt they are," he said, the corners of his mouth twitching a few times. "Had a bit of wine, did you?"

"Just a little," I said, nodding, unfortunately smacking my forehead on his when I did so. "Ow."

"Mrs. Avrabos?" Iakovos called as he tossed aside a cocktail napkin that he'd been using to mop up the spewed whiskey on his shirt. The woman I'd met when Ziggy and I arrived at the apartment emerged from a side hallway. "Coffee, please, and lots of it. The ladies appear to have been celebrating a bit hard."

"Am I interrupting?" I asked, watching with concern when Dmitri and Theo followed Iakovos out to the patio.

"No, we were done. They were telling me a few things—but I think that should wait until later, when you're not quite so ..."

"Not drunk," I said, nodding, then got to my feet and padded my way barefoot after the men, feeling that I might have to defend my new almost relations in case their respective husbands were not understanding.

"Perhaps just a little buzzed?" Neo asked, his hand warm on my back when he helped me get past a tricky part where the carpet ended, and the bare wood floor began.

"Not really, just relaxed. Really, really relaxed. Ziggy's out cold, though. You might have to carry her. Would you mind if I put my hand on your dick?"

Neo stopped, his eyebrows rising. "Right now?"

"No. When some woman thinks she can get it on with you. Harry goes after toes, and Kiera rubs herself on Theo's front, and Thyra grabs ass. So all that's left for me is to go straight for your package. Would you mind if that's my standard hussy-removal-system response?"

"I think that's something we'll also talk about later," he said, an odd look on his face.

"OK, but it's that or shove my hands down your pants, and copping a grope just seems like the quickest way to send a message. Ladies! Good news, Neo is OK with the dick plan."

Three cheers met my announcement.

"Wife, you are shit-faced," Theo said, helping Kiera disentangle her legs from the lemon-tree planter.

"Barely, husband. Just a tiny bit. It's a celebration," Kiera said with another of her soft, breathy giggles. I watched Theo for a moment, prepared to defend Kiera if he appeared angry, but he did nothing more than hoist her out of the chair before seating himself and pulling her down onto his lap, where she curled up happily. Judging by the way he kept kissing her neck, it appeared all was well there.

"Comfortable?" Dmitri asked Thyra.

"Yup. Join me?" she asked, patting the floor.

"Always, Princess," he said, and lay down next to her after moving the wineglasses out of the way. Immediately, she rolled over and snuggled up next to him.

"Do I want to know how you ended up like this?" Iakovos asked, standing over where Harry and her chair were still on their backs, her feet now doing a little dance in the air.

"Wine. Blame the wine. We didn't get enough of it for the party. Next time we'll need a couple of cases. Are you going to just stand there looking down at me with your sexy, sexy thighs, or are you going to help me up?"

A half hour later, several cups of coffee had been consumed, and I stood with Neo at the door saying goodbye.

"Thank you for a lovely party," I said, holding up Ziggy when she started to sag again. "Ziggy and I had a lovely time."

Harry emerged from where she'd been to visit the bathroom, complaining about the way her children had ruined her ability to hold wine, saying, "You're leaving? It's so early. Well, no worries, now you're part of the good side of the family, so we'll see each other often. Did Yacky tell you about his island? Theo and Kiera live just down the coast from it, and Dmitri is going to build a house along there, as well. You and Neo will have to see if there's something in the area you like, so we can all visit each other. All right, all right, stop prodding me. I'm saying good night."

"I'll be in contact with you about what I find out from my mother," Neo told Iakovos, who had wrapped an arm around Harry, the pair of them leaning against each other in the way couples did.

It made me happy for them, but at the same time filled with yearning.

I stared at Neo.

"What?" he asked.

"I yearn," I told him.

"As do I, sunshine, but now is hardly the place to fulfill such things. We have to get Ziggy home first."

"I'm awake," Ziggy said, snapping upright from where she had slumped against the wall. "I'm fine. Li'l sleepy, that's all."

"Let us know when your wedding is," Harry said as Mrs. Avrabos handed Neo his jacket, and me my shawl. "As long as you don't mind us being there."

"Oh god. I'm never drinking again," Thyra said, coming out of another room, a wet cloth on the back of her neck, Dmitri helping her as she weaved a little. "Wait, what was that about the wedding? Do you want the mountain? Dmitri can help with that." She froze, her eyes wide, then spun around, saying as she ran for the room she'd just emerged from, "Nope. Nope, nope, nope."

Dmitri sighed, gave us a wry smile, then said, "Let me know if you need anything from me regarding the Sri Lanka situation. If you'll excuse me, I'd better make sure Valentino doesn't try to help Thyra again. He almost drowned her by jumping on her back when she was vomiting."

"I hope you're proud of yourself," Iakovos told Harry.

"Bah. This was nothing compared to the Christmas party last year. Thyra couldn't get out of bed for three days then." She took me by surprise by kissing first Ziggy, then Neo, and finally me on the cheek. "Welcome to the family, all of you."

"I'm so glad you're nice and not evil," I told her, then allowed Neo to hustle Ziggy and me out of the apartment to where the elevator was waiting.

FOURTEEN

"Did you have a nice time with your cousins?" I asked Neo a few minutes later, when we were smooshed together in the back seat of the car, since Ziggy insisted she couldn't sit in the front seat without getting carsick.

"I'll have to get my car back from my mother," Neo answered above me. I was draped partially across his chest, holding on to Ziggy as she slumped against me, evidently having dozed off again.

"Isn't this your car?" I asked, startled, staring at the back of the head of the man driving. "I thought this was your car. Holy shit, maybe I really am drunk if I got into a stranger's car. Why didn't he say anything? Why didn't you?"

His arm tightened around me. "You are drunk, and this is my car, sunshine. But I have a bigger car, one with more seats, and that might be more comfortable to ride in when we have Ziggy with us. My mother uses it, though."

"Ugh," I said, then realized how rude that sounded. "Sorry, didn't mean that like your car had cooties. Did you have fun?"

"Fun?" I could feel him thinking about that, parsing out the full meaning of the question. "Yes," he said finally, his voice rumbling around in his big chest. "Yes, I did enjoy my-self. It was nice to talk to my cousins and get a few things clear. I liked knowing you were bonding with their wives, although I don't remember you imbibing too much before. Is that something you do often?"

The question was gently asked, but it drove home the point that although I'd known him for more than half my life, there was still so much to learn. "No. I seldom drink, to be honest. Alcoholism tends to run in my family, so normally I don't indulge. Do you?"

"Drink? Sometimes. Like you, I don't make a habit of it, and mostly in social situations. I think one of my cousins has a problem with it. He didn't have any whiskey, and no one asked him if he wanted it—they simply handed him a soft drink instead."

"Theo," I said, nodding to myself when I remembered the scene when I had interrupted them.

"Yes. You liked the princess and the others?"

"I did. They're nice. Thyra isn't at all what you think of when you think royalty. She's just like anyone else. Harry said there was a story about why she was that way, but we didn't get into it." I pushed Ziggy a little farther down so she rested on my legs rather than my side, and sat up so I could look at Neo. He wasn't overly visible in the darkness until occasional lights filled his side of the car as we drove through the streets. "Are you going to tell me what you guys talked about?"

"If you like," he said, tipping his head toward the front of the car. "Are you coming back to my boat with me?"

"I have a hotel room," I pointed out.

"Yes. My boat is more comfortable, not to mention much more quiet."

"All right, but I'll have to tell Ziggy I'm with you."

"That's OK," she said, her voice muffled as she snuggled into my leg. "I figured you guys would be gettin' it on after the way you were looking at each other."

"Go back to sleep," I told her, stroking her hair back off her face, feeling alternately so full of happiness I could sing and dance, and mildly unsettled.

I couldn't figure out why I was feeling unsettled, unless it was too much wine, so I waited until we dropped Ziggy off at her residence hall—and Neo saw her safely to her door given the late hour—and were almost to the marina before asking him, "Have you heard from your mother?"

"The phrase 'blowing up my phone,' I believe, would describe the situation."

I sighed. "She's going to give you hell about me. Also, why did you go on a rampage at Pi if you weren't furious with me? I mean, I assume you weren't furious with me. You wouldn't have asked me to marry you—again—if you believed all those things your mom said."

He was silent for so long that I wondered if he'd gone to sleep, or simply didn't want to answer in front of the driver. "I wasn't furious at you. I was hurt at first, yes, but that's because you didn't tell me why you'd sought me out. Then I realized that I'd never asked you about that in private, when my mother wasn't there making the most ridiculous accusations, and that if I had done so, you would have told me."

I shifted a bit uncomfortably, my Housewife raising her eyebrows at me because she knew full well I'd had the opportunity to be forthcoming, and hadn't.

"My rampage, as you call it, was nothing more than removing those people who either directly took orders from my mother or had an arrangement with her that I felt superseded their allegiance to Pi."

"And Chase? I thought he was your friend. You said you'd known him for a long time."

"I have. He was." Neo's gaze flickered toward the driver. "That's a more complicated story, one that I suspect will take a little time to tell. The end result is what matters. I told you I was cleaning house, and that's exactly what I did. Three board members were removed a few hours later. Why didn't you wait for me?"

I was confused for a second before I realized he was talking about earlier in the evening. "I thought you were mad at me and didn't want to see me again."

"But you went to my cousin's apartment."

"Yes. I promised I would support you, and I was going to do so unless you kicked me out."

He fumbled around next to me until he found my hand, then held it in his while lights from the various marina buildings flickered by us. "I've done a lot of things in my life, Beam, but somewhere, I had to have done something especially good to deserve you having my back."

I squeezed his fingers. "It's kind of humbling, huh? Part of me wants to feel all smug with myself because you love me—me, a poor girl from Nowhere, New Mexico, one who couldn't possibly model any underwear—and the other part wants to rant and scream at myself for not finding you earlier."

"No ranting. No screaming," he said, opening the door when the driver deposited us at the parking lot. Neo said something briefly to him in Greek, then helped me out. "And why couldn't you model underwear if you wanted? Your body is perfectly made for it."

"Right, that's earning you another round of Make the Dishy Greek Moan," I said, leaning against him as we strolled down the dock toward his ship.

"Oh no. It's my turn tonight. I get to make you … er … you don't really get sticky."

"I do, but only after parts of you have been visiting. Man. I don't remember that being so narrow."

He paused at the narrow white gangplank that led onto the lower deck of the boat. "Are you so wobbly you can't make it?"

I wrinkled my nose at the black water that gently slapped against the wood of the pier. "Maybe if you hold on to me, I'll be OK."

"I have a better idea." He scooped me up, and before I could protest that he'd have us both in the water, he ran up the gangplank, depositing me on the deck.

"Show-off," I told him, then stretched, and breathed deeply of the salt air. It had a pleasant tang that helped drive out the last dregs of my wine haze. "I could get used to this environment."

"I'm glad to hear that." He unlocked the door to the living area, then stood at the entrance and watched me as I peered over the edge into the water, still enjoying the slight breeze. "There are lots of things we have to talk about, Beam, where we will live being one of them, and what my cousins told me about my parents, but right now, all I can think about is stripping you naked and kissing every square inch of you."

I turned slowly, filled with a sense of feminine power as I strolled toward him, trying to exude seduction and anticipation. "Oooh. I like the sound of that. Will it involve you touching me, Neo? Will you rub your stubble on my inner thighs? Will you let me tickle yours with the tips of my hair?"

He gave a little shiver as I reached him, pushing off his suit jacket. "Christ, I hope so. What do you want to do?"

I allowed him to pull me inside, waiting while he locked the door again. I didn't know much about yachts, but assumed there was some sort of security system that prevented people from getting on board without him knowing. "I thought you said it was your turn to be bossy tonight? Do I get to pick?"

"It is my turn, but I was asking you if you preferred to talk now, or if I could make love to you all the ways I want to, first."

"Definitely sexy times first, then maybe some enlightening pillow talk later."

He started toward me, but I got past him before he could so much as lay one stubbly whisker on my sensitive self, and hurried down the spiral staircase, unzipping my dress as I ran. By the time I hit his cabin, my clothing was strewn in a path that led to his bed.

"I can't help but notice you're fully dressed," I said, panting a little as I tried to arrange myself on his bed in a manner that didn't make me look quite so much like a forty-two-year-old woman who needed to lose twenty pounds. I went for the Little Mermaid pose, sucking in my stomach while thrusting forward my breasts. "Are you going to do a strip-tease for me this time?"

Neo's hand was on his already loosened tie as he entered the room, but he paused, looking down at himself before settling a highly speculative gaze on me. "Do you want me to?"

"Oh, yes," I purred, and pulled a few pillows over to prop myself up while I watched him. "Dance for me, Neo."

"That I won't do. I can't dance to save my life. But if it would make you happy to have me remove my clothes slowly, I will do so."

"Just wiggle your butt a little as you do it," I told him, watching with great pleasure as he unbuttoned his shirt, revealing that lovely chest. "Oooh. And maybe flex a bit. Mmrrowr!"

"I feel silly," he said, tossing his shirt on the same chair where he'd deposited my clothing that he'd collected on the way into the cabin.

I twirled my finger in the air. "Turn around for the pants. I want to watch your butt cheeks."

"You are an odd woman, Beam," he said, giving me what I'm sure he thought was an extremely effective stern look, but he turned and dropped his pants. "You never used to demand I perform for you. I wonder about that. Is this some new, strange side to you? And if it is, will you promise to let me be just as demanding?"

"Absolutely," I said, applauding lightly when he flexed his cheeks a couple of times.

He turned to pull off his shoes and shuck the pants gathered at his feet, then stood with his hands on his hips, his underwear bulging in a meaningful way. "Right. What next?"

I eyed the bulge. "Dammit, you could be a male underwear model. How do you feel about thongs?"

"On you or me?"

"You. They'd just get stuck on me. But you … hmm."

"It's not something that sounds comfortable," he said, then started to pull off his underwear but, with another speculative look at me, gave a little wiggle, and whipped the undies off, tossing them onto the chair with the other things. "Now, I believe something was mentioned about whiskers on sensitive, quivering thighs."

"Yes, please," I said, then held out a hand when he took an ankle in each hand. "Wait, we're doing this face-to-face again, right? Because I really have doubts about the scenic quality of my backside."

"You are very wrong in that regard, but yes, if you want to do this without any frills, I'm happy to oblige."

"I didn't say no frills," I answered, allowing my gaze to admire the display of very fine man body.

He had been kissing his way up my leg from my ankle to the back of my knee when he paused, and waggled his eyebrows. "Oh really?"

"What does that look mean?" I asked, suddenly a bit wary. "You're not into kinky things that will shock me, are you? Not that I want to kink shame. To each his own. But other than the hammock that you swear isn't a sex swing, I'm not sure I'm going to be comfortable with things like whips, and submission, and … and …" I thought through the few snippets of porn videos that I could recall. "… sexy plumber role-play."

"Stay there," he said, sliding off the bed and disappearing into the hallway.

"What? Wait, you do have a kinky habit?" I hurriedly got beneath the duvet, worried what he might return with.

"It's not kinky unless you don't like chocolate and hazelnuts," he said, reappearing with a jar of chocolate spread. "I have a weakness for this stuff. How about you?"

"I like it," I said, watching with approval as he pushed the duvet off and retook his position. "Both your plan and the actual spread. But it's going to make us awfully sticky."

"That, my tender little morsel, is my plan. Let's just dab a bit here …"

He smeared a bit of chocolate on my inner knee, then snaked his tongue in to lick it off.

A shiver rippled up my back and down my arms.

"... and some here ..."

His fingers brushed a bit on my left inner thigh. His breath was hot on the now highly erogenous flesh, making another wave of shivers cause goose bumps.

"... and I think we'll forgo this spot just because I don't want to cause any sort of infection, not that I think chocolate would do that, but better safe than sorry, eh?" he asked, then dipped his head and let his tongue go wild on my now quivering intimate parts without the benefit of chocolate spread.

A dull ache started inside me, all my inner muscles tightening in anticipation of him.

"As for your breasts ..."

"Too much," I said, grabbing him at the same time I slid down, wrapping my legs around his hips so his penis pressed against my now slick parts. "My breasts can have chocolate fun another time. Now is the time for hip action, Neo. Dive deep and hard. And keep diving deep and hard because to hell with foreplay tonight."

His eyebrows rose for a moment. Then he set the chocolate on the nightstand and pulled one of the pillows to rest under my hips. "I like how you think, Beam. I like how you are demanding and, at the same time, let me know what you're feeling. You're sure your breasts won't mind if I do them later?"

"Positive," I said, taking him and positioning him where I wanted him.

"All right, but you have to act as an intermediary later if they won't talk to me because I didn't pay them due homage. Christ, Beam, you're so tight around me ... Please, just a second," he said as he paused and seemed to try to catch his breath before slowly moving inside me again.

"Stop going so slow," I told him, trembling on the edge of an orgasm. "I told you, deep and hard."

He had obviously been trying to hold back, because he lost control at my words, and did indeed indulge in the full, hard thrusts. He plunged and plumbed my intimate depths, and I bucked and writhed and urged him on with every frantic beat of our hearts.

And when the race was over and we lay panting, sweaty, and boneless on each other, the cooling breeze from an open window touching flesh so heated I was willing to bet there were scorch marks on the sheet, I drifted down from my postorgasmic daze, and looked over at him. "What did your cousins tell you about your parents? What's the story with Chase? What did your mother say in all the messages she sent you?"

"Mrf," he said, cracking an eye open enough to pull me over until I was snuggled up against him, and yank up the duvet so we were covered. "Tell you later."

I listened to his breathing deepen and slow as his body relaxed next to me, and for the first time in a very long time, I felt safe, protected, and cherished.

There was Neo's mother to deal with, but I had confidence that together we could face anything she threw at us.

My inner Housewife shook her head, but said nothing, just left me with a faint worry flitting around the edges of my mind.

FIFTEEN

"I could get used to a life like this." Ziggy lolled back in the hot tub that sat on the open deck. "Imagine having a hot tub on a boat. I mean, there's decadent, and then there's decadent. Hey, does that mean we're rich now, Aunt Beam?"

To Neo's amusement, Beam, who had been sitting at the dining table next to the hot tub tapping quickly on the laptop keyboard, looked over at her niece with a horrified expression. "What? No! Ziggy, you ought to be ashamed of yourself. Neo's money has nothing to do with us other than he kindly had his … er … housekeeper turn on the hot tub for you, not that I think anyone needs to soak first thing in the morning. But that aside, no, we are most decidedly not rich."

"Damn. Some of my friends are going to Berlin for the break, and I was hoping to go with them."

"I'm sure an allowance can be arranged that would allow you to travel if you wanted," Neo told her, ignoring Beam's sputtered objections. He cocked an eyebrow at the love of his life and asked, "Or do you expect me to not support you and Ziggy?"

She looked righteously indignant, something that amused Neo even more. He had a pretty good sense when people were trying to use him for monetary gain, and Beam had never triggered that warning system. He ignored the thought that it hadn't always been so, telling himself he would spend his life making Beam as happy as was possible.

"We are not leeches," she told him before turning to glare at Ziggy. "Stop cheering, you boob. Neo isn't giving you an allowance. I give you enough money to do things like take trips. So long as you are careful with your money."

"Is a thousand a week enough?" Neo asked Ziggy.

She pursed her lips for a few seconds. "Dollars or euros?"

"Euros."

"Sure. That sounds about right." Her grin was as cheeky as ever.

"Over my dead body will you give her that sort of money!" Beam said, transferring her glare to him.

"More, then?" he asked, knowing full well that he was about to be sparked at. "Fifteen hundred euros a week, it is."

Ziggy whooped with joy and jumped out of the hot tub, dripping water everywhere as she snatched up her phone and dashed inside, into the cabin he'd told her she could use. "You're the bestest almost uncle ever! Gotta tell my friends that Berlin is a go!"

"Neo, that was uncalled-for," Beam said, her eyes just starting to glint at him. "I told you that I give her money—"

"Sunshine, do you really expect me to not love and support Ziggy like you do?" he asked, knowing just how tight the bond was between them. He knew it might take Beam a bit of time to be willing to let him have a part of that relationship, but if he was patient, she'd see that he was devoted to them both.

"Well … no, of course not … but there's supporting and *supporting*. What you're doing is bribery, pure and simple."

He considered that, genuinely confused. "Do you think she only likes me for my money? She didn't strike me as more materialistic than any other young woman her age, but you know her best."

"No!" Beam reached across the table and gave his hand a squeeze. "I didn't mean she's after you for what she can get.

Ziggy is exactly what you see—charming and quirky and silly, but she doesn't use people. She never has."

"I believe there's a phrase about the apple not falling far from the tree," he said, watching with delight her attempt to both graciously accept the compliment and decry it at the same time. "Beam, I won't say that you should by rights have become completely and utterly used to my financial situation by now, because we've agreed to let the faults of the past lie where they are, but I am going to think it quite vividly at you."

She laughed, just as he hoped she would, her cheeks still dark with pleasure. "I'm not going to argue about whether or not you're situated well enough to support us, because everyone has heard of how popular Pi is, but I do want to point out that although of course I want you to love Ziggy, you don't have to pay her to return that affection. She really is the most loving person I know. She's always falling for people—actors and singers and even a few professors, who thankfully have had no idea of her passions—so I'd suspect she'd fallen for you, as well, but she has you firmly in the uncle role. Kindly, possessor of a fancy boat and a tech company that makes her mouth water, but nonetheless avuncular."

"Is that another word for old?" he asked, not being familiar with the term.

"No. Yes." She gave a little shrug. "Kind of depends on the situation."

"I will accept avuncular, then. Did you contact your landlord?"

"Yes. Luckily, my apartment lease is up in four months, and since this month has been paid for already, she said she'd let me off without having to pay for the rest. I would like to go back home to pack up my things, though. That is … I assume you don't want to live in a one-bedroom apartment over a beauty salon?"

"We can live wherever you'd like," he said easily, wondering if she would want to live in the States.

"I don't mind it there, but I do like Greece. It's so pretty here. And there's water." She slid a look up at him. "I think

I'd like to live here, and I know Ziggy loves Greece, but I do have a couple of friends back home that I'd like to see. Maybe we can visit every few months?"

"As often as you like," he said, then added, "And your friends will be welcome to stay with us anytime, if you think they would travel this far."

She gave a short laugh. "Oh, yes. My friend Daria—she's also my therapist; I've known her since I was in grade school—she's the one who helped Ziggy get her internship at Pi. Her husband works for a university that arranges for international internships, and she's always trying to get him to go abroad with her, but he's terrified of flying. I bet she'd come out here like a shot to see us, and meet you. She's heard a lot about you."

"I wondered how Ziggy found herself at Pi. And more, why you let her come here." He kept his tone light despite the stab of guilt. He could only imagine the things Beam's therapist thought about him.

She made a face. "Don't think I didn't try to talk Ziggy out of the internship. The irony of her wanting so badly to work for your company … but in the end, I couldn't tell her no. The opportunity to go to school here and work for Pi was about her, not me, or even us. It was the best offer she had, so I told her to take it."

"You are a very good parent, even if you are technically only an aunt. Now that our future living arrangements are decided, what have you found?"

She blinked at him a few times before understanding what he was asking. "Oh, not much." Those wonderful black brows pulled together as her attention returned to the laptop screen. "I don't see any signs that some of the tendrils have been removed, but I saw more yesterday than I'm finding now. I've checked multiple change logs, and there's nothing, but I know there were a few more rabbit holes than I can find now."

"Rabbit holes as in … ?" He moved around the table to stand next to her, one hand on her bare sun-warmed shoulder, the scent of her teasing him, making him want to carry her off to his cabin so he could ravish her again, just as he'd done when they woke up that morning.

"Different locations in the various codes where I found bits of Beowulf," she answered, flipping through a few screens. "I don't understand how someone could make changes without any footprints. Are you sure that your mother doesn't have access to this server?"

"Quite sure. She doesn't have the know-how to access it, even if she did." A growing idea demanded his full attention, so he missed what she asked next. "Hmm? Sorry, what was that?"

"All those people you let go yesterday." She slanted a look upward at him, shading her eyes from the morning sun. "Could any of them have done this before they left?"

"Doubtful," he said, the growing idea taking hold. He wondered what was the best way to deal with it—the legal department? He gave a mental headshake. He might be many things, but he refused to be a coward. He'd have to face the problem head-on. "Are you ready to go?"

Her eyebrows rose. "Go as in you want to get rid of me and my embarrassingly mercenary niece? Or go somewhere with you?"

He bent, her lips warm and soft on his, her breath making his balls tighten with need. "The day will never dawn when I want you out of my life. I hope that someday you'll understand that."

"Oh, I understand," she answered, smiling a little before she nipped his bottom lip. "It's just that this is still kind of new, and I forget now and again that we really are getting a happily ever after. You want to go to the office to dig up more on Beowulf?"

"I want to go to the office, yes, but I'm going to call a meeting with my mother and Chase. Something is going on with them, and I want to know what."

She stood up when, after one more kiss, he moved into the interior of the boat to change from knee-length shorts and tank top to something a bit more fitting for the office. "Goddess! You think they're having an affair?" she asked, following him.

He paused at the head of the stairs, the thought one he hadn't considered before. "Christ. No, they couldn't. Could they?"

Her shoulders did a little bobble that he interpreted as a noncommittal shrug. "You know them better than me, but your mom looks pretty good for someone who is in her sixties."

"I don't know whether to be outraged at the idea, angry that they would do something like that behind my back, or indifferent because it's none of my business what my mother gets up to with her dalliances."

"She is married to that red-haired guy, isn't she?" Beam asked as they went downstairs to his cabin. The sound of Ziggy chatting from her cabin drifted out. He tapped on the door, opened it a crack, and said, "We're leaving in twenty minutes, if you want to come with us. Otherwise, I'll have my driver take you wherever you want to go."

"Be there!" she called, then said, "I'm going to have to go, Roma. My new uncle wants us to go somewhere, and I have to keep an eye on my aunt. She's prone to drama."

"I heard that, you unnatural child!" Beam called over his shoulder as he closed the door. "Honestly, she seesaws from being the most mature, wise person I know to annoyingly twenty. I never know which part of her is going to speak next."

"I like her, too," he said, pulling his shirt off as soon as he entered the cabin. "Ah, Luca, good, I didn't see you come on board. This is Beam, my ex-wife and current fiancée."

The wiry young man who emerged from the bathroom smiled, and greeted Beam with congratulations. "It is welcome to see you," Luca told her.

"Luca is Yianna's son," he said, naming the woman who acted as cook and housekeeper. "He and two cousins rotate shifts in taking care of the *Athena*. He doesn't speak a lot of

English, so if you need something and he has a hard time understanding, go to Yianna."

"Hi," Beam said, her eyes, which had been staring at Neo's bare chest, flickering over to Luca. She gravely shook his hand. "It's nice to meet you. I feel a bit weird having a person picking up after me, and doing things like making the bed and cleaning the toilet, so if you want me to help out, just let me know."

"He won't do that," Neo said, telling Luca quickly in Greek that Beam was delighted to meet him. "He is going to college, and the wages he gets for working here cover his weekend band hobby. If you do his job for him, then I won't have a reason to pay him."

"You could just, you know, give him money," she told him.

"I could, but if I did that, where would I stop? There are a lot of people who work for me who are just as worthy as he is, some more so. Don't confuse generosity with stripping people of their dignity, sunshine. Pi was set up to benefit its employees, and I make sure that wages are increased each year in excess of the cost of living. I extend the same policy for those people who work for me, personally."

"Sorry," she said, holding up her hands. Luca had returned to cleaning the bathroom, leaving them in possession of the cabin. "I didn't mean to sound accusatory. I know your company is good when it comes to how it treats employees. It's one reason why Ziggy wanted to come here, so she could intern for you. Well, Pi, but that's really the same thing as you."

"It was once." He peeled off his shorts and pulled out a suit, feeling that the more formal his appearance, the better the meeting would go. "I don't know what it is anymore."

Beam had sat on the edge of the bed, but rather than watching him, as he'd half expected, she was staring at the floor, clearly puzzling out something. "What do you want, Neo?"

"Right now? Other than stripping you naked, and covering you in oil so that you can slide all over my body?"

She waggled a hand. "Oiled-up sexy times are a given. What do you want for Pi?"

He thought about that as he finished dressing. "I wanted Pi to return to what I originally made it to be—a company that developed tech beneficial to people who need it. I thought it was going to make a difference in the world, but now I'm not so sure. Somewhere along the line, I lost the vision."

"Well, you did have a few hard years," she pointed out, rising so that she could straighten his tie. "You can't be blamed if you lost focus while you battled cancer, and afterward, you were celebrating being alive. I would have done the same thing. Besides, there's nothing to stop you from taking charge of the company again."

"I'm not sure I know where to start." He held her hips, relishing the feeling of her leaning into him, her being lighting up his soul. "I've worked so long on my own projects that Pi seems like a different entity. And I'm not sure I have the energy to reinvent the wheel."

"Do you have to?" she asked, her hands warm on his chest through the thin material of his shirt.

"I don't know." He pushed aside the niggling worry that he might be out of his depth with Pi, and allowed her to see all the love that filled him. "And yes, you can help me, assuming that was the next thing you were going to say."

"I was," she said, smiling as she reached behind him and pinched his ass. "Also, you're entirely too gorgeous in that suit. I mean, you in shorts and tee is sexy as the day is long, but you in a suit, with your hair swooping back off your forehead, looking all *GQ* cover … whew! I can see why you are the number two bachelor of the universe."

"If you put your hand on my cock, I will not be responsible for my actions," he warned her.

Her eyes widened even as her pupils flared with awareness; then she shot a quick glance at the closed bathroom door where Luca was working. "I'm not saying that I would object to doing that, but I assume you don't want to be walking around sporting wood."

"I don't. I was referring to your plan to dissuade other women from flinging themselves on me." He held the door open for her, relieved to see that the door to Ziggy's cabin was open and the room empty, although he noticed that she'd managed to spread the interior with not only various garments he had no memory of her bringing with her when he'd sent his driver to fetch her from her room, but also sundry items near and dear to the hearts of young women. He studied the cabin for a few seconds, then looked at Beam.

She leaned back to look in, then *tsk*ed, and gave another waggle of her shoulders. "It doesn't take her long to make any room look like a tornado hit it. I will tell her to pick up after herself."

"No, I want her to feel at home here." He admired Beam's ass as she ascended the stairs ahead of him, fighting to keep his hands from straying. "Although if we dispossess my mother of the penthouse on Pi Tower, we could stay there. You might like it better. It has a decent view, and a swimming pool, and eight bedrooms. There's plenty of room for Ziggy to stay there if she would prefer that to her student digs."

"Your boat is fine for now," she reassured him. "Although … do you normally just keep it parked here?"

"Docked, and no. It would be a waste of such a nice yacht to keep her moored when she loves to travel."

"We're going sailing?" Ziggy asked, straightening up from where she was helping Yianna put the cover back on the hot tub. "Can I snorkel? Wait, do you have one of those water-jet things that go way up in the air? Or Jet Skis? I've always wanted to Jet Ski. Can I bring a friend if we're going for a cruise?"

"You have another three weeks before the end of the semester," Beam told her, shooing her toward the gangplank. "There will be no snorkeling or Jet Skiing for you until then. Er … do you have a Jet Ski?"

"I have three, and yes, Ziggy, I'm happy to take you and your friends when I show your aunt my favorite islands. But I need to settle a few things here, first."

"Does that mean you'll reinstate my internship with Pi?" Ziggy asked as they headed down the dock.

"You were reinstated yesterday," he told her.

"Nope. I checked this morning, and I was still persona non grata with Pi."

He swore in Greek, wondering who had countered his order to reinstate Ziggy for the second time.

"Sorry," Ziggy said, shooting him a worried look. "Didn't mean to harsh your mellow and all that."

"Harsh … ?"

"That's something Aunt Beam says my grandma always used to say," she answered.

"My mother fully embraced the hippie life," Beam said with a twist of her lips.

"Regardless of my mellow, you should have been reinstated yesterday. I'll look into it once I get to the office," he told them both.

Beam took his hand as they headed for the parking lot where he'd ordered the car that his mother normally used to be available. He had taken a few minutes earlier in the morning to reassign his driver Christos to another position. He wasn't sure if Christos had some involvement with Chase, but he wasn't comfortable around the man, and now with Beam and Ziggy to be driven around, he wanted someone he could fully trust.

"This is Dag. He's taking over as my driver. Dag, this is Beam, my former wife, who has kindly agreed to marry me again, and that's Ziggy, her niece, who is attending the University of Athens."

"So this is the one you let get away," Dag said, giving Beam a grin that both annoyed and amused Neo. He shook her hand, adding, "I've known our boy Neo since my mother used to work for his mom. And before you ask what a Norwegian is doing here in Greece, my wife is a doctor here."

"Dag's mother has a couple of stores in Athens that cater to women with more money than fashion sense," Neo explained as they got into the car, Ziggy claiming the full length of the seat that faced them.

"That's an awfully rude thing to say," Beam told him with a little frown.

"Ah, but it's true, so very true," Dag said, buckling his seat belt and giving Beam another grin in the mirror. "Mum makes money hand over fist from the women who are desperate to hang on to their youth. We going to the office?"

"Yes. Ziggy?"

"No classes today," she said, lying on her back, holding her phone over her head. "And I finished my project in the middle of the night, so I'm golden for today and the weekend."

"Pi Tower it is." Dag, with a wink at Neo, hit the button for the privacy window before setting off.

"He seems nice, but what happened to the other guy?" Beam asked.

"I wasn't sure I could trust him," he said slowly.

Beam slid a glance toward Ziggy before settling back beside him, saying nothing, but putting a hand on his leg in a way that warmed him.

It took some time to get to the bottom of the situation with Ziggy's internship, but as soon as he forced the head of the program to admit that Camilla had been behind the problem, he demoted the former to a lesser position. He then went on to reinstate Ziggy, saw her to the interns' shared office, and ordered HR to find someone to head the program who would answer only to him.

"Thank you," Beam said when they left the HR department, her eyes filled with admiration, making him feel like he could move heaven and earth if it gave her pleasure. "I know you're tired of issues with Ziggy's internship, but it's very important to her."

"It's important to me, too, and not just because she's your niece. It's becoming increasingly clear to me that the rot I thought had touched just a small part of Pi has much deeper roots than I imagined." He glanced at his watch. "And speaking of that, it would appear that the showdown is nigh. Do you wish to stay out of it? I won't blame you if you want to keep clear. My mother has said unforgivable things to and about you, and although I won't tolerate her abusing you, I do need to ask her a few questions before I banish her from the building for good."

"Remember when I said you might want to try setting boundaries first, before you go to outright banishment?" Beam asked, taking his hand. "That still applies. She's your mom, Neo. No matter what she thinks of me, she loves you, and is just trying, in a horribly twisted way, to protect you."

"That doesn't mean I'm going to let her try to hurt you or Ziggy. You can go to my office if you prefer. Work on the Beowulf problem."

"Do you want me with you?" she asked, a shadow of hesitation in her expression.

"Yes," he said simply. "But not at the expense of your feelings."

Her smile was as bright as the noon sun, filling him with hope and love and warmth. "I'm a big girl now, Neo. I may not have acted like it yesterday, but I can stand up to your mom. So lead on, Macduff."

"*Macbeth*, Beam? Really? I thought you preferred *Hamlet*."

"I do, but 'Hie thee to a nunnery' doesn't have the same impact."

Neo entered the small conference room, determined to settle several things. He braced himself to face his mother's tirade, but the room was empty of everyone but a startled secretary who was setting out tablets of paper and bottles of chilled water.

"Where is everyone?" he asked the young man. Beam, who had taken possession of his office laptop as her own, moved over to one end of the oval table and extracted the laptop from its bag.

"I don't know," the man answered in Greek, giving Beam a curious look out of the corner of his eyes. "Kyria Zola came in a little bit ago, but she said she was not a dog to answer to her master's call."

Neo gave a mental sigh. Of course his mother was going to be difficult. "And Chase? Has he been admitted to the building?"

"I don't know. Should I know? I was just told to prepare the room," the man said, looking like he was about to dash off.

Neo waved him away, turning to Beam to tell her that he was going to have to go rout his mother out of the penthouse when the door opened and Camilla walked in, followed immediately by Lancelot Zola.

"There you are," Camilla said, giving him one of her wounded sniffs that told him she expected him to apologize. She ignored Beam, who obviously decided to keep her head down lest the storm break on her. "I wondered if you'd have the nerve to face us after what you said yesterday. Lancelot, my pills."

"Mother," he said, holding out a chair for her. He waited until his stepfather hurried forward, extracting a pill bottle from his jacket, and shaking out a couple on Camilla's waiting hand. Only after she'd taken the pills did she deign to take the seat.

Neo nodded at Lancelot, then took the chair next to Beam before turning his attention back to his mother. "Thank you for coming."

"Darling, you act as if me being here is something extraordinary. I am always happy to see you. I realize this woman has turned you from us out of spite, but I'd like you to remember that I have always been on your side," she said, her voice silky. "Never once have I complained. Never once have I stopped you from pursuing your little projects. I've always supported you, and done my best to keep Pi from floundering while you were away. I'm sure she has brainwashed you into thinking you've been poorly served and abused at our hands, but I want you to look deep into your heart to see the truth."

"I don't need to look deep into my heart to recognize truth," Neo told his mother, remarkably calm despite the drama that he knew was on the horizon. "I've always been grateful for your support of my projects. They were important to me, then and now."

Camilla smiled. He had never noticed before how artificial her smile appeared. It was as if she strictly confined it to her lips, with no sense of pleasure or joy or even mild interest reaching her eyes.

Beam was just the opposite. When she smiled, her whole body expressed happiness. He felt warm just being the recipient of her smiles. He looked forward to years of them lighting up his life.

"You've always been such a caring, thoughtful man," she said, still obviously pretending Beam wasn't sitting next to him. "It's one reason why I've been happy for you to take your little trips, so that you can spread happiness to those who need it."

Beam blinked a couple of times. He knew just how she felt. His mother, while normally a very verbally gifted woman, had never got the hang of subtle flattery. "All that said, recently I became aware that something was wrong with Pi."

"Wrong, how?" The faintest of lines appeared on Camilla's forehead. "If you're talking about that silly business with the intern—"

"I'm talking about the systematic restructuring of Pi's core philosophy," Neo interrupted. "When I started the company, I told you and Dad that I wanted to make a difference in the world. I wanted to use the growing tech world to benefit people, rather than profit from them. You both agreed."

"You were a visionary," Camilla said, giving a little wave of her hand. "Your father always said so, and I agreed. It's why your father set you up with the company, and why I hate now to see you forget how much you owe us just because a chaotic force has returned to your life."

"I will always be grateful for the help you gave me to get Pi going, but as I've paid you back several times over, we can both agree that there is no further financial debt between us regarding the company."

Beam watched Neo, her eyes filled with mingled worry and admiration.

Camilla's mouth tightened, causing a number of tiny lines to form around her lips, which were tinted a delicate shade of coral. "I won't say that I'm not hurt by this new attitude toward your family, but as I have never paid any attention to the acquisition of wealth, it's not as if your intention to cut me off has any impact on my life."

"I didn't say I would cut you off financially," he answered, tracing a pattern on the table and wondering how much of his morning's speculation was actionable, and how much was never going to be proved. "I will, naturally, make sure you continue to have an income on par with what I've given you in the past. What I intend to change is the focus of Pi. Where I started it to help people by providing tech solutions to impoverished peoples and regions, in the last few years it has apparently been shifted to financial investment concerns."

"But darling, of course it has!" Camilla's expression, which had frozen for a second, now melted into one of her cold smiles. "How do you expect to go jaunting all over the world, pouring money into this place or that, helping all those needy natives, if Pi wasn't making money for you?"

"Oh, man," he heard Beam whisper to herself.

"The term 'native' when used in that respect is problematic, Mother," Neo said, keeping a good firm grip on his annoyance. He was determined to prove to Beam that he could deal with his mother without losing his temper.

"Pish," she said, dismissing his correction. "It's what they are. Natives. Indigenous people. My point is that they need help, and you give it to them. And you can't do that without money. I don't know how you expect to fund your pet projects if Pi isn't turning a profit."

"It was never intended to be a cash cow," he argued. "You know that. And yet, when I dug into the financial history of the last few years, I found that the yearly statements were deliberately misleading."

"You'll have to talk to Chase about that, then," she said smoothly, then paused and pressed two fingers to her forehead as if she was thinking. "Oh, but wait. You fired him, did you not?" Her gaze shifted for a second to Beam. "I certainly hope you don't regret such a rash action. I would hate to think that listening to rumors led to you irreparably harming Pi."

"I would be grateful if you'd stop implying that Beam had anything to do with my decision to clean house," he said, keeping his voice even. "Because other than making me realize how insular and isolated I've been, she has had no influence on my actions. And as for speaking with Chase, I plan to do that. But first, I wanted to make sure that we had an understanding."

"No influence?" Camilla's lips tightened again. "Have you forgotten the fact that she deliberately sought you out in order to benefit her and her bastard child? I'm just surprised that she hasn't tried to convince you that the child is yours."

"Right, I've told you before, and I'll tell you again, since you obviously are having memory issues," Beam said, her eyes sparking at Camilla. "Ziggy is my niece, not my child. And I will thank you to leave her out of any references you make about me. She's young and hasn't had the experience I've had in dealing with problematic older women."

Camilla slammed her fist onto the table. "You spew lies with every breath. I won't have it. Lancelot, call security and have her removed."

Neo sighed. "Mother, stop it. Beam is staying where she is."

"I'm sorry," Beam told him. "I shouldn't have let it get to me, but I get a little protective when she goes after Ziggy."

He turned his head so only she saw his smile, and said in a tone pitched for her ears only, "The phrase 'mama bear' comes to mind."

"I'm her aunt," she said just as softly.

"Biologically, but I think you're her mother in every other sense."

"What are you whispering to each other? What are you saying? Is she maligning me again? I won't have this, Neo. I won't have her spilling lies into your ears without being able to dispute them."

"We weren't speaking about you, actually. But that does bring up a point I'd like to have cleared up. Just how did you find out about Beam using a detective to locate me? I assume the information came from Chase?"

"Yes, of course Chase told me about the information he had regarding that woman. And why shouldn't he tell me?" Camilla tapped at the table with her long, pink fingernails before flicking them, dismissing the issue as if it was of no importance. "He knew how worried I was about you falling into her clutches again. So he told me what he found out about her."

"Does he tell you other things?" Neo couldn't help but ask.

A flicker of consternation passed over his mother's face at the same time she slid a look at Lancelot from the corner of her eyes. Neo had an uncomfortable feeling that she would have preferred he not see any of that. "What sort of question is that? Of course we speak frequently. He is the CFO. I am acting CEO—"

Neo didn't interrupt her, although he'd never officially designated her to act in his stead. It was just one of the many ways he'd let her slip into running things that by rights he should have handled.

"—and naturally, he reports to me anything he thinks will have an impact on you. He is your oldest friend, after all," she added, with a hard stare at Beam.

The latter rolled her eyes, and leaned back in her chair, not even pretending to be working at the laptop any longer.

"Since you brought the subject up, has that person explained to you just why she, a woman with no job and nothing of any value, spent so much time and money pursuing you?" Camilla asked.

"Yes." Neo didn't take any pleasure in the moment of consternation visible on his mother's face, knowing she was just firing up the bulldozer. "What I want to know is why Chase told you what he'd found out about Beam."

"Why?" Camilla gave a dismissive shake of her head. "Why do you think? I'm your mother, and he hoped I'd have some pull with you. He hoped that I'd be able to stop you from doing any more damage to Pi. But you have always been headstrong, just like Aris, always jumping without considering where you'll land."

Neo felt like he had the answer he sought to that question that had been tickling the back of his mind. "Yes, we need to have a discussion about just what exactly Dad and Uncle Okeanos did to their brothers."

"What they did? Darling, have you let this person give you drugs? You know what happened. Your father and uncle were abused by their brothers, horribly abused and cheated. And when your father died, they refused to help us—"

"I was twenty-eight when Dad died, and Pi was six years old. It was the first year it turned a profit, so I fail to see what sort of help you expected from anyone," he pointed out.

"There are other ways to be supportive other than mere money," Camilla said with great dignity, which effect she ruined when she slapped the table when turning to Lancelot. "Get me a drink! I need one after having to listen to my own son accuse me of trying to rob him."

"I have not accused you of any such thing," he said, watching when Lancelot got up and went to the small bar at the far end of the room, where several crystal carafes sat with a number of short tumblers.

"No, but you clearly believe it to be true," Camilla said with enough acid to etch the glass that Lancelot handed her.

"On the contrary, I don't think you care overly much for money, other than what you need to keep the lifestyle you have." He thought for a moment, a bit surprised to find that it was true. "You never did ask for more money, or want me to buy you new cars and houses."

"Of course not," Camilla said, slightly muffled as she tossed back the whiskey and handed the glass to Lancelot, obviously expecting a refill. "I have sufficient."

Neo nodded, recognizing the truth in that statement. His mother had a large wardrobe, and enjoyed the social scene, as well as visiting the three houses his father had owned and which were hers to use during her life, but other than wanting to use his *Athena* for jaunts around the Mediterranean, and occasionally redecorating the penthouse, she had not pestered him for increasing amounts of money. "Which leads me to believe that any help you might have received from Dad's family was one of emotional support. But how could you expect that after what happened?"

"Naturally, I had hoped that they would see the error of their ways and reach out to make up for what they'd done to us. They shunned your father and uncle, but when Aris died—and Okeanos was off in America trying to start a business there—I had expected, had *hoped*, that the family would reach out to make amends."

A thought startled him as he watched his mother tell Lancelot to get her another drink. He turned to Beam, once again making sure that his voice was low enough for just her to hear. "Am I crazy, or is she telling the truth?"

Beam nodded, her gaze solemn on his. "I think so, too. I don't know what your dad did, but is it possible he didn't clue her in?"

"I'm beginning to think so," he answered, feeling as if the world had somehow shifted imperceptibly. Was everything he believed to be true wrong?

He'd been wrong about Beam being at fault.

He'd been wrong about his mother's complicity in dealing with the cousins.

And he'd been wrong about Chase. The question was, now that he could see the truth, was there any way of keeping everything from crashing and burning around him?

SIXTEEN

I wondered if the day would ever end, or if Neo and I were stuck in some sort of hell. One consisting of his raging mother.

"You can keep the penthouse," Neo told Camilla, obviously taking her by surprise. "Beam thinks you would like to keep it since you've lived there so long. If that's so, then I will arrange for you to have a life tenancy. I will also continue to provide you with a yearly allowance. But beyond that, you have no financial claims on me or my company."

Camilla didn't like being given an ultimatum. "Why are you doing this to me? Is that woman demanding that you cut me out of your life? I am your mother! I have always only ever thought of your welfare—"

Neo held up his hand. I was more than a little startled when it actually stopped her from continuing.

"Beam has done the opposite, actually. She believes that we would all be happier if we could work out a relationship based on mutual respect and boundaries that are not to be crossed. And I will ask you to stop referring to her as *that woman* or *that person*. Beam and I are going to be married. I won't ask that you give us your blessing, but I do ask that you treat her with the respect due my wife."

"I knew it!" Camilla's eyes narrowed on me as she all but crowed the words. "I just knew she'd try to trap you! Well, it didn't work the first time, and I will not allow her to pull the wool over your eyes—"

"Stop!" Neo shouted, slamming his palm down on the table, startling everyone present. "Just stop! If you continue treating Beam that way, then I will have no option but to limit contact with you. I don't wish to do this. You are my mother, and I love you, but I also love Beam. She makes me whole. She is the light of my life, and nothing you or anyone else can say will change that. About this, Mother, it's my way, or we will live our lives without you."

I'll say this for Camilla, she knew how to pivot. "Darling, the words coming out of your mouth! If I were any other mother, I would be prostrate at the attack against my character, but I know that you don't have a vicious bone in your body. Although, really, I would have thought that you would know that I did not mean anything but the most loving interest in your life." She leaned across the table and patted one of his cheeks while shooting me a toothy smile. "You can be so smart about computer things, and yet utterly ridiculous about others. You seem to think I have a vendetta against Beam."

It took an effort, but I managed not to make a face when she waved a hand at me in an airy gesture that could mean either inclusion or dismissal.

"You made it fairly clear you think she's bent on using me, yes," Neo said.

She brushed off the history of our previous conversations, just as, I suspected, she refused to acknowledge everything else that didn't fit in with her personal worldview. I had to admit, I admired her turnabout.

"That couldn't be further from the truth," Camilla said with a beatific smile at him. "Naturally, given what Chase told me, I was concerned about her motivation in seeking you out, especially since she didn't seem to want to explain herself to anyone's satisfaction. However—" She ignored the noise of protest that Neo made, steamrolling over him to say with a slightly louder volume, "However, I see now that you have developed an attachment to her, and of course, as your loving mother, I can do nothing more than to welcome anyone you love to our little home. Marriage, is, of course, a wonderful thing, but you are young yet, and I hope you will take whatever time you need to make sure that you are ideally suited to each other. An engagement party, I think, would be an excellent start. Naturally, I will host it, and of course, you will both come and live with us. You can't want to stay on your boat forever, nice though it is. Beam will want to join us in the penthouse, where she will be welcome with open arms."

I stared at her in stark amazement for a few seconds, then said softly out of the side of my mouth, "She's good."

"Always thought she should have been on the stage," Neo agreed in a whisper, which fortunately Camilla didn't hear because she was too busy planning an engagement party.

It took a few more minutes before Neo managed to regain control of the conversation.

"In the spirit of this détente, I believe it's right to mention that I've recently had a long conversation with Iakovos, Theo, and Dmitri."

Camilla made a face, but instantly smoothed it over, obviously taking Neo's threat of no contact well to heart. "Darling, how brave of you. I take it they didn't spurn your attempt at friendship outright?"

"Far from it." He gave her a long look. "They filled me in on quite a few things about which I'd been kept in the dark, most notably, the deal that Dad and Uncle Okeanos pulled on the cousins' fathers. I know how Dad promised money to help them start their business, encouraging them to take out loans using their own property as security."

"That doesn't sound right," Camilla said, frowning a little. "I'm sure Aris said it was the other way around."

"Despite what Dad told you, he and Uncle Okeanos promised to invest in their brothers' business, but not only cut off the source of their funding; they also spread rumors about the new business's insolvency, causing several banks to refuse to help them, as well as calling due their loans rather than extending credit, as Dad promised."

"No. I can't believe that. Your father would not have been so ruthless ..." She stopped, a hard look flashing in her eyes. "Not to his own family. They were the ones who wronged us."

Neo took a deep breath, his fingers twining through mine. I relished the fact that he sought me out for comfort, even though I knew he didn't need it. He was dealing admirably with his mother. "I also know how—when Dad's two brothers were facing nothing but economic loss after loss, the destruction of their business, and foreclosure on their homes—he bribed the man who they'd convinced to sell them a property that was their last chance to save themselves from complete financial ruin."

Camilla's protests started even before he had finished. "That can't be true, darling, it's just not reasonable. Your father and uncle were the ones who were hurt. They were always picked on because they were twins. All their brothers disliked them. Aris always said that he and Okeanos made a pact that they would prove to the family that they were just as successful as the rest of their brothers. If the brothers lost a valuable property, it was their own fault. Your father would never have stooped to anything so underhanded."

"The cousins told me how you begged your father to give you a sizable amount of money so that Dad and Uncle Okeanos could buy the property themselves, turning it to a substantial profit. And when the rest of the family members sided against you three, they spun a web of lies making themselves the victims, and keeping me ostracized from the family."

"Holy shit," I said, slapping a hand over my mouth when I realized just how rude that was. But if I was worried about Camilla coming unglued on me, I was mistaken.

She looked momentarily as gobsmacked as I felt, which surprised me. I hadn't been entirely sure when Neo asked if he thought his mother was innocent of the family's history, but there was no denying that he had hit home.

"My father?" she asked, her voice faltering for a second, before she straightened up her back, obviously gathering her emotional resources. "That money was for Aris's company, the one that he had to start after his brothers sided against him and Okeanos."

"Was it?" Neo asked, his voice gentler now. Obviously, he'd seen the stark emotions pass over his mother's face at the realization of what he was saying. "I've seen the documents, Mother."

Her jaw worked a couple of times, before she made another last-ditch attempt to cling to a false version of the past. "Manufactured, no doubt, just to confuse you and turn you against me."

"Manufactured just as you and Dad manufactured proof of the lies you told me about Beam?" he asked, his voice oddly neutral, but I could hear an undercurrent of anger.

"Darling, that was so long ago … How can I remember what he did or did not do?" She turned her head to bare her teeth at me in what I could only assume she intended for a smile. "I'm sure dear Beam has long since forgiven us for whatever misunderstandings happened in the past."

"I can't speak for her, but I certainly haven't forgiven Dad for what he did." Neo got to his feet, walking to the window to look outside for a few seconds before he turned back to add, "I'm not saying you knew what was going on, but I can't help but be angry for what was taken from me."

"What have I taken from you?" Camilla leaped to her feet, almost snarling the words, her mood changing instantly to that of a tiger on the attack. "All I have done is work for you, my entire life—"

"At best, you allowed Dad to take my love away from me," Neo answered. "You saw how devastated I was. You knew how much I loved her."

"You were young," she said, her gaze flitting around the room like she was looking for an exit. "You didn't know your own mind. You had an infatuation, yes, but Aris and I knew that you would soon outgrow it."

"I didn't," he said, irony dripping from each word. "Then there was the family. I don't hold you to blame for that, since it's become evident that Dad and Okeanos deliberately isolated us from the rest of the family, but did you never once question the decision to cut us off from them? To encourage me to remain isolated and alone?"

"You were always a solitary boy," she snapped back. "You didn't want friends."

"Didn't want them, or wasn't given the opportunity to have them?" Neo checked himself, adding, "No, that's not fair of me. I had a few friends when I went to college. But I did not know my family because Dad didn't want us to know them. And then later, when I should have been paying attention to Pi, you encouraged me to pursue interests that took me to remote areas."

"You wanted to go," she countered.

"The idea of doing so never occurred to me until you pointed out how much good I could do tackling projects that had no other way to be funded. I don't blame you for the lack of my awareness of what was going on with Pi— in that, I am wholly responsible—but you deliberately encouraged me to go off to different countries, and I can't help but think it was because you liked the idea of being in control of Pi."

"I was an excellent CEO while you were gone," she answered, stabbing a finger in the air at him. "I took control in ways you would never have. Chase and I ensured that the company was steered properly to reasonable goals, ones that would fund you, and keep the company afloat."

"Chase," Neo said slowly, in a way that had me wondering what he knew about his friend. "Yes, I thought we'd circle back to him. What was he to you, Mother? Confidant? Counselor? Lover?"

"How dare you say that to me!" Camilla slapped him before I realized what she'd done. But the second Neo's head snapped back, I was pushing my way in between them, shoving her back.

"Stop it!" I yelled. "That's the same cheek I hit three days ago. And what sort of mother hits her son, especially one who has been as nice to you as Neo has been?"

"I appreciate you defending me, sunshine." Neo's voice was warm in my ear as he gently pulled me back to his side. "But it's not necessary. What I said was out of line. I apologize, Mother. And to you, as well, Lancelot. But beyond that, I believe my mother and I understand each other."

"I understand that you are beyond all reason," Camilla said, her nostrils flaring in the same manner they had so many years ago. "But I am not the monster you are so eager to paint me. I'm sure you expect me to refuse to accept your decision to marry this woman, but although I believe you are making a mistake, and will one day realize that I have only had your best interest at heart, I will accept her to the family. And since she will be busy taking my place at Pi, I will find other things to do. There are my charities, and friends, and of course, Lancelot and I have wanted to travel, but I've always felt duty bound to remain here, to keep an eye on Pi."

"No, you are not a monster," Neo agreed, and, after rubbing his cheek for a moment, actually summoned up a weak smile. "I wish I could say as much about Dad, but he's dead, and there's not much I can do about his actions. As for our relationship, I appreciate the olive branch. I don't believe that Beam and Ziggy and I will want to live in the penthouse, but I am pleased that you are willing to accept that Beam is the woman with whom I intend to spend the rest of my life."

"So be it," Camilla said, and underwent an obvious struggle before she addressed me. "I'm sorry that you have had to witness our respective shows of temper. I assure you that normally Neo and I are in perfect harmony. Regardless, I will be in touch about the engagement party." Her gaze raked me from head to toes. "I will be happy to take you to my favorite designers and shops. Lancelot, we are due at the museum meeting, are we not?"

The redheaded man hurried to open the door for her, his gaze moving between Neo and me as she strolled through it. He gave what I thought was an apologetic smirk, opened his mouth to say something, but closed it quickly and hurried out when Camilla barked his name.

"She really is something," I told Neo when the door closed behind them. "I hate to sound callous, but that man—your stepfather?—is he ... er ... aphasic?"

"Lancelot?" Neo looked momentarily surprised. "No. He talks all the time when he's not around my mother."

"Gotcha." I put my arms around him and kissed his jaw. "Do you feel better?"

"For making my peace with my mother? Yes and no." His eyes were clouded, telling me that all was not well in his world.

"The yes I understand, but the no? Does it have something to do with Chase? Or with Pi? Or is it Beowulf? I noticed you didn't ask your mom about that."

"She doesn't have the slightest idea what code is. There's no way she could do anything to Beowulf or the proprietary Pi programming."

"No, but she might be able to get someone to do something with it," I pointed out, gathering up the laptop and placing it into the bag.

Neo held out his hand for me. We left the conference room and walked to the elevator, the hum of business proceeding around us. "It's possible, but I doubt it."

"Chase, then?"

"He doesn't have the access to the programming side. He just handles—handled—the financial aspect. Which reminds me I need to dig a little deeper than just the last two years that I accessed this morning."

"Do you think he's ripped you off?" I asked, aghast at the idea. Chase had seemed so devoted to Neo.

"No. The first thing I did when I realized that Beowulf was buried in the code was to access my financial accounts. Everything is fine there. More than fine; evidently I've been making money hand over fist while I was in South America. Likewise, the financials on Pi itself appear normal."

"Have you talked to him? Chase, that is."

"Not yet." Neo's body language read discomfort. "I know I need to talk to him, but I'm waiting until I have some time to go through everything."

"You're not regretting letting him go, are you?" I asked, concerned.

"No." He looked away, definitely avoiding me. I chalked it up to him not wanting to talk about being so wrong in his estimation of a friend.

I decided to return to a safer subject. "Someone has to have stuck that code throughout your programming." I was more than a little bit exasperated that I hadn't done what I'd said, and dug out all the bits of it. "Someone who knows something about twenty-year-old code."

"We'll find them," Neo said with a grim note to his voice that echoed within me.

I made a mental promise as we rode the elevator up to his office that I would do whatever it took to find out who had stolen my code and used it to damage Neo. And when I found them … "Hell hath no fury like a programmer annoyed," I murmured to myself.

SEVENTEEN

"Anything?"

"Anything. Whatever she wants."

"Dude. This is, like, an Amex black card. An actual black card. One that has no spending limits. I could rack up a million dollars on there, and you'd have to pay it."

"Get her whatever she likes. I don't care if it's seven figures. I want her happy. And don't tell her that I gave you the card."

"Do I get to keep it?" Ziggy asked, hope filling her voice.

"No. But you can buy yourself whatever you want for the ceremony, too."

"OK." Ziggy gave a little giggle. "That's some pretty big guilt about Aunt Beam that you're trying to assuage."

"Not guilt, love. Well … perhaps a tiny bit of guilt. But ninety-eight percent of it is adoration, love, and a deep and abiding lust. Erm … how old are you?"

"Twenty," Ziggy said with a grin.

"Pretend I said nothing about lust. Just remember that I love your aunt more than anything, and see to it that she gets whatever she wants."

"OK, but she's not going to believe that I saved up enough money to buy her a nice dress to get married in. Unfortunately, she knows me and my weakness for manga all too well."

"Of course she won't. Beam is smarter than both of us, but she can't very well refuse a gift from her own niece, even if she suspects I am the source of the money. Did Yianna give you the money I left for your first month's allowance?"

I leaned against the partially opened door of the galley, biting my lip to keep from laughing as I listened to Neo and Ziggy scheming together.

"Yeah." Reluctance filled the air. I took the risk and peeked around the edge of the door. Ziggy was standing just beyond the small table, her face twisted with a familiar expression, part regret, part obstinance. "You know, I think maybe Aunt Beam is right, and you shouldn't give me so much. I mean, it's not fair you pay for me to go to Berlin and stuff. So maybe I should give you back some of it."

It was obvious that she'd made that offer only after an almighty inner struggle, a fact that just made me beam with pride. I hadn't thought she'd let Neo's wealth turn her head, and I was relieved to know I was right.

"Hmm?" Neo had been looking at his phone, but he had good hearing and must have heard my intake of breath when I saw him lounging against the table clad in nothing but a pair of board shorts, because he turned to glance toward the door. "What did you say?"

"I thought maybe I should give you back some of the allowance. It's an awful lot. ..."

He dismissed her concern just like I knew he would, his eyes lighting up when I pushed open the door and walked into the room. "Don't be ridiculous. It's barely enough to get in trouble with. Ah, there you are. I told Dag you were going shopping before meeting the cousins' wives for lunch, so don't worry about sending him back for me."

"Ah, the infamous stag party?"

"Such as it is, yes." His eyes laughed at me. I hugged myself, both over our secret that we'd let only Ziggy into and for the upcoming celebration. "Dmitri's going to pick me up. He's promised that since we are having the ceremony this afternoon, we won't get even a quarter as drunk as you were the other night with Harry and the others."

He accepted the kiss I pressed on his lips, his mouth warm enough that I thought seriously about dragging him back to bed, but the knowledge that Ziggy wanted to get something for the ceremony had me keeping my smutty thoughts to myself. "We weren't drunk, just having a good time."

"You were that. I'll see you this afternoon, then?"

"You will, with bells on." I bit my lip for a second, waiting until Ziggy trotted down the gangway before asking, "You're sure you want to do this?"

"Have the ceremony at Iakovos's apartment?"

"Have Ziggy be our officiant. Not that I want to disparage her choice of religions, especially one that worships a spaghetti monster, but I don't want you to think I view marriage with you as anything but serious and permanent this time."

He kissed me, then walked me over to the gangplank, saying, "I don't care about the religious aspect of the ceremony, as you well know. Since it means a lot to Ziggy to put her status as an ordained Pastafarian minister to good use, then I'm happy to have her officiate. Have fun shopping, sunshine."

"Have fun stag partying, sexy former number two most hunkalicious bachelor," I told him, and hurried after Ziggy.

Two hours later, we were both exhausted. "Let's find somewhere we can get a tall, cold beverage, and maybe some nibblies," I told Ziggy, handing Dag our bags before asking, "Can you pick us up in about half an hour?"

"Sure. I'll get some lunch. Text me if you want me earlier," he said, then with our various bags in hand whistled as he joined the throngs of shoppers and tourists.

"Right," I said, glancing up and down the street. "There has to be a nice café around here where we can spend a little more of Neo's hard-earned money—"

The squeal of tires, followed by a horn pressed in obvious anger, interrupted me. I looked over to the traffic, surprised to see a car window roll down and Kiera's head pop out of it. "Beam! Ziggy! We were just shopping for your wedding. Did you get a dress yet?"

"We did. We're a bit worn out, so I thought we'd have a few snacks at that café," I said, pointing at tables set out on the sidewalk half a block ahead of us.

Kiera's head popped inside; then the door opened and all three ladies piled out, Harry pausing long enough to give the driver orders.

"We'll join you," Thyra said, wearing an oversized pair of sunglasses, her cat on a harness and lead. "Although I am not drinking anything. Two times in ten days just about did me in. Plus, Dmitri is starting to make noises about me teaching bad habits to Valentino."

"What did you buy?" Kiera asked. "I got a cute dress that I know Theo is going to love because he always wants me to show my legs, which is ridiculous, because he's the one who looks good in shorts, not me."

We spent a pleasant half hour discussing the various garments we'd purchased, taking over two small sidewalk tables, and ordering a number of appetizers. By consensus, after our bachelorette dinner the night before on Neo's boat, we collectively shunned anything alcoholic.

"What I want to know is what the men are doing," Thyra said, handing a bit of plain chicken to her cat, who occupied his own seat. I had to admit, Valentino had exceptionally nice manners. He also had yellow eyes that were strangely disconcerting when they locked onto you.

"Strippers," Ziggy said, sucking a bit of feta out of a stuffed olive before popping it into her mouth. "Pole dancers. Beer pong. Maybe a little weed."

"It's not legal here, and the day Iakovos authorizes strippers and pole dancers to visit our apartment is the day hell freezes over," Harry told her. "Although the beer pong is a possibility."

"Theo would play beer pong, but he doesn't drink," Kiera told me. "I'm not sure if the others would play a game with alcohol, though. They're fairly protective about him, which is really sweet, when you think of it."

"I don't normally indulge, either," I told them. "Wine tends to make me sleepy, which is why I fell asleep last night while you were trying to play the cucumber game."

"Which I won, even though I don't have a man whose dick I was re-creating," Ziggy said, chomping on a bit of naan. "If beer pong is out, then they're probably watching porn. Or maybe playing naughty virtual reality games."

"We should see what they're doing," Thyra suggested, lifting her shades to squint at a bit of hummus before tentatively dipping a finger into it and tasting it. Silence greeted her statement. She realized we were all looking at her, and let the sunglasses slide back down. "What? You guys were thinking it, too, right?"

"I wasn't, but it's not a bad idea," Harry said thoughtfully. "I don't say that Iakovos would actively promote porn to Neo, but the guys are still getting to know each other. Maybe he thinks that Neo would like it?"

They all turned to me.

"Your guess is as good as mine," I had to admit. "He wasn't like that when I first knew him, but twenty-four years have gone by since then. Maybe he got into it?"

"It doesn't seem likely," Kiera said slowly.

"We won't know till we see for ourselves," Ziggy said, and, waving Neo's black credit card in the air, caught the waiter's attention.

Which is why, almost half an hour later, we were clustered outside the door to Harry's apartment.

"This is ridiculous, but I feel really empowered," Thyra said in a whisper, clutching her cat's leash. "Also, I kind of want to giggle."

"Me too, and I'm so not a giggler," Kiera said, holding on to a bag that contained the leftovers from our abundant appetizer spread. "It's almost like I'm giddy."

"'Giddy' is a good word," I agreed, feeling joyous and bubbly and so happy I wanted to sing.

"It's because we're all madly in love, except for Ziggy, and she's too young to be this deeply in love yet," Harry whispered, then unlocked the door and opened it a crack before peering in. "Love makes you giggly and giddy. OK, living room is clear. Everyone, be quiet. The room with the theater that Yacky insists the children will die without, but really is because he loves movies on a big screen, is to the left."

"I could be madly in love if I wanted," Ziggy said, and all four of us shushed her until she got a case of the giggles, too.

We crept into the room after Harry, but hadn't taken more than two steps before a figure loomed up, startling me. Thyra shrieked, but Kiera clapped a hand over her mouth before much of the sound got out. Harry jumped a good six inches, clutching her chest as she said, "Oh, Mrs. Avrabos. It's you. Man, it's a good thing the kids keep my heart strong. We … uh … we're …"

"You are here to check the arrangements for this afternoon?" the older woman asked, a little twinkle in her dark eyes.

"Yes," Harry said, nodding. "That's it."

"Nothing has changed since you checked this morning. The tables will be set an hour before people are to arrive. The caterers are preparing the meal now. And the champagne is cooling."

"Excellent," Harry said, still nodding.

Kiera and I giggled.

"You ladies have had some already?" she asked, eyeing us.

"Nope, not a drop," Thyra told her, holding her hands up. "We're just giddy because we're so in love."

"Papaioannou men have that effect," Kiera said, and giggled again.

"They do," Mrs. Avrabos agreed, a hint of a smile on her lips.

"We stopped by because … because we … er …" Harry stopped, obviously searching for a reason to be there ahead of the ceremony we'd agreed to hold at their place at five o'clock. Her gaze fell on Ziggy and me. "Because I haven't shown you around, have I? You'll want to see Elena's room, which we've set aside for the bridal party. Oh, that's … er … on the other side of the apartment."

"You can show her the gym, where Dmitri likes to use the punching bag," Thyra suggested.

Harry nodded vigorously. "Yes! I'll show you the gym! And the kids' former playroom, which now acts as a small study when they have to do distance learning. And … and … other things down here."

Mrs. Avrabos said nothing, just disappeared in the opposite direction, which I gathered was the kitchen area.

"You are so devious," Kiera told Harry with obvious admiration. "I would never have come up with even a remotely reasonable story."

"I *am* an author," Harry said with much modesty.

Ziggy started to say something, but I pinched her arm, and gave her a gimlet look that told her we were not going to rain on our new relations-by-marriage's parades. She grinned in response.

"This way, ladies! And remember, be quiet. We'll just peek into the gaming room and the theater, and see which one the men are in."

We crept in single file down the hallway that led at a right angle from the living area. I had to admit that the silliness of the moment led me to stifle a couple of snorts of laughter. I knew full well that even if Iakovos had arranged for a showing of porn, or something similar in VR, Neo would not have more than a passing interest. Other than his determination to have a hammock strung up in his cabin, and his love of sticky chocolate spreads, he seemed as boringly white-bread as I was when it came to sex.

"I'm going to have to introduce him to some toys, though," I said softly to myself, mentally sorting through my bedside toy box.

I was so intent on deciding which one—if any—he might enjoy that I bumped into Kiera, who was ahead of me.

"Toys?" she asked in a whisper. "Sex toys?"

I nodded.

"Reeeally," she drawled, and looked thoughtful. "Do you have a particular recommendation?"

"Ladies!"

We snapped to attention when Harry turned back to face us. She stood outside a door, her hand on the doorknob.

"Sorry," I mouthed.

"Beam mentioned getting sex toys for Neo," Kiera explained to Thyra.

"Oh really?" She picked up her orange cat and, leaning out, asked, "What brand?"

"Ahem," Harry said pointedly, then made a little face, and added, "Someone start up a messaging thread with toy recs and add me to it. Right. Let's see if they're in here."

She eased the door open, but the room, set up with a couple of old 1990s arcade machines and more modern gaming consoles, was empty.

"So much for the VR stuff. Porn it is," she said, closing the door and pointing to the end of the hallway.

We snuck up to it, stifling various giggles as Harry carefully turned the doorknob.

The room was dark and completely empty.

"Well, hell," she said, turning back to face us, slapping her hands on her legs. "Where can they—"

She stopped, an odd expression coming over her face, as if she just remembered she left something boiling on the stove.

"Could they have left?" I asked the others.

"Went to a strip club, no doubt," Ziggy said, making kissy noises at Valentino, who was graciously allowing her to scritch him behind his ears. "Men are dawgs. Well, most are. The ones I've met are, present company's husbands excepted."

"Maybe they went to your house?" Kiera asked Thyra.

"I don't know why. This is where we're having the wedding. It makes more sense for them to do it here—"

She'd turned around as she spoke, and she, too, froze.

I knew at that moment what I'd see. I pursed my lips, smiled at Harry, then casually swung around.

Four men stood at the end of the hallway, all clad in swim trunks, all clearly having been in the water, their hair plastered down, and silver streams of water moving lazily down their respective bare chests and legs. Each man had his arms crossed.

"The pool," Harry said, sounding exasperated. "Why didn't I think to check the pool first? Er … hello. We got done a little early."

"Which is why you were skulking around the apartment, rather than coming out to find us?" Iakovos asked, breaking rank and strolling forward.

"We were merely being respectful of Neo's stag party."

"We didn't want to interrupt the strippers," Ziggy said, happily taking Valentino when Thyra handed him to her in order to move over to Dmitri like he was a lodestone.

Kiera giggled. Theo wiggled his eyebrows at her and mouthed something that I pretended I didn't see.

Iakovos wanted to roll his eyes, I could see, but instead he just took Harry by the hand, pulled her up for a loud, fast kiss, and said he knew better than to let her lead others astray.

She protested all the way out to the patio.

"Did you really think there were strippers here?" Neo asked when the others followed suit, Ziggy promising Valentino that she would take good care of him while his parents were busy snogging.

I strolled toward him, my soul singing at the joy of knowing he was mine. His skin was wet, warm from being in the sun, and oh so tempting. "No. But the others kind of ran with that idea, and I didn't want to be the party pooper."

"Cousin Harry told me to tell you that Neo isn't supposed to see the bride," Ziggy said, appearing behind him. "I told her you guys slept together last night, so you could hardly get up in the morning without being seen, but she said it's still a tradition, and she's coming back in exactly seven minutes to take you away from Neo, and to finish your smooching by then. She also said there's a hairdresser and a lady to do our makeup coming in an hour. Can I get a henna tattoo? The makeup lady knows how to do them, evidently."

"Yes," I told her, my lips against Neo's. He kissed me, then spun me around and, with a gentle buffet on my butt, sent me to Ziggy.

"I'm going to return to the pool, since I don't want a henna tattoo, and my hair doesn't need a specialist," he said as he headed out toward the patio. He paused and added, "My mother is coming after all. She said that in the spirit of proving that she holds no grudges, she will be here to watch us get married."

"Oh, lord," I said, glancing at Ziggy.

"Goody," she said, and would have rubbed her hands, but they were full of cat. "I hope she likes the ceremony I wrote."

Neo said nothing, just shot me a look full of meaning, and returned to his pool party.

"Come on, Harry told me which room we're supposed to use. Thyra said I can let Valentino down, because he's used to roaming around the apartment, and they have a litter box and food for him here, but he likes to be held, don't you think? Aunt Beam—"

"I'll ask, but I don't think having a cat on a yacht, even one as nice as Neo's, is a great idea," I told her, forestalling the request that I knew was coming. "Maybe if we get a place of our own, then we can have one."

"Deal," she said, and bustled me off to the room set aside for us.

EIGHTEEN

Four hours later, suitably dressed in a gorgeous ruby-colored liquid jersey, bias-cut, A-line floor-length dress, with a neckline that was so plunging it made me a bit nervous, and clutching a small bouquet of wildflowers, I approached an aisle that was created by the arrangement of a dozen wooden folding chairs out on Iakovos and Harry's patio.

"Are you nervous?" Ziggy asked in a whisper, walking beside me.

"No. Should I be?"

"Neo's mom is here. I would be worried she was going to create a scene, given the shit show you said went down. Oh, I forgot to tell you, Neo's friend came with her."

I stopped and looked at her for a second, before craning my head to see over the people waiting. All the men, I was not surprised to see, were in dark suits, not tuxedos, but nice enough to almost be classed as such. Dmitri wore some sort of a royal order, and Thyra had on a dazzling necklace of amber and diamonds. I had to remind myself that Thyra was an actual princess and, as such, no doubt had a ton of killer jewelry.

It wasn't until Theo shifted to the side that I saw Camilla and Chase at the front row. All the guests were standing and waiting for me to complete my walk down the aisle. My gaze moved to Neo. He stood next to a small table that was serving as a podium, with Iakovos and Harry flanking him. He'd decided on them as his best man and best woman, since he felt that honor should go to the oldest member of the family. Harry, naturally, was thrilled, and was wearing a truly outstanding midnight-blue silk pantsuit studded with beads that made it look like she was wrapped in the night sky.

"Shit," I said, then realized the polite "waiting for the bride" looks had turned a bit pointed. "OK. Well, Neo must have known he was coming. He doesn't look upset."

"He said not, but I didn't really get to talk to him," Ziggy whispered back, and we resumed our slow walk toward the others. She held Valentino's leash, and he marched out in front of us, his tail crooked at the top, a bow-tie collar making him look particularly dapper. Ziggy had insisted he fill the role of flower girl, since she was acting as both the family member who was giving me away and the officiant.

"And even I can't do three things at once," she'd told me an hour earlier when she demonstrated how well Valentino walked on a leash.

I didn't particularly care. I just wanted the ceremony over, so Neo and I could get down to the business of fixing all the things wrong with Pi.

Everyone smiled as we passed them, except Camilla and Chase. The former had a tight-lipped look that warned she was in a bit of a brittle mood, while the latter kept his gaze on Neo.

And Neo … "Damn, he's fine," I said under my breath, wondering what I'd done to deserve him. As he had said about me, it must have been something exceptionally good.

"Neo," Ziggy said, her lips twitching as she bowed to him, her dress fluttering around her legs. She'd chosen to wear a lime-green-and-yellow cotton print, thigh-length, tiered summer dress highly representative of those I could remember my mother wearing. She ceremoniously took the flowers from me, handed them to Harry, and then gestured toward me. "I bestow upon you my aunt."

He bowed in return, taking my hand, his fingers warm and strong.

I stifled a laugh at the seriocomic attitude he had struck.

"Thank you. I am happy to receive her hand—and all the rest of her—in marriage."

A noise came from behind me, a *tsk*ing annoyed sound that I figured had to come from Camilla. I knew full well she was going to hate the ceremony, but I didn't care. This was for us.

Ziggy handed Valentino's leash to Thyra, then moved around to stand at the makeshift podium.

"Be seated, please," she said with great dignity.

People sat. Kiera giggled.

"Gathered loved ones," Ziggy began. "New relations by marriage, friends, acquaintances, and kitties, we are gathered here today to marry my darling aunt to her ex-husband, who, because he's my uncle, I can't comment on whether or not he's a thirst trap, but I will say that I'm totally open to meeting any junior members of the Papaioannou sexy-bachelor club."

"Ziggy!" I said, giving her a look intended to quell. She just smiled in return.

"If anyone here has a problem with this union, then you'd better take it up with my new uncle, Neo, because he is obviously perfect for my aunt, and she makes him go googly-eyed with happiness."

Behind me, Camilla heaved a dramatic sigh.

"Right, this is the part where you guys consent to be married to each other from here on out. Moonbeam Swiftcloud Nakai, do you promise to take care of Neo when he's hale and hearty, as well as those times when he's on his knees puking up his guts? Do you promise to love him, and hold him forever in your heart, and swear that you'll support him no matter who gives you a hard time?"

"I do," I said, smiling at the love of my life, my eyes getting a bit weepy despite the silliness of Ziggy's idea of wedding vows.

"Yay! OK, Neo Aristeidis Okeanos Papaioannou, do you promise the same thing—you'll take care of Beam when she's feeling great, and when she's upset and angry? Do you swear you'll love her forever and ever, and will stop beating yourself up about the past, because you know she loves you and forgives you? Do you promise before everyone here that you will put her wishes first above your own? Will you consider buying us a house so we can have a cat, too, because I really like Valentino, and I can't steal him from Thyra because she might have our heads lopped off or something?"

Neo burst into laughter, as did everyone but Camilla and Chase. The latter, at least, had cracked a smile. Camilla looked like she wanted to smite Ziggy.

"I do," Neo said, taking my other hand in his, and kissing both of them. "Although the cat is subject for negotiation."

"I'm going to hold you to that," she told him, then smiled broadly at us both. "I have before me the two rings that Beam and Neo have chosen to exchange. They are shaped in the endless circle of love that wraps around them both, and which may never be broken. Aunt Beam?"

I took the ring, and slid it onto Neo's finger, whispering to him as I did so, "If your mother had lasers for eyes, my head would have exploded by now."

"Awesome. And Neo?" Ziggy handed him a ring.

He slipped it on my finger, choking when his gaze slipped past me to where his mother sat. His chest and shoulders shook for a moment, but he managed to keep the laughter inside this time.

"And now, by the power vested to me by the online Pastafarian website, duly recognizing me as an ordained minister, I pronounce you wife and husband, aunt and uncle, and best friends forever. Go ahead and kiss the bride, Neo."

Applause swept over us as Neo kissed me, although he kept it relatively tame, no doubt for his mother's benefit.

We turned to the guests, accepting congratulations and good wishes. Ziggy, who had discovered Iakovos's sound system, hit a button, and the patio was flooded with bouncy dance music.

"Best wedding ever," Thyra said as Dmitri took her hand and hauled her toward a clear spot where Kiera and Theo were already dancing with abandon.

"It was charming, and I'm so happy you let us be a part of it," Harry told us, sobering a little when Iakovos spoke briefly to Camilla. Neo, with a glance at me that I answered with a nod toward them, moved off to join his mom and Chase.

"How did that go?" I asked Harry in an undertone.

"Not as bad as you might imagine, actually." She smiled, and nodded when Mrs. Avrabos obviously asked a question about the food. "Iakovos and Dmitri had a little chat with her while we were waiting for you, and they said she was nothing but polite. Of course, no one mentioned the past, but all in all, I think this is a good omen."

My gaze swiveled to where Neo was standing. For some reason, he looked rigid, far too rigid for a man who'd just gotten married.

"Do you mind if I ask you a nosy question?" Harry asked.

"Not at all," I said, a little startled nonetheless.

"You guys wouldn't have happened to have already gotten married, would you? That is, recently, not in the distant past."

"How did you know?" I asked, amazed.

"You weren't nervous at all. Even the most laissez-faire bride gets a little case of the nerves, but you were rock solid, which made me wonder if that's because this was just window dressing, so to speak."

"Don't tell anyone," I warned her. "We were married at the registry office yesterday morning, with just Ziggy and a stranger Neo roped in to witness us. That's all we really wanted, but Ziggy had her heart set on officiating, and then you mentioned we could have the wedding here, and … well, I wouldn't want to ruin it for anyone."

"I won't tell anyone but Iakovos, and I think he already knows. There's not a lot you can get past him. Now, I'd better go deal with the food and drink, because that's the third time Mrs. Avrabos has come out to stare at me. Happy marriage, Beam."

"Thank you," I called after her as she hurried off. My heart was full as I looked at all the new friends and family who were present ... until I looked toward Neo.

Iakovos had moved off to help Harry, and ended up swinging her into the dance that was going on with the others. I moved over to slide my hand through Neo's arm, forcing a smile to my lips.

"—such an irreverent ceremony. I'm surprised that you would want such a thing, but of course, you have your own way of doing things," Camilla was telling Neo before turning a brittle smile on me. "And there's the bride. What an interesting dress."

"I bought it because I could wear it to parties," I told her. "And Neo asked me to get something red, since that's his favorite color. Hello, Chase. It's nice to see you again."

"Congratulations," he said, inclining his head. "I hope you don't mind that I gate-crashed your wedding, but as I told Neo earlier, his stepfather is a bit under the weather, and I couldn't turn down Camilla's request for my presence."

"I believe I will go sit down inside," Camilla said, one hand fluttering around her chest. "It's so loud out here with the music blaring. Neo, darling, come inside and see me before I have to return to your poor, sick stepfather?"

"In a few minutes," he told her, watching her silently as she made her way inside. He turned back to Chase, saying, "I've been meaning to get in touch. I didn't think you would come to the wedding if I had invited you."

His words were somewhat stiff. I wondered what was up. I hadn't seen him since we'd interrupted his pool time, and wondered if he'd spent some of the afternoon working.

"Of course I would have come—you are my friend, no matter what has happened in the last ten days," Chase said, his face expressing no emotion. "You may think I harbor animosity for you, but I assure you that the opposite is true. I don't understand what you've been told to make you throw away so many years of friendship and, yes, devoted work, but I hope we can straighten matters out."

"Maybe this isn't the moment to have this out," I suggested, getting more worried about Neo.

"I'm not sure it can wait," he said softly. "What have you done, Chase? Why have you tried to destroy Pi?"

"Are you insane?" Chase looked astonished. "I've spent the better part of my life working for you. Working for Pi. I've always had your back."

"You helped my mother turn Pi from a company that tried to benefit others to one whose sole purpose was to line the pockets of investors. You dumped Beam's old code into my system, siphoning money to an account that you set up, and then told me it was going to her."

"He what?" I made a fist, but remembered in time that it was impolite to punch out a guest at one's own wedding. "You bastard."

Chase rolled his eyes, actually rolled them in response to me. "Oh, please. Like your code was anything to write home about?"

"How would you know that unless you were the one to work it into Pi?" Neo asked. "Honestly, I'm surprised you had the wherewithal to install it."

"I didn't," Chase said, a cruel glint to his eye making me extremely nervous.

"You had to," Neo argued, the muscles in his arm tensing. "You knew about Beowulf. You knew what the code did, and that it originated with Beam. No one else was aware of the code's existence, since it was archived on my personal laptop. You had access to that computer. You had to have put it on the servers. Nothing else makes sense."

"You're so literal," Chase said, rolling his shoulders like he was bored and wanted to get going. "You always were. That's why it was so easy to do what I wanted—all I had to do was lead you into making an assumption, say that your mother was meddling with Pi, and you swallowed it whole."

"You had one of the devs do it," Neo said, a muscle in his jaw jumping.

"That's right. Do you remember Gio? That Italian who was so good with debugging? He had other talents, including encryption. Once I found the bit of code that had a unique way of siphoning money without anyone tracing it, I knew I had to utilize it. Not use it as it was," he told me. "It was crude at best, but with some modifications, it served the purpose."

"Uh-oh." My stomach turned, leaving me feeling mildly sick to my stomach.

"It's all right," Neo told me. "You don't have to stay here, sunshine. Go be with our guests while I deal with Chase."

"No." Slowly, I pulled Neo a little to the side, so he was partially facing me. "He's telling you what he did."

"Yes." Neo's eyebrows pulled together. "If you'd prefer to leave—"

"No, you don't understand." My mouth went dry as I tried to make him see what my inner Housewife was screaming about. "He's pulling a Bond villain on you."

"A what, now?" Neo asked.

"I believe your new wife is referring to the fact that I'm freely admitting my actions of the last thirteen years." Chase looked me over before returning his attention to Neo. "And you have not asked yourself why. But she has. I see now that I was wrong to underestimate her. There's something of a brain behind that rather messy head of hair. Kudos, madam, for seeing what your obtuse husband hasn't."

"He's not obtuse," I said quickly. "He has a straightforward way of thinking, that's all."

"So you admit stealing from me?" Neo asked, his voice as harsh as stone. "Why?"

"Money, why else?" Chase said with a mirthless bark of laughter.

"But I paid you well as CFO. Very well. In fact, I noticed this afternoon that you seem to have accrued quite a bit of Pi stock during the last few years. By my calculation, you own roughly eight percent of the available stock. Was that bought with money you stole from me?"

"Champagne?" Iakovos appeared at my side bearing a tray with several flutes of bubbling golden liquid.

I took one automatically, but Neo and Chase appeared oblivious to him.

"Eight percent?" Chase gave another little laugh and shook his head in what struck me as faux regret. "Oh, Neo, how very clueless you really are."

Iakovos, who was about to leave, turned back, his eyes narrowed on Chase.

The latter smirked and told Neo, "I don't own eight percent of Pi. I own sixty-two percent."

My fingers tightened on Neo's arm. A sudden surge of nausea had me setting the untouched glass down.

"You can't," Neo said, his eyes narrow slits of silver as he faced his friend. "You can't possibly have that much stock. Only I own that much. My mother is the next largest shareholder, and she has ten percent."

Chase picked up my glass and drained it in one swig. "I don't know if this new level of obtuseness is due to Beam, or if you've just gotten soft in the head. You've never been one to be led around by the cock before, so I'm going to have to believe it's the latter."

"This is a wedding, a celebration," Iakovos interrupted, pinning Chase back with a look that I wouldn't want turned on me. "This discussion can surely be conducted another time."

"Yes, I'm sorry," Neo said, rubbing a hand across his brow. "I shouldn't have started it."

"You know, I think so long as you've opened this particular can of worms, we might as well finish it," Chase said, pulling a couple of pieces of paper from his suit inner pocket. He slapped them against Neo's chest. "These are copies, naturally. The originals are filed with the appropriate authorities."

Neo stood as frozen as a statue, although one hand clasped the papers that Chase had thrust on him.

"I'm happy to help you find the front door," Iakovos said after a quick look at Neo.

"There's no need. I'll see myself out. Congratulations, again." Chase's lips curled in a smirk that I badly wanted to remove in a highly violent manner. "Since I didn't come with a wedding present, I'll leave you with this bit of advice: you might want to be a bit more observant when your next CFO asks you to sign papers. It's been remarkably easy to have you sign things that you are too distracted to read."

"You're done now," Iakovos said in a voice that brooked no argument.

Theo, who had strolled up, took one look at our faces and asked, "What's going on? Why do you all look like you want to punch someone?"

"I'll leave you all to explain," Chase said, and, with one last smirk at Neo, sauntered off.

"Make sure he leaves," Iakovos told his brother, who turned and immediately did as he was asked.

"Neo?" I moved to stand in front of him. He was staring at the papers Chase had given him. "Is it true?"

"Yes." He took a long, deep breath.

Uncaring that Iakovos was still next to us, even now trying to catch Dmitri's eye, I put my arms around Neo. "I want to tell you I'm sorry, but I know you'll just tell me it's not my fault, and then you'll go off into a tirade about how you are a horrible person for not realizing that your friend betrayed you and stole your money and your company."

"I would, and I would." He sighed, his breath ruffling my hair. "You're the only good thing to come out of the mess of my life."

"What are you going to do?" I asked, wanting to cry for the despair I knew he must be feeling.

"About Pi?" he asked.

I nodded, kissing his neck, enjoying the smell and feel and heat of him.

"I hope your first step is to consult with your lawyers," Iakovos said, having finally gotten Dmitri's attention. Theo returned, the three men blocking us from the rest of the party. "I don't know if there is something that can be done about the sale of your stock, but assuming he falsified documents, then it is reasonable to expect you can regain it."

"What's going on?" Theo and Dmitri asked at the same time.

In a soft tone that wouldn't carry, Iakovos told them. Both men's eyes widened as they watched us.

"I'll definitely consult my legal team," Neo said. "Then I'll talk to the board members."

"They like you, right? They'll no doubt be on your side." I wondered how rude it would be if I gathered up Ziggy and took her and Neo home to his boat.

"We'll give you whatever help we can," Dmitri said. "Our area of expertise is real estate, not tech concerns, but you can count on us to help you."

"Thank you," Neo told them. "Normally I'd rather deal with this by myself, but if there's one thing I've learned in the last two weeks, it's the power of friends, so I will gladly accept your help."

"How desperate a situation will it be for you if you can't get the stock back?" I asked, needing to know the worst.

To my surprise, Neo didn't look devastated by the question.

In fact, he brightened up. "Actually, I don't think that Chase realizes a few things that keep the situation from being the calamity that he imagines. For one, I've never formally initiated a license for the software that runs Pi. Chase will find it impossible to keep the infrastructure running without the core programming."

Theo burst into laughter. "I am willing to bet that your board will have a thing or two to say to him about that."

"They will," Neo agreed, then gave me a little squeeze. "And as soon as I spread the word that I've pulled all support—monetary and otherwise—from Pi, I expect other businesses to take note and reconsider their interests in the company, as well. My biggest concern is for the employees who may be impacted, but I will see to it that they find other jobs, if that's what they desire."

"You were supporting Pi financially?" Iakovos asked.

"Yes. Have been for the last fifteen years. I didn't mind because it was serving the purpose for which I'd built it, but once my mother and Chase changed things ... well, dumping funds to keep it going ends now." Neo looked almost cheerful.

"You own the software?" I asked, realizing what that meant. It would be almost impossible to rebuild that without a substantial investment. "Not Pi?"

"Not Pi." He smiled, and my stomach settled down and gave me the go-ahead to kiss him as I'd wanted to do earlier.

"Is the building in your name, or the corporation's?" Dmitri asked. "Not to be nosy, but ... well, inquiring minds and all that."

Neo's smile grew. "Alas, that is also in my name. I'm thinking that it might very well be time to get some new occupants."

"But it's your company," I protested, wanting to sing and dance and rip off all his clothing to molest him in a way that I knew he'd approve. "Your precious company that you love above all things."

"Whatever gave you that idea?" he asked, kissing me the way I'd been wanting him to kiss me ever since I set eyes on him again. "The employees were, on the whole, excellent, but as I said, I will make sure they are taken care of. But Pi itself changed because I had other interests. It started out good, but I didn't put the time and energy into keeping it on track. I don't intend on making that mistake again."

"And this, I believe, is where we leave the bride and groom to enjoy a dance by themselves," Iakovos said, herding his brother and cousin back to where the others were celebrating.

"Oooh." I wiggled my hips against Neo, feeling his arousal beginning to stir in response. "You're going to start a new company?"

"No, I meant with you and—" He stopped, frowning at me. "Another company?"

I grinned, doing a belly roll that I hoped would have him wanting to leave the party early. "Why not? You're the computer genius. Ziggy is very gifted when it comes to programming. And I'm willing to take some classes in computer languages so I can help you both. Wait ... are you sure Chase didn't wipe you out? Will you have to sell your pretty boat?"

His hands skittered down my back, stroking along my bare flesh. "Would you still love me if I had to sell it?"

I punched him on the chest. "You take that back!"

He laughed, and bent to kiss the protest right off my lips. "Pax, sunshine. I know you don't care if I have any money, but I do. And since I just checked my accounts this morning while you were showering, I can assure you that I not only have enough money to keep you cruising around the Mediterranean in style, but also enough for Ziggy to have sufficient pocket money. Although I want my black card back. Happy?"

"Despite your asshole friend? Yes."

"Good. Because I need you, Beam. I've always needed you, and now you are officially mine."

"I am so not an object to be owned," I said, moving out of his grasp, and pulling him toward the dance floor. He looked confused for a moment until I added, "You, however, are mine, all mine, and I'm not going to let any of those hordes of women who think that just because you're the second-most adorable bachelor in existence, they can have you ... wait, I lost control of that sentence. It doesn't matter. The end result is that you, sir, are mine, and after we do the minimum amount of celebrating that politeness requires, I am going to race you back to your boat."

"The last one to get there has to be on the bottom," he said, pulling my hips to his as a slow song drifted out across the warm evening air.

An hour later I stood at the door of the apartment, thanking Harry, Thyra, and Kiera, all of whom were saying goodbye.

The men, who evidently had a quick conference while Neo was supposed to be gathering up the things Ziggy and I had left, started toward us down the hallway.

"Hoo," Harry said, watching the four men.

"Seriously, the genes in this family," Kiera said, fanning herself.

"Someday, I'm going to have kids, and by god, they had better take after Dmitri, or I'm going to want to know why," Thyra said, clutching her cat.

"I can't wait for some woman to make a move on Neo," I announced, my heart beating fast at the sight of him. "I'm going to have a great time proving he's mine."

"Kind of makes you wonder what the number one bachelor looks like if these guys are considered lesser numbers, huh?" Ziggy asked.

We all looked at her for a few seconds, then turned back to the men.

"Wow." Harry blinked a few times. "Yeah."

"Boggles the mind," I agreed, smiling when Neo approached. "But on the other hand, perfection is overrated. Give me a man who is sexy as sin but has the sort of personality that appreciates what's important in life any day."

"Amen, sister-cousin," Harry said, as I went to meet Neo.

It had taken a long time to get my man, but this time, I wasn't going to let him go.

"Ready, sunshine?" he asked, shepherding Ziggy and me out the door.

"For you? Always," I said.

And so I was.

A NOTE FROM KATIE

My lovely one! I hope you enjoyed reading this book, which I handcrafted from the finest artisanal words just for you. If you are one of the folks who likes to review books, I'd love it if you posted a review for it on your favorite book spot. If you aren't a reviewing type, fear not, I will cherish you regardless.

I'd also like to encourage you to sign up for the exclusive readers' group newsletter wherein I share behind-the-scenes info about my books (and dogs, and love of dishy guys, and pretty much anything else that I think people would enjoy), sneak peeks of upcoming books, news of readers'-group-only contests, etc. You can join the fun by clicking on the SUBSCRIBE TO KATIE'S NEWSLETTER link on my website at www.katiemacalister.com

PAPAIOANNOU NOVELS

- It's All Greek to Me
- Ever Fallen in Love
- A Tale of Two Cousins
- Acropolis Now

ABOUT THE AUTHOR

For as long as she can remember, Katie MacAlister has loved reading. Growing up in a family where a weekly visit to the library was a given, Katie spent much of her time with her nose buried in a book.

Two years after she started writing novels, Katie sold her first romance, *Noble Intentions*. More than seventy books later, her novels have been translated into numerous languages, been recorded as audiobooks, received several awards, and have been regulars on the *New York Times*, *USA Today*, *Publishers Weekly*, and *Wall Street Journal* bestseller lists. Katie lives in the Pacific Northwest with two dogs, and can often be found lurking around online.

You are welcome to join Katie's official discussion group on Facebook, as well as connect with her via TikTok and Instagram. For more information, visit her website at www.katiemacalister.com

Made in United States
Orlando, FL
06 September 2022

22050202R00152